Beguiled

ELIZABETH
ROSE

OLIVERHEARTBOOKS

0 9 8 7 6 5 4 3 2 1

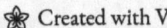 Created with Vellum

Foreword

*I have attached a map of the land of Mura for your convenience. If you'd like to see a much more detailed map that is in color and also shows the lands from my Elemental Magick Series, please click **HERE** to see it.*

When the darkness of despair casts shadows on life, the spark of hope flickers, just waiting to burst into flame once more.

One

CASTLE GLINT – THE ELVEN QUEENDOM OF MURA

QUEEN LIRA PENTSTONE bolted upright in bed, screaming at the top of her lungs. Her heart drummed in anticipation, making it hard to even breathe. Her body quaked like a leaf in the wind, brought on by the dream that woke her from a sound slumber. This time, the dream was a nightmare so vivid that she was sure it was more than the normal mindless nonsense often experienced in a sleep state. She was sure it had to be a premonition.

"Valindra," she gasped, jumping from her bed, grabbing the nighttime candle and running through the halls of Castle Glint. She hurriedly made her way to her four-year-old daughter's bedchamber. Lira had just seen her sweet Valindra being kidnapped, as she had on several other occasions lately. This time, it was clear and there was no doubt in her mind. In her vision, it hadn't been an enemy from Mura taking her child away. It was something different that she couldn't explain. To her, it looked like a man emerging from a swirling portal. And it was inside the castle!

"My lady?" came the voice of her handmaid, Nima, poking her head out the door of her chamber. She was an older woman, but very spry and alert for her age. "Is something wrong?"

"It's Valindra," she said, not stopping her pace, and barely able to speak. Her heart lodged in her throat.

"The princess is in danger?"

"I believe so." Lira pushed open the door to her daughter's room, stopping in her tracks. There, at the side of the little girl's bed was a portal with swirling colors of blue, white, and red. In the center of the portal was the silhouette of a man. He wore a long cloak covering him from head to foot. The hood of the cloak covered his face, so she wasn't able to see his identity. He reached out of the portal, his fingers closing around Valindra's arm, and he started to pull her toward him.

"Nay! Leave her alone!" Lira raced into the room, dropping the candle and lunging for the bed. She grabbed Valindra, yanking her, trying to break the hold of the mysterious man. The action woke her daughter and she started crying. Lira felt the tug of the abductor's hold working against her. She used one hand to pry his glove-covered fingers off of her daughter's arm.

"Mama, I'm scared," cried Valindra, clinging to her. Her eyes filled with terror.

"My queen!" Two of her guards barged into the room, both calling to her as they slammed the door open against the wall. They held torches high above their heads. Their swords were drawn and gripped tightly in their hands as their eyes scanned the area, stopping on the portal. Lira's handmaid peeked out from behind them, keeping half-hidden in the shadows.

Lira's action, as well as the arrival of the guards, must have done something to disrupt things. The portal man's head snapped around and he jerked backward. Then he released her daughter, and pulled back his hand. The portal quickly snapped closed, taking him and all the swirls of color with it. In the blink of an eye, all danger was gone.

"W-what was that?" asked her head knight, Argis, making his way into the room. The man was only a few years older than her own age of three and twenty. He was one of her most devoted warriors as well as a good friend.

"We heard you screaming and came right away," said her guard, Rivikyn, who was Argis' younger brother.

Lira got off the bed, cradling Valindra in her arms as the girl continued to cry.

"Everything is fine," she said, pressing her lips in a kiss against her daughter's head, and brushing back her strawberry-blond curls.

Looking down to the bed, Lira noticed a leather gauntlet covered with dirt that had fallen atop the covers. She realized it was from her daughter's attacker. It must have been left behind in the struggle, before he disappeared through the portal. She picked it up, then quickly hid it from her daughter. If Valindra saw the glove, it would only upset her. Lira took a deep breath and slowly released it, calming her emotions and regaining her control before speaking to her soldiers.

She knew how important it was to keep her composure since she became queen. If she was to be an effective leader of Glint, it was better to hide her emotions.

"I'm sorry to have caused alarm," she told the others. "It seems as if a portal was opening, but I was able to get to Valindra in time. The attacker and the portal have disappeared."

"Thank the gods. Was it your premonition again that alerted you?" asked Argis. "Was it the same one you've been having lately, my queen?"

Lira took a deep breath. It was exactly that, but she didn't want to speak of it in front of her daughter.

"Mama? Is something bad going to happen to me?" asked the little girl, looking up to her with terror in her wide, blue eyes. Lira did her best to hide her concern, trying to calm her daughter. She also didn't want to cause alarm within the queendom yet, until she could figure out just what was happening here and what to do about it.

"Everything is fine now, sweetheart. Just go back to sleep."

"But I'm scared, Mama. I want to stay with you."

"Nima, take my daughter to my room to sleep for now. Stay with her until I get there, please," commanded Lira.

"Aye, my queen," said the handmaid, reaching out and taking the child from her. Nima was more to Lira than just a handmaid. She had more or less raised her as well as Lira's twin brothers, and was like family to her. With a positive attitude and always a smiling face, Nima was the balance to the worry that resided within Lira for many years now.

"Nay! I don't want to leave you, Mama," cried Valindra, reaching out for Lira once again. As a mother, Lira wanted to keep her daughter close to her. As a queen, she knew she had other duties to perform.

"Valindra, what have I told you about staying strong?" asked Lira. "You are the princess of Glint and someday will be queen. You cannot act this way in front of your subjects. You need to control your emotions."

"She's just a child, my queen," said the handmaid, sticking up for the girl. Pity showed in the woman's eyes. "It is much to ask of her, especially during this trying time."

"Aye, but she must honor what is expected of her as Princess of Glint, and act accordingly," Lira reminded her. "My daughter might be young, but it is important for her to start her training now."

"Of course, my lady," said the handmaid with a nod. "I understand."

Lira looked over to her soldiers. "Argis, post two guards at my bedchamber door and keep your ears open. If there is trouble, my handmaid will call out for you."

"Of course, my queen," answered the man with a deep bow.

Glint was a matriarchal society where the line of succession continued through the female lineage rather than the male like the other kingdoms of Mura. Instead, the women were more powerful in Glint. The realm was considered a queendom as was proper in this case.

Lira, being the only daughter of the king and queen, inherited the title of ruler upon her mother's death four years ago. Valindra, being Lira's only daughter so far, would inherit her title someday as well.

Once the handmaid left with the little girl, Lira spoke to the guards in a low tone.

"Summon Elric, the sage," she commanded, opening her hand and looking at the leather glove she clasped. It was long, up to the elbow, and really more of a gauntlet. It seemed familiar to her, yet she didn't know why. She needed to know from where it came.

"Summon the sage?" asked Rivikyn, his eyes opening wide in surprise. He and Argis exchanged confused glances. "Are you sure you want him here, my lady?"

"With all due respect, Elric's been nothing but trouble, my good queen," Argis reminded her. "You were the one who banished him to the high cliff of Glint in the first place."

"I don't need you to remind me what I did or didn't do," she ground out. "Now, I said, summon the sage!"

Lira lost her temper and found herself yelling since she was so angry and upset by the events that had just transpired. Panic lodged within her. It was getting harder and harder to hide it. Her men had no right to question her word. What happened in the past regarding the sage was a sore spot to her but she could no longer dismiss it. She needed help. "My daughter's life was in danger tonight. I must speak to the sage anon to request his wise counsel."

"If you are sure, my lady," answered Argis. "I'll send a messenger up the cliffs to the sage's home right away. However, he is often not there. I am told he spends much of his time on the other side of the mountains lately. Amongst the humans," he added, wrinkling his nose and making a face.

"He needs to be found immediately, so do it! Report to me as soon as he sets foot inside the castle. Summon my Aunt Sasha as well. Since she is my advisor, I'll need her help with this matter, too." Lira pushed past them and headed down the hall following Nima's path to her own chamber.

"Aye, my lady," answered both the men in unison.

"My lady, are you . . . sure about the sage?" Argis tried once more to discourage her.

"Yes. I'm sure." She let out a breath of frustration. "Send a messenger up the cliffs to his home, and do not question me about it again."

"Aye, my queen. I will carry out your orders at once."

Lira hoped she was doing the right thing by sending for Elric. Suddenly her confidence started to waver. Her soldiers were most likely only looking out for her best interest, and she appreciated their concern. It was true that the sage had only caused her trouble and heartache in the past. Lira had been the one to banish him from

Glint four years ago after a horrendous battle with the giants from the nearby Isle of Denwop. But she was a widow now, and needed family around her during this trying time for support.

What happened tonight was serious. It shook her up so much that she needed to ask the sage for his advice. Elric was irritating to be around, but the eccentric little man did on occasion have extreme wisdom. He was not only wise, but held powerful magic. That magic could be of assistance to her since all her magic, except her power of premonition, had vanished not long after the birth of her daughter. Lira never thought she'd ever welcome Elric back inside the castle's walls. Then again, she felt so alone right now that she didn't have a choice. Being alone was the basis of many of her nightmares. Too many people, especially family members, had disappeared from her life in one way or another. Lira would not lose Valindra, too. She both needed and wanted the sage here right now, not only for his advice, but also because he was her father.

Two

EVANDORM CASTLE

STANDING in the courtyard of Evandorm Castle, Zann Blackseed threw down the spoils of his hunt at the feet of King Drustan Grinwald, getting a dissatisfied grunt from the man in return. Evandorm was one of the three kingdoms on the south side of the Picajord Mountains of Mura.

King Grinwald was a big man, built like a castle's retaining wall, with a wide chest and thick arms and legs. His brown hair had been turning gray over the years, and his skin was baked from the sun and looked like tanned leather. A long mustache joined with his beard, hanging down to the top of his chest. While the man wasn't overweight, he was solid, and liked to eat. He was also very particular about his food.

"A half dozen rabbits, three pheasants, and two squirrels? That's it?" snapped the king.

"I also delivered a deer to the door of the kitchen earlier this morning, sire," answered Zann, who was the king's huntsman. "Not to mention, I collected a few dozen arcine eggs as well. I gave them to the cooks to prepare for the main meal."

"Arcine eggs? Yuck!" spat the man, making a sour

face. "I don't like them and don't want them on my table. You know I hate those slimy things," he complained, talking about the snake-like animal's eggs that were slimy on the outside as well as the inside. They became so chewy once cooked, that it was better to eat them raw. It was an acquired taste, and unfortunately not one the king ever got used to. "They are no better than eel eggs, although I'd even welcome some of those right now since I am so hungry," the king continued with his rant. "What is the matter with you, huntsman?"

"Pardon me?" asked Zann with a shake of his head. "I don't know what you mean, My King. I've provided food for the occupants of the castle, just like I always do."

"I want more. More, I say! Do you hear me?" bellowed the king. "This isn't enough food to feed me, let alone my soldiers."

The kings of Mura were greedy and selfish, only thinking about themselves. They had been battling each other, fighting for total control of the kingdoms on the south side of Mura for what seemed like forever.

Just recently, King Osric of Kasculbough had perished. Zann's brother, Rhys, had inherited his title. Rhys now ruled Kaculbough along with his new bride, Medea de Bar at his side. Rhys wasn't greedy or petty at all, but King Grinwald as well as King Sethor of Macada Castle still cast shadows of evil and hatred over the land of Mura.

"I understand, my king," said Zann, holding back from lashing out at the man with his true feelings. Zann was a shapeshifter and often spent time in his wolf form, especially during his hunting sessions. He had a hard time controlling the wild side of himself when in human form. Of course, the king didn't know he had magic like this. Nor did Zann ever want him to discover the fact. Magic was still banned on Mura by two out of the three kings who ruled the land. Anyone caught using magic was executed. Nay, it would do him no good to share this tidbit of information . . . ever.

"I'm going to starve, I tell you. My people are going to die hungry," the man continued his nonsensical conversation in an over-dramatic tone, waving his hands in the air.

Zann almost laughed out loud at this ridiculous statement. Evandorm had more food growing inside the castle's walls than both Kasculbough and Macada Castles put together. Evandorm had a bustling village right inside its courtyard. Tiny cottages for the villagers dotted the area. Market tents were set up, and brought in much trade from all over the land.

The castle had orchards, a vineyard, and plentiful fields of crops of all kinds. Animals filled the pens. Only the finest horses were stalled in the stables. The mews were filled with many coveted birds, ranging from doves to falcons. In the kennels were housed at least a dozen dogs, even though the animals weren't used much to hunt since they weren't needed. Zann was the castle's huntsman and brought in most of the food all by himself.

"If I may speak freely, my lord?" Zann bowed his head, waiting for permission. At the same time he bit his tongue, trying not to spew out words that would be laden with contempt.

"What is it? Spit it out, Blackseed. If you have something to say, then do so," commanded the king. "My time is precious, and you are wasting it right now."

"Thank you, my king," Zann answered through

gritted teeth. "I just wanted to point out that I hardly think starvation is possible with Evandorm's orchards all laden heavily with ripe fruit. Besides that, the crops in Evandorm's fields are even more bountiful than ever before, and nearly ready for harvest."

"That's not real food. I want meat! Have you been afraid to hunt lately, influenced by that damned fae wife of your sin-eating brother, by any chance?" The king spoke of Zann's eldest brother, Darium, who was the sin eater of Mura. He recently married a fae named Talia-Glenn. She was also an Elemental of the Earth. Talia and her kind didn't eat meat at all. They cherished and protected all wildlife of the Goeften Forest.

Zann's head snapped up. He wasn't afraid of anything, especially not a woman. He didn't appreciate being accused of such a thing. Talia was his sister-by-marriage, and a fae, that was true. She had often tried to stop Zann from hunting the animals of Goeften Forest. Mayhap he did feel a little guilty lately doing it, but still he didn't let it stop him from completing his job. Or at least he didn't think so. Zann performed the task that was required of him, always being loyal to the king.

"I assure you, my brother's wife has not influenced me in the least as to how I perform my duties, my good king," he answered.

"Then is it that witch that your brother, Sir Rhys recently married? The one who rode the dragon and almost burnt us all to a crisp? Is she the one scaring you from bringing me what I want and need? After all, magic is banned in Mura, but the Blackseed family doesn't seem to think this applies to them."

The king's further accusations didn't sit well with Zann at all. It was getting harder and harder not to lash out at the man with not only his words but also his sword. King Grinwald was goading him, and Zann knew it. Still, he found this verbal attack hard to condone.

"My brother, Rhys, is King of Kasculbough now, and can make his own decisions," he reminded Grinwald. "That witch, as you refer to her, is his wife, Queen Medea, if I must remind you."

"Hmph," sniffed the king. "Your brother killed King Osric and claimed the throne for himself. He's not a real king. He only has the title because he stole it." The man's words dripped with jealousy and contempt.

"Nay, that is not true. King Osric named my brother his heir. Everyone knows that. And you know as well as I, that Rhys did not kill him," Zann said, holding back from punching the man now. "If I were you, I wouldn't let it be known that you're slandering my brother's name in public and calling his wife a witch. Medea won't like that. And I don't think I need to remind you that she has a darkness inside her that cannot always be controlled. In all due respect, my king, I'd think you'd be best to choose your words more carefully."

"Well," said Grinwald, clearing his throat, shifting from foot to foot. It seemed as if he were considering Zann's warning. "Mayhap we'll just keep this conversation between us, shall we?"

"I believe that would be best, sire," agreed Zann, giving a nod of his head.

"Blackseed, I want you to cross the mountain and hunt in the lands of Glint," ordered Grinwald with his hand to his chin in thought. As he spoke, he fingered his long beard. The words that came out of this man's mouth never ceased to amaze Zann. This, by far, was the stupidest order he'd ever given.

"You want me to hunt in Glint?" Zann shook his

head, not able to believe what he'd just heard. No one ever went there. The other side of the Picajord Mountains was the land where the magical beings lived. The kings of Mura stayed on the south side of the mountains, and the beings of magic stayed put for the most part, on the north. It was better that way. "Glint is the elven realm, my lord. Surely, you don't want to anger them. I suggest I continue hunting in the Goeften Forest, right here instead."

"Nay. I hear the elves have lots of animals in their woods. More than we do. I'd like to try something exciting, so bring me some new game that I've yet to taste. And while you are at it, stop by the Whispering Dale and bring me back some of those prized pazzleberries. I've heard they grow abundantly there, and are twice as big as the scant ones on this side of the mountain."

"The Whispering Dale? But that's the land of the fae folk, my king. I can't go there." Now that Zann found out recently that he, along with his two brothers, was part fae, he didn't want to upset the fae folk. It wouldn't bode well for him at all.

"Of course, you can," scoffed Grinwald, dismissing the fact that the idea was absurd, swiping his hand through the air. "You will go wherever I tell you to, because I am king and you will follow my orders. This is not a suggestion, it is a command, huntsman. Do you understand?" The king's mouth turned up into an evil grin. Zann couldn't read minds like the fae, even though his mother's fae blood flowed through him. However, he didn't need to do so to know that the king was trying to rile him. Grinwald knew damned well Zann's connection to these magical beings. He was only trying to start trouble. "Your mother is one of them, is she not?"

Zann cringed. Why did Grinwald have to bring this

up? "You know that she is, my lord," Zann answered through clenched teeth. The last thing he wanted was to talk about his mother. It only made him angrier than he already was. Zann still couldn't forgive her for abandoning him and his brothers when they were children.

"Then, get her to give you some of that magical food they eat. I want to see it on my table by the morrow."

"Their food isn't any more magical than what you have right here," Zann explained, splaying out his arm at the kill spread out at their feet. "I also suggest that we do not anger the gods by going to the other side of the mountain. After all, the Pyramids of the Gods, the temples of our deities, are found right next to where the fae folk live."

Before the king could answer, a guard approached, bowing his head. "My king?"

"What is it?" snapped the king. "Can't you see that I'm busy?"

"I apologize, sire. I just wanted to report that a new cook has been hired and has just arrived, as you have requested. He wants to get started on the meal anon."

"Is he any good?" asked the king. "Can he cook? Is he fast? I am tired of the bland food served lately that takes my cooks too long to prepare. I need someone who can produce quickly, and make it taste exciting."

"I believe he's just what you're looking for, my lord. Your head cook tells me that this man can prepare food faster than all the rest of them combined."

"Really? That is good. Very good," said the king with a chuckle. "He'll be my new head cook then. Inform the others in the kitchen of his position. Now, I'm sure to get my meals prepared faster, served hotter, and tasting better. Aye, it is a true blessing that this man is here in Evandorm at all."

"I will tell him to start on the meal anon, my lord." The guard bowed once again.

"Fine," said the king. "I want you to also help my huntsman bring this meat to the kitchen. Deliver it into the hands of my new head cook. It'll be a meager meal but mayhap my huntsman will do better providing us with food in the future."

"Aye, sire," said the guard, bending down to pick up the kill.

Zann didn't answer. Nodding his head in a slight bow, he started picking up the food from the hunt as well. All he wanted was to be away from the king before he ended up hurting the man. He hated doing King Grinwald's bidding. He also despised bowing to this fool. Zann would have to talk to Rhys again and convince him to give him a position at Kasculbough. The only reason Zann was still here was because his brothers thought it would be good to keep a foot inside Evandorm to know at all times what Grinwald was doing. Too damned bad it was at his expense.

Zann and the guard carried the food to the kitchen. They unloaded the kill from the hunt onto the large wooden counter where the food would be prepared by the kitchen's cooks. The guard left, and Zann turned to go, but stopped in his tracks when he heard a voice from behind him that he knew only too well. It was one that he didn't want to hear right now – or, for that matter, ever again.

"Not there, you big oaf! Bring the food over here to me, where I can reach it."

Zann slowly turned to see the elven sage named Elric standing on a stool. His head and chest just cleared the tall kitchen counter. He was a full-grown man, but had the height of a youth, and often acted worse than a child at times. He had given Zann and his brothers a lot of trouble recently.

"Elric? What are you doing here?" asked Zann, wondering what the elf was up to now.

"I'm the new cook at Evandorm, what do you think I'm doing here, you fool?" Elric slammed down a meat cleaver into the wooden surface, then waved his hands in the air. "I said, bring that food over here. Right here. Didn't you hear me?" He slapped his open palm down on the table in front of him now.

Zann sighed and pushed the kill closer to the short, irritating man. He glanced around quickly, and then walked to Elric's side. He talked to him in a voice not much above a whisper, not wanting to be heard by the others in the room.

"Elric, you shouldn't be here," Zann warned him. "If anyone finds out that you're a . . . what you really are, your life will be in danger."

"Nonsense," spat the elf, plucking the feathers from a pheasant so fast that his hands were naught but a blur. "No one is going to know unless you are planning on telling them." He threw the plucked bird to the side and picked up another, finishing off all three before Zann knew what happened. "Besides, Blackseed, you are magical, too. Yet, here you stand."

"True, but I don't use magic in front of the king," Zann explained in a whisper from the side of his mouth. "If I did, he'd execute me."

"But he knows you come from fae blood."

"He only knows my mother is a fae. Remember, my father was human. The king doesn't realize that I have any magic at all. Now, we are going to keep it that way. Got it?"

The little man looked ridiculous wearing the tall white chef's hat that was pulled down low, covering the tops of his pointy elf ears. It fell partially over his eyes. Zann wondered how he could even see. He also wondered how Elric could think no one would notice that he was different from the rest of them. Even without seeing his ears, he was as short as an adolescent, and that wasn't normal. Also, his motions happened so fast, that when he moved it was naught but a blur.

"Are you?" The elf scowled at him and put his hands on his hips.

"Am I what?"

"Are you going to say anything about me to the king?"

Zann thought about it for a minute, being tempted to do just that. Then he sighed and shook his head before he answered. "Nay. Of course not," he answered. "But why in the name of Zoroct are you even here? It's not like you need the job," Zann cursed, using the name of the main god of the land. There were many gods and goddesses of Mura, and no one wanted to anger a one of them or they'd have to pay the price. Zann's sister-by-marriage, Medea found out the hard way when she didn't give an offering before breaking in and entering one of the pyramids that was used for worshipping them. Of course, stealing from the gods hadn't been wise of her either.

"I was bored, that's why I'm here. Not that I have to explain my reasoning to you or anyone." The elf picked up the heavy meat cleaver, holding it with two hands. "I am a sage. My actions are not to be questioned." He used the cleaver like a madman, chopping up and preparing all the meat in a matter of minutes. Zann's eyes roamed around the kitchen. Thankfully, the rest of the cooks were busy at the hearth, baking bread, or sweeping up. They didn't notice the elf's actions.

"Fine, then," said Zann. "Stay here if you want. I don't really care what you do. I'm leaving."

"Wait, Wolf, I want to talk to you." The sage threw down the cleaver, wiping his hands on his apron.

Zann turned around, speaking through clenched teeth, his voice coming out like a low growl, much like a wolf. "Don't call me that! What is the matter with you? Someone might hear you."

"Oh, stop your worrying. You are worse than an old alewife, I swear."

"I'm done here," said Zann, his hands balling into fists. He turned and left because he wasn't sure he could stop himself from strangling the blasted elf if he stayed a minute longer.

Zann rode his horse to Darium's home. It was a small cottage in the Goeften Forest where Zann and his brothers, Darium and Rhys had grown up. There wasn't much room in it, but it had sufficed. He dismounted his horse and went inside without even knocking.

"I have had it with that damned elf!" Zann spat, stopping in his tracks when he saw his brother, Darium, in bed with his new wife, Talia. Their naked bodies were pressed together, with Talia's long, chestnut-colored hair falling around her shoulders, hiding her bare breasts from him.

"Zann!" growled Darium, pushing up in bed. "Why do you insist on always entering without knocking first?"

"Ooops," he said. "Sorry about that." He turned his head to give them privacy. "How was I to know you'd be in bed at this time of day?"

"It's early morning. And I am still on my honeymoon," Darium reminded him. "Although you and Rhys don't seem to care."

"Where's Mother?" asked Zann, looking around the darkened room.

"She's not here." Darium stood up naked, starting

to dress. Talia wrapped the sheet around her and scooted off the bed, disappearing into an adjacent room. "Mother decided to reside at the Whispering Dale instead, even though I offered for her to stay with us. Haven't you heard the news?"

"What news?" asked Zann.

"The news that the fae have elected her as their queen."

"Fae Queen? What? Mother?" bellowed Zann, walking over and sliding down atop a chair. "Why would they do that? She's not even really from Mura, since she's lived so long on Lornoon." He spoke about another magical land across the waters from Mura where some of the most powerful elementals lived.

"She is from Mura, even though you don't want to admit it," said his brother.

"I have trouble acknowledging anything from a woman who abandoned her own children." Zann didn't accept the absence nor the sudden presence of their mother back into their lives, even if Rhys and Darium had easily done so.

"The fae haven't had a queen in the Whispering Dale for some time now," Talia explained from behind a partially closed door. She stepped out of the adjoining room, completely dressed.

"Mayhap not, but why would they choose Mother to be queen?" asked Zann. "I still don't understand it."

"Well, it's probably because she is the most worthy and the most powerful fae in the Dale," explained Talia, padding across the floor with bare feet, placing dishes on the table.

"Most powerful, mayhap, but surely not the most worthy," commented Zann. "She'll end up abandoning the fae, the way she did to us when we were children," he told his brother. "They shouldn't give her the title, and neither should they trust her."

"Zann, you are overreacting. You'll need to make amends with Mother someday." Darium, tied his breeches and pulled a tunic over his head. "It's not healthy for you to stay angry with her for this long."

"I'll do what I want, and not have you telling me how to act, brother." Zann heard the anger in his own words, but he didn't care. He had a right to how he felt, even if it was different than the attitudes of both his brothers.

"It's not the way of the fae folk to stay angry," Darium told him, slipping his feet into his boots.

"That's right. Fae are happy, carefree people," added Talia with a giggle that was a strong characteristic of being a fae.

"Well, I'm not a fae like you two!" Zann shot up off the chair and started pacing the room. He always paced nervously when something was troubling him, which seemed to be often lately.

"You have just as much fae blood in you from your mother as Darium or Rhys do," Talia pointed out. "You just are not in tune with it yet, that's all."

"And neither will I ever be, because it's the last thing I want!" Zann headed for the door.

"Zann, will you join us for breakfast?" Talia called out.

"Aye, stay," said Darium. "Talia has baked a fresh pazzleberry pie." Pazzleberries grew freely on the north side of the mountain, and some were found in the Goeften Forest as well, but those amounts were scarce. Pazzleberries were purple berries that had an exotic taste of sweet and tart at the same time, exploding into a delicious mixture in the mouth.

"No, thank you," said Zann knowing that since the

fae didn't eat meat, anything Talia would offer would be naught but weeds and roots. "I almost forgot to tell you." He headed back to the table. "King Grinwald expects me to move my hunt to Glint and the Whispering Dale."

"What?" Talia looked up in surprise, dropping a spoon. "You can't do that. It wouldn't be right." Her eyes shot over to Darium as she looked to her husband for support.

"I have to agree with my wife," said Darium, bending down and picking up the spoon. "Now that we have connections to these magical beings, we can't go in there and start killing off their animals just for a greedy king."

"What difference does it make?" asked Zann with a shrug. "We have no connections to the elves. I'll leave the Whispering Dale alone if it makes you happy, but if I don't bring back what the king wants, I'll be out of a job. Not that I mind, but you and Rhys seem to think it's important I stay there."

"Yes, we need a spy, so you can't leave. However, it's not your job to kill the animals on the other side of the mountain," Darium told him, helping Talia bring food to the table.

"Well, if the damned elf thinks he can show up in Evandorm and chop up our animals that I hunted right here in the Goeften Forest, than why can't I hunt on the other side of the mountain?"

"The elf?" asked Talia. "Are you speaking about the sage, Elric?"

"Aye, that's the one," Zann answered with a sigh.

"Elric is in Evandorm now? Are you sure about this?" Darium placed a pazzleberry pie on the table and licked off the juices from his thumb.

"He's there, I tell you. The damned elf showed up

and is somehow the castle's new head cook," Zann explained with a shrug.

"Really." Darium chuckled lowly. "First he's the jester at Macada Castle, then the assistant advisor to the King of Kasculbough, and now a cook at Evandorm? My, he gets around."

"Head cook," Zann corrected him.

Darium chuckled again and shook his head. "I wonder what he's up to?"

"It does sound odd," agreed Talia. "I'll see if I can find out what is going on. Darium, I'll send your raven over to the Whispering Dale to ask your mother about it. Mayhap she can shed some light on the situation." Talia could communicate with animals and all nature, just using her mind.

"Murk's not going to like that." Darium looked over to the corner of the room where his pet raven was pecking around on the floor.

"Murk will do it for me," said Talia with a smile. "We have a connection. Besides, there is some exciting news I want to send your mother anyway. I am going to tell my mother and sisters about it today, too."

"Exciting news? What do you mean?" asked Darium, this information seeming to surprise him.

Talia smiled and put her hand on her belly. "I'm pregnant, Darium," she announced.

"You're what?" Darium's head shot up. "Really? How do you know? I mean, it's too soon. We just got married and we just . . . it's too soon to know, sweetheart. You must be mistaken."

"Nay, I'm not, husband. The fae know right away when they've conceived. Our gestation time for birthing a baby is only four months long."

"Four months?" gasped Darium. "That soon?" He ran a hand through his long, black hair and started pacing the floor like Zann now. "That's so fast. I'm not ready yet to be a father."

"Hey, you've got it easy, brother," Zann told him with a chuckle. "At least it's not as fast as Medea and Rhys had a baby. You'll have at least a little time to get used to it."

"True," said Darium. "No one has a baby as fast as Medea."

"Well, congratulations," said Zann. "Darium, mayhap you'll have a baby girl like Rhys and Medea. After all, the Blackseed curse of just having boys seems to already be broken."

"We're having one of each," announced Talia with a smile, looking down and rubbing her flat stomach.

"We're what?" The shock on Darium's face was worth the trip here just to see it, Zann decided.

"We're having twins, dear. One boy and one girl," announced Talia with a satisfied sigh.

"You can't possibly know that." Darium shook his head in denial and looked pale and as if he were about to faint.

"I do know it," insisted Talia. "Fae have the ability of just knowing the sex of their babies right from conception."

"It seems there is still a lot I don't know about the fae. I need to sit down." Darium collapsed atop the bed, flopping back, staring up at the ceiling with his arm thrown over his eyes.

"Aren't you happy, Darium?" Talia's smile turned into a frown.

"Of course, I am, princess." Darium bolted to an upright position and held out his arms. "I'm just in shock, that's all. Come here."

Talia went to him and sat on his lap. When they started to kiss again, Zann knew this was his cue to leave.

"If anyone is looking for me, I'll be hunting in the forests of Glint," Zann announced, leaving the house and closing the door. "I'll never be so taken by a woman that I act like that," he mumbled, mounting his horse and heading to the Picajord Mountains to carry out the orders of his insane king.

Three

LIRA PACED the floor of the great hall two days later, still waiting for word from her messenger about her father.

"My queen," said the messenger, entering the great hall and bowing in front of her.

"Did you find the sage? Where is he?" she asked anxiously, looking up and around the room but not seeing Elric anywhere.

"I'm sorry," her messenger answered, shaking his head. The young boy seemed worried, as if he thought she would yell at him. "Elric has still not returned to his home atop the cliff."

Lira let out a loud sigh, and nodded. "All right. Thank you," she said. "Just keep an eye on his home and tell me as soon as he returns."

"Aye, my lady."

"You are dismissed."

"Lira, have they found Elric yet?" asked her Aunt Sasha, walking up behind her.

"Nay. He's still not home," she answered.

"Perhaps we don't need him, my queen," said the woman.

Sasha was Lira's late mother's sister. The woman had never liked Elric. It was at her suggestion that Lira banished him to the top of the cliffs in the first place. While Lira appreciated and valued Sasha's advice, sometimes she wondered if the woman had misled her, just because of her dislike of the man.

"It's been two days now, and still there is no word of my father," Lira told her. "Perhaps I should go to the other side of the mountain to look for him myself."

"Nay!" said Sasha, raising her hand and shaking her head. "It is not safe, my queen. This is your realm and you need to stay here. If you have to send a soldier than do so, but you will not be protected outside of Glint. You are too vulnerable, especially since you have lost your powers."

"Shhhh." Lira quickly scanned the great hall where her soldiers and the villagers sat eating at the long trestle tables. "I don't want my people to know that I haven't had magic for years now. I am sure my powers will return eventually . . . won't they?"

"I'm not sure," said Sasha. "I've never seen the likes of this before. They've been gone too long. It is not looking promising, my queen."

"It must have something to do with birthing my baby," said Lira. "That was when my powers disappeared, although I don't understand why."

"As I've told you years ago, you should ask the gods about it. Go to the pyramids and seek an audience with Hapsren, since she is Goddess of the Hearth and Home."

"Nay, I don't think so," said Lira, fearing the deities and not wanting to have to confront them. The gods were known to be ruthless and cruel at times to those who displeased them. Or so the stories went. She had never had contact with them personally and wasn't eager to put herself in that position. Great power such as the gods had, could do great damage. There was enough sadness and hardship in Lira's life. She didn't need to tempt the fates by purposely putting herself in a potentially compromising position. With her luck, she'd say or do something to make them angry and bring their wrath down on her head. Nay. Even though the Pyramids of the Gods were close by, Lira had only seen them from a distance, and she didn't want to go there now or ever.

"Then how about contacting Cnoir, Goddess of Love and Wealth? Mayhap she can help you."

"Nay," protested Lira. "I have wealth and don't need love in my life, if that is what you mean, Aunt Sasha. And before you suggest another god, I don't want to see any of them."

"Whatever you wish, my queen," her aunt said with a deep sigh. "May I speak freely?"

"You always do," mumbled Lira.

"My dear, your husband has been gone for many years now. Don't you think it is time you remarry, and start producing more heirs?"

"Only the eldest daughter is an heir, as you well know, since you are my mother's younger sister," Lira pointed out, hoping that would keep her quiet.

"True, but you have been having premonitions that involve your daughter lately. I don't want to alarm you, but if something happens to Valindra, it would be good to have another daughter to inherit your crown. It is always good to be prepared for whatever might happen."

"You really think something is going to happen to Valindra, don't you? Well, I assure you, that isn't true. I will protect her. She is the only heir I need."

"Of course," said Sasha, softly. "I'm sure she'll be fine." Her aunt tried to calm her, but Lira knew she was right. She should take another husband and get pregnant as quickly as possible. It was the only way to ensure the line of succession would stay with one of her off-spring. But after the death of her husband, Laeroth and the disappearance of her twin brothers, Korack and Kee-van, it wasn't easy to want to remarry and care about someone that she might lose in the future. "I only say it, because perhaps a man is what you need in your life," continued Sasha.

Lira released a deep breath. She didn't want to think of this right now. "What I need is to find my father! He is the sage. Mayhap he can answer questions about the man I saw in the portal. I am going out riding, Aunt Sasha. Perhaps I'll find Father in the forest. If not, at the very least, I can clear the cobwebs from my head."

"Take a guard with you. Do not venture out un-escorted," Sasha warned.

"Nay. I will be fine. I promise to stay in the forests of Glint. Besides, I want to be alone. Now, please keep a close eye on my daughter. I am afraid whoever it is trying to abduct her might reappear in the portal again. The faster I find my father and seek his counsel, the better."

"As you say, my queen." Her aunt said the words, but Lira could hear the disapproval in her voice.

Lira hurried to the stable, saddling her own horse, liking to do things for herself. It was already getting late in the day and she wanted to ride out and return before nightfall. If the portal was going to reopen, she had the feeling it would be at night.

Mounting her horse, she made sure her bow and ar-rows were at the ready since they were her only means of protecting herself now. Until her full powers returned, she was truly vulnerable. Lira had always been independ-ent, and didn't like this feeling. Riding from the castle, she headed to the woods where hopefully she could find an answer to all the questions rolling around in her head.

Lira had a flash in her mind – another premonition as she rode. She had the vision of a white wolf, killing off animals in her forest. This was not a wolf of Glint. There were no white wolves in Glint to her knowledge, and certainly none as big. Something seemed sinister or odd about it. As if it was up to no good. It didn't belong here and needed to be stopped.

Riding to the clearing where she'd seen the wolf in her vision, she stopped her horse and looked around. Then she pulled an arrow from the quiver on her back, nocking it in her bow. Sure enough, a big, white wolf bolted out of the brush, snarling and jumping at a roakan, one of the peaceful, deerlike animals that roamed freely in the woods of Glint. While it was similar to a deer in many ways, it was much bulkier, and had long shaggy hair down to its feet. Its ears were droopy and hung down around its shoulders, reminding her of a floppy-eared rabbit.

"Nay, you don't!" she shouted, releasing the arrow just as the wolf lunged for the roakan. The arrow struck the huge, white wolf in the backside, taking it to the ground as the animal cried out in a half-yelp, half-snarl. The roakan darted off through the brush, thankfully unharmed.

"That will teach you!" she spat, directing her horse closer to see if she'd made a clean kill. When she approached where the wolf fell in the brush, she gasped aloud. There was no wolf. Prone on the ground was a naked man instead.

"Oh!" she cried, jumping off the horse, and hurrying over to the man who was moaning in pain. Her arrow was embedded in the man's back end. "I'm sorry," she apologized, not knowing how this could have happened. "I was aiming at a wolf, and I –" She stopped in midsentence when the man looked up at her and she saw his orange, wolf-like eyes changing into those of a human. The man's long blond hair, so light it almost looked white, framed his face like a mane. His features contorted, his nose and snout turning from a wolf into that of a man. He glared at her and snarled, sounding much like a wolf even if he did look human.

Lira jumped back, nocking another arrow and aiming it right at his heart. "Who are you and what do you want?" she yelled.

"Me?" The man breathed through his mouth, panting like an animal. He looked normal now, but she remained cautious, not sure what to expect. He lay on his stomach, her arrow piercing his butt cheek. "Who in the name of Belcoum are you and why did you shoot me?" The man used the name of the god of underworld in vain.

"Y-you were a wolf," she said, the tip of her arrow still aimed directly at him. "You were about to kill one of my roakans. I couldn't let you do it."

"Put down the bow and arrows, wench! Or are you blind to the fact I am a defenseless, naked man, with an arrow stuck in my ass?"

"Oh, I'm sorry." She slowly lowered the bow and released the tension from the bowstring. "I – I'll help you." She quickly put the bow and arrows on the ground, gingerly walking over to the man, reaching out for the lodged arrow. She stopped, and pulled her hand back before touching him. "Before I remove the arrow, tell me who you are."

"I am Zann Blackseed. Who are you?"

"Blackseed?" Her head snapped up and she looked him in the eyes. "The new fae queen is Alai Na-Dae, but she was once married to a sin eater with the surname of

Blackseed. Do you know her?" The elves and the fae were allies and worked closely together. They were a lot alike in many ways. Their realms were next to each other, making them neighbors.

"What does it matter?" he asked with a grimace, putting his hand on the shaft of the arrow. From his position on the ground, he couldn't get enough leverage to remove it without breaking it off. "Aaaargh," he groaned in frustration.

"Tell me," she demanded to know. "Tell me the answer to my question before I help you."

"I've had enough of your kind of help. After all, look where it's gotten me so far. If you won't tell me who you are, I don't believe I owe you an explanation at all."

"You do owe me an explanation. You were hunting in my forest, and you are not from Glint or mayhap I'd show you a little mercy." One slip up might be able to be ignored but not two.

"Your forest?" he asked, making her realize she had just given away her identity. She sighed, figuring she might as well tell him who she was even if she was vulnerable. After all, he was at more of a disadvantage than herself at the moment. "All right, I'll tell you. I am Queen Lira Pentstone of Glint."

"Queen?" He squirmed a little, trying to get a better look at her. His eyes settled on her pointy ears. "Oh, damnation and hellfire, you're one of those blasted elves!"

Zann watched the beautiful woman's brows dip when he called her a blasted elf. She didn't like the fact he referred to her in such a manner, but neither did he care. The wench almost killed him with her arrow! If he hadn't shifted back into his manly form, he was sure he'd be dead at her feet right now. She wouldn't have hesitated to finish off a wolf. Thank goodness she stopped when she realized he was a man.

"You're from the other side of the mountain, aren't you?" she asked, cocking her head and eying him up and down, still trying to get answers.

"Who cares where I'm from? Remove the arrow. Now!"

"I don't take commands from anyone, and certainly not from the likes of you," she spat, throwing her nose in the air. "You were hunting in my forest, and you deserve to die. I might just walk away and leave you."

"This is nonsense. I haven't killed a thing. Yet. However, that could change soon."

He watched as her green eyes opened wide, when she realized he'd just threatened her. She was surprisingly pretty, and much taller than he figured an elf would be. He'd never seen an elf before in person, except for that irritating little sage. He didn't have much to compare her to. This one was the size of a human. She seemed nothing like that short little sage that he and his brothers despised.

The wench had long, strawberry-blond hair that hung down past the curvy swells of her perky breasts. The elven queen was dressed in a short brown skirt with leather boots up to her knees. She wore a frilly white tunic and a green bodice, laced so tightly that the tops of her breasts spilled out. It excited Zann. He couldn't stop wondering what it would be like to bed an elf. He'd had many women in his time, liking the act of coupling just as much as any man – mayhap even more so. This wench was comely and intriguing. Even though he was wounded, he still felt his libido growing, fed by her image and his thoughts.

"Well, Zann Blackseed, if your words are so sharp, then I think I'll leave you here to fend for yourself." She picked up her bow and arrows and turned to mount her horse again. He was at a disadvantage, and wasn't going to be able to ride his horse back over the mountain with an arrow sticking out of his back end.

"Wait!" he called out to her as she prepared to leave. "You've got to help me."

"Why?" She stopped momentarily with her toe already in the stirrup. "I don't believe I need to do a thing."

"Because, I do know the fae queen. You were right. Alai Na-Dae is . . . she is my mother."

That seemed to change her mind about him. She slowly looked back over her shoulder. "Are you telling me the truth? Or are you just trying to trick me into helping you so you can take advantage of me?"

"Hah!" he said, blowing air from his mouth. "I'm lying here wounded and naked. I'd think it is more likely that you'll be the one to take advantage of me instead."

"Are you really who you say you are?"

"I told you my name before you asked about the fae queen, didn't I?"

"Yes. But what does it matter?"

"Well, how could I have known you were going to ask about her?"

The woman eyed him curiously, seeming to consider things and then gave her answer. "All right," she finally said, leaving her weapon and coming back to help him. "But I don't like being called a blasted elf!" She put the bottom of her foot on his rump and used both hands to yank the arrow out in one quick jerk.

Zann felt the sting, the burn, and the pain, and couldn't keep from crying out. "Aaaaaaaah!" he screamed, closing his eyes tightly, and clenching his jaw, trying to ignore the pain. When he opened his eyes he saw the elf girl cleaning her arrow with a piece of cloth, not worried at all that he might be bleeding to death right now. All she seemed to care about was her bloody arrow. "That hurt," he snapped, getting to his knees. His hand went to his backside to feel the blood.

"Stop whining. You're alive, aren't you?"

"Barely," he scoffed.

"You're lucky I didn't decide to put a second arrow through your heart." She bent down and yanked up a handful of weeds and approached him. She bent over and spit on his backside and then slapped the weeds against his wound, rubbing his ass with the greens. It was an odd thing to do. In a way, it was almost alluring. He wasn't sure if he hated it or liked it.

"What the hell are you doing?" he grunted.

"Hell? What is that word?" she asked him. "I don't know it."

"It's a word I was introduced to recently from my brother's wife who is a witch. It is what her people call The Dark Abyss."

In England, Medea's people had a religion that referred to God and the Devil and Heaven and Hell. In Mura, they had their own deities. When people died, they went to the Land of the Dead, and eventually ended up either in The Haven, or down in the underworld of The Dark Abyss.

"Witch?" Lira stopping rubbing and looked over at him. "Are you talking about the woman who rode the dragon and almost killed us all?"'

"Yep. That's the one." Zann got a bad feeling about mentioning this at all. Mayhap he should have stayed quiet about Medea.

"Y-you're friends with her?" This seemed to frighten her, and rightly so. Medea's dark side was plenty evil.

"She's my sister-by-marriage. Does that concern you?" Then again, mayhap, it wasn't a mistake after all, he started thinking. This could work to his advantage. If nothing else, it might knock the haughty queen off that high pedestal she seemed to put herself on.

"You really are the son of the fae queen, aren't you?"

"I told you I was. Now tell me why you're spitting on me and rubbing weeds on my ass? Is it meant to make me randy?"

"I'm treating the wound, so don't make it sound like it is anything other than that," she retorted. "It'll stop the bleeding until we get back to the castle and I can see to cleaning your wound properly and stitching you up."

"Don't bother." He stood up and turned around. Her eyes traveled down his body and stopped below his waist. Her jaw dropped.

"What's the matter?" He looked down to realize he had an erection the size of Mount Catskulp – the tallest peak of the Picajord Mountains. "Like what you see?" he asked in a cocky manner, smirking and raising a brow. It wasn't a smart thing to do, but he couldn't help himself from being a little playful. Plus, he wanted to see her reaction.

"Oh! You mongrel-headed, conniving, furrowing saddle-goose!"

"What?" Zann scratched his head. "I'm guessing that's not a compliment, but something elves say as an insult? At least get it right. I'm a wolf at times, not a goose."

"You, Zann Blackseed, will answer for hunting in my forest, I promise you that." She turned and looked the other way, speaking to him over her shoulder, not wanting to look at his nakedness. She crossed her arms over her chest. "You'll be tried and punished as is appropriate."

"Punished? Now just a minute. I told you, I didn't kill a thing." He looked back at his rump, trying to see his wound. It still hurt like a demon. Surprisingly, when he touched it, it was no longer bleeding. It seemed the girl hadn't been lying about the weeds after all. "I am here on a mission for King Drustan Grinwald of Evandorm. He commanded me to hunt in the forest of Glint against my will. I couldn't disobey the king's order."

"You are the son of a fae queen and yet you answer to one of those greedy, murderous, human kings?" She glanced back over her shoulder. "Why?"

"More questions?" he asked, walking right up behind her, taking directly into her ear. "I'm not telling you another thing and neither am I going anywhere with you, elf." He turned to make his way back to his horse, but his head dizzied and the world spun all around him. Before he knew it, he felt himself falling, and his world went black as he hit the ground.

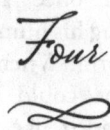

Four

ZANN AWOKE to find himself lying in a bed with his hands and legs tied together. He was clothed, which surprised him. He also found it interesting that his ass didn't hurt as much as it had before.

"Let me out of this," he ground out, pulling at the ropes, realizing these elves knew how to tie a mean knot. These were tight and strong. He figured it wouldn't be hard escaping the wench, but since she obviously had her guards helping her, mayhap it wouldn't be so easy.

Zann rolled over and fell off the bed, ending up on the floor. Surprisingly, no one was around. He decided to use this to his advantage. Closing his eyes, he pushed away his exhaustion and concentrated, using what little energy he had left to shapeshift back into his wolf form. It wasn't usually that hard to do, but with his wound it made things more difficult. He felt the shifting of his bones and the shrinking of his body. Fur started to emerge atop his skin. His nose and ears grew longer. It was an odd feeling, but he'd gotten used to it over the years. The animalistic urges started to fill his body, making him want to howl or at least run.

Finally shifted into his wolf form, he released a

breath and started to pant. His plan had worked. The ropes binding him were now much looser and he was able to slip right out of them, setting himself free.

Then he focused once again, controlling his breathing and visualizing his human self in order to shift back into his manly form. When it was done his heart pounded so loudly he could hear naught but the banging of what sounded like drums in his ears. It wasn't a good idea to shift back and forth so quickly. Usually it took some time for his body to adjust and adapt to his new form. If he didn't allow himself at least a few minutes, he'd pass out. Zann lay naked atop his clothes since his clothes didn't transform with him through his shifts. With his eyes closed he focused on slowing down his breathing.

The door to the chamber made a squeaking noise. His eyes popped open and he looked up to see the elf queen scowling down at him again. She had entered the room and brought two guards with her this time. He groaned.

"It seems you like to flaunt your nakedness, Mister Blackseed." Lira nodded, sending her guards over to get him. "I assure you, no one wants to see it."

"Now, wait a minute," said Zann, holding up his hands in surrender, still not sure he wouldn't pass out from shifting so quickly and with a wound draining his energy as well. "I am unarmed and harmless. And wounded," he added as an afterthought, but it made no difference to the shrew.

"Be careful, he might try to fight you," warned Lira. "Or bite you," she added with a sardonic grin.

"Nay, I won't," Zann answered. "I am at a disadvantage since it takes me a few minutes to get my bearings again after I shift."

"Oh, so that's how you got out of the knots I tied." The queen glanced at him from the corners of her eyes.

"You are the one who tied me up, not your guards?" It impressed him that she had the ability to make such ferocious knots.

"Shall we throw him in the dungeon, my queen?" asked one of her guards, reaching out for him.

"Nay. Let him dress," she commanded. Once he was clothed, she gave her guards instructions once again. "Leave us."

"My queen, it is not advisable to leave you alone with a stranger," protested one of her guards.

"He's dangerous. We need to protect you," said the other.

"I'm sure he's harmless enough," she answered. "At least for now."

"But my lady, what if he is one of those . . . from the portal?" the guard asked in a low voice.

"The portal?" That took Zann's interest. He finished dressing and stood up, still feeling a little dizzy. Reaching out to steady himself, he sat down on a chair. The clothes he wore were those of an elf, and it wasn't to his liking at all. They were too small and rubbed on his wound. They felt tight and uncomfortable. Plus, he looked like a blasted dolt!

"Do you know anything about portals?" asked Lira.

"That depends." Zann saw a pitcher and goblet on the table, and poured himself a drink. "Which portal are you talking about?"

"Go," the woman commanded her men. "And close the door behind you."

"Aye, my queen." The guards left them, closing the door as instructed. Lira walked over to join Zann at the table.

"Well?" he asked, taking a drink of the liquid and making a face. "Damn. Is this some of that dandelion wine like the fae drink?" he asked, peering into the goblet. "Don't you have any ale or mayhap whisky instead? This tastes awful."

"That isn't dandelion wine," she answered, looking as if she knew a secret.

"It's not?" He took another sip but it still tasted like dirty stockings to him. "Well, whatever it is, it is not appealing at all. How can you elves drink it?"

"We don't drink it," she told him.

"Huh?" He looked back to the goblet in his hand. "Well what do you do with it then?"

"That, Mister Blackseed, is the liniment potion I used to cleanse your wound with. It is made from herbs and mixed with spit and a just a touch of spirits. Since it's already been used to clean your wound, I wouldn't suggest using it for anything, let alone drink it."

"Egads, now you tell me!" He quickly put the cup down, not wanting to think where that liquid had been. Not to mention, the thought of drinking spit was repulsive.

"Your wound is mostly healed. The herbs worked quickly and you didn't even need stitches after all. Still, you'd better try to relax for now."

"I didn't need stitches? Those must be some powerful, magical herbs you used." He turned his head to look down to his butt. "How bad was it?"

"You'll live. Now, tell me all you know about portals." She pulled out a chair and sat across from him at the table, leaning forward with interest.

"Why do you ask about them?"

"I have my reasons." It was obvious she wasn't going to tell him anything more.

"Well, what will I get in return for giving you information?" He figured it wouldn't hurt to try to strike some kind of deal since he had something she now wanted.

"I'll spare your life," she told him.

"I see." He picked up the goblet and stared into it again. "Are you sure you don't have any ale?"

She sighed and got up and walked across the room, coming back with another pitcher and goblet. She poured him a cup and handed it to him, thumping the pitcher down on the table and sitting back down. "You've got your ale, now talk."

"My, you are a bossy one, aren't you?" Zann sniffed the contents of the cup, not sure the wench wasn't trying to trick him into drinking spit or vile liquid again. It smelled like ale and looked normal enough. He supposed it was drinkable after all.

"My daughter was almost abducted by a man coming through a portal," she told him.

He was taking a sip and stopped, slowly lowering the cup. "Really?"

"Yes."

"You have a daughter?"

"Aye," she said, rolling her eyes. "Now tell me everything you know about portals."

"Well, let's see. There was the portal to the Land of the Dead. That was pretty horrifying and not easy to close. There were lots of dark spirits wailing and basically possessing the dead, and that sort of stuff." He chuckled and took another drink.

"Was it red and blue?"

"I'd say it was more murky and dark."

"Nay, that isn't it. Plus, I didn't see any wailing spirits. I don't think that's what this one was. Are there more portals?"

"Well, sure. There was the portal that Medea came through. The one that led to England."

"England? Where is that?"

"I'm not exactly sure. But the portal had lots of bright swirling colors. Mainly yellow and pink I believe."

"Nay, this one wasn't that bright. It was basically red and blue. What else can you tell me?"

"Well, one thing about portals that I've learned is that they don't last long. Plus, one never knows where they will open or when they will close. It is also a mystery as to where they lead.

"I found this, after the man disappeared." She held out a gauntlet for him to see.

"Really. Interesting," he said, putting down his cup. He reached out for the glove, inspecting it closer.

"I need to track the man that the gauntlet belongs to. Can you do it in your wolf form?"

"Me? Nay," he said, shaking his head and pushing the glove back across the table toward her. "I don't want anything to do with portals anymore. Each time, they've been nothing but trouble."

"Please. I need your help since you've already had experience with portals. I need to know where it leads, and why someone is trying to abduct my daughter. I'm afraid it might happen again."

"Sorry. I'm not for hire. Besides, I already have a job." Zann chugged down the rest of the ale and got up off the chair. "Speaking of that, King Grinwald will be expecting me. Now, if you'll be kind enough to return my weapons and horse to me, I'll be on my way. That is, unless I'm still your prisoner."

"Prisoner? Nay, of course not," she answered, the idea of him being her prisoner seeming to bother her. "If you must leave, your weapon belt is on the table and your horse is tethered outside the stable," she told him.

He saw his weapon belt on a table and walked over to don it.

"My clothes were in my travel bag. You might have dressed me in them, instead of these jester-looking thin rags that you elves wear." He looked down at his brown and green vest and green trews that ended just above his knees. He supposed on an elf the trews would reach their ankles. He wore a white tunic open at the top and his chest hairs stuck out. And his feet were crammed into soft green, pointy-toed shoes. "I think you forgot the hat with bells on it."

"Don't be silly. We don't wear bells. That would give away our presence," she answered.

"Mama, you're back." A little girl with strawberry blond curls burst into the room, running toward them. She stopped suddenly when she noticed Zann. A handmaid was right behind her.

"I'm sorry, my queen, she got away from me," apologized the handmaid, hurrying after the girl, reaching out and pulling her back.

"Who are you?" asked the little girl with wide blue eyes, breaking away from the handmaid and running over to her mother for protection. She crawled up onto Lira's lap.

"I'm Zann Blackseed," he told the child. "What's your name?"

The little girl hid her face against her mother's chest. "I'm scared," she whimpered.

"Her name is Valindra. She is four years old and very impressionable," explained Lira. "So please, do not frighten her."

"Mama, is he going to try to take me through a portal like that other man?" asked the little girl, peeking out at him. "I don't want to go."

Zann's heart went out to the child. He could see how frightened she was, and he didn't want her to be scared of him. He saw her looking at his weapons, so he lowered his hands to try to cover them.

"Don't worry, Valindra, I'm not going to take you anywhere," said Zann. "I'm here to help you, not hurt you."

The girl looked directly at him when he used her name. "You are?" she asked, sounding cautious yet curious at the same time.

"So, you will help us, then. Good," Lira said, making Zann want to kick himself for saying that since he had no plan to help anyone other than himself. He especially didn't want to get involved with elves.

"Nay, I didn't mean it like that. Not really. I'm leaving for Evandorm, like I said." Zann felt the need to get out of there quickly and headed for the door.

"If I find you poaching in the woods of Glint again, I'll not be so forgiving next time, Mister Blackseed," the queen warned him.

"Just call me Zann, Queenie," he said with a chuckle. "And don't worry, I don't plan on hunting here anymore because there doesn't seem to be anything worth the chase." He turned and headed out the door, making his way quickly out of the castle, down a long, covered walkway that led to the courtyard.

Once out in the open, Zann got his first look at Castle Glint. He had been unconscious when they brought him here. He turned around, taking in the sight of the building that looked more like a gigantic temple of some sort instead of an actual castle.

The place was surprisingly pretty. Made of stone, it had long walkways lined with pillars that seemed to lead all the way around the keep. There were several balconies on each side, overlooking the tall walls and the village. The roof was steep and covered with bright green tiles. There was a lot of green everywhere he looked. He decided it was an elf thing since they were said to be very earth oriented.

Nighttime was closing in fast. It would take a while to get over the mountain and back home. Zann didn't want to be traveling on the steep cliffs at dark, so he had to hurry.

He noticed several buildings lining the bailey, recognizing one of them as the stable so he headed in that direction.

"Wait," he heard from behind him, seeing the elf queen running out of the keep after him, with her daughter trailing a little ways behind her. "You haven't told me anything yet about the portal."

"I don't know what you want me to say," he ground out, not liking the wench's persistence. This wasn't any of his concern, and neither did he want it to be. He wanted to distance himself from this elven woman's problem quickly before he got talked into doing something he had no intention of doing.

He made his way to the stable, seeing his horse tethered outside of the building just like she'd told him. Good. This would make it easier for a fast departure. His horse was also still saddled, so he was ready to ride. Zann mounted his steed, looking down at the woman who stared up at him with pleading eyes that were just as green as everything else in this land of elven magic. Suddenly, a chill travelled up his spine and he had the undeniable feeling that something was wrong.

"Mama!" cried little Valindra from the center of the courtyard. Her voice held fear.

Zann's head snapped up to see a portal in swirling colors of red and blue opening right in front of Valindra. A man dressed in a dark cloak reached out, grabbing for the little girl.

"Valindra! Nay!" shouted Lira, turning and running

to try to help her daughter. From atop the horse, Zann could see the portal flickering and starting to get smaller already.

"Damn it!" he swore, kicking his heels into the sides of his horse, speeding toward the portal. He had to save the queen's daughter. If the child was taken, there was no telling where she would go, or if they would ever see her again. He had no idea if there was someone or something evil on the other side.

Zann made it to the portal before Lira. He reached down, grabbing the little girl's arm. She was already being dragged in, and the portal was starting to close. The man held on tightly to Valindra, pulling her back to him as Zann tried to tug her the other way. Valindra screamed and cried as the portal started to dissipate with the little girl half in and half out of it. This wasn't good. He needed to move faster. Holding on to his horse with just his legs, Zann reached down with both arms to scoop up the little girl. He thankfully managed to snatch her away from her abductor, bringing the child up atop the horse with him. The girl landed with a plop across his lap. He looked back to see the portal close with a snap, taking the abductor with it, and disappearing from sight.

"Valindra!" screamed the queen, running to join them.

The little girl clung to Zann, crying. He pulled her closer to him, wrapping his arms around her in a protective manner, trying to calm her.

"It's all right. I have you, sweetheart," he said, running his hand over the girl's back. Her whole body shook in fear. She clung to him so tightly that he found it hard to breathe. His eyes closed and he wavered, feeling like he was about to retch. He still hadn't settled himself from his shift. Now, with this and his wound still draining his energy, he felt lightheaded as well.

"Give her to me. Hand over my child!" shouted Lira, reaching up for her daughter.

"All right. Calm down, Queenie," said Zann, handing the girl to her.

Lira clutched her daughter to her chest, rocking her, trying to calm her. Zann saw the tears in Lira's eyes. He also noticed that her body shook in fear. So did the child's. Damn it, he couldn't leave now. It wouldn't feel right if he just turned and rode away. These people needed him. He was their only chance of figuring out what was going on. Part of him wanted to leave here and never return after the wench shot him. Another part of him didn't want to go anywhere until he was certain Lira and her daughter were safe. Releasing a deep sigh, he got off the horse.

"All right. Let's go inside where we can talk," he told Lira, reaching into the travel bag attached to the horse, pulling out his own clothes to wear. "I'll answer any of your questions I can concerning portals. Mayhap between the two of us, we can figure out what is going on here."

Five

AGAINST ZANN'S BETTER JUDGEMENT,

he decided to stay at Castle Glint for now, instead of heading home. Little Valindra clung tightly to her mother, too frightened to let go. Zann's heart went out to both of them after what just happened. He'd seen a dark figure snatch up the girl and nearly sweep her away into who-knows-where. It had been truly frightening. He was only glad he had been there to help save the child.

After returning his horse to the stable and changing his clothes, he glanced out the open gate, getting his first look at the elven village beyond the castle. Glint was adjacent to the Whispering Dale, but there was a forest between the two realms, blocking their views of each other. While the home of the fae folk was filled with flowers and fauna of all kinds everywhere you looked, the elven village was quite different.

Little cottages spotted the landscape, and each of them had a circle of bushes enclosing each house into a private space. He wasn't sure if this meant the elves were unsociable or just liked their privacy. Or perhaps it was somehow done for protection, he decided. Mayhap magic was interwoven in the circles around each home making a barrier from outsiders. He could only imagine the purpose since this was all new to him and he knew nothing at all about elves. There were also lots of trees and bushes everywhere, and rolling hills of bright green grass. Everything looked so alive, healthy and vibrant.

As he headed back to the keep, he realized the castle of Glint was smaller than those he was familiar with from the other side of the mountain. Still, it was fortified with a high brick wall around it to keep out unwanted people. This land of Glint seemed to be a tidy place. Everything looked neat and in order. Every little thing seemed to have its purpose. Fields of crops could be seen up on the hillside, as well as an orchard filled with colorful trees laden with fruit.

"Thank you, Zann," came Lira's sweet voice. "If it wasn't for you, my daughter would be gone right now."

"I have never seen that portal before," he explained, walking next to her.

"Did you get a good look at the warrior trying to take my daughter?" she asked.

"Nay, I didn't. I'm sorry."

"Lira! Lira, what happened?" An older woman ran to them from the keep, being followed by an army of elves. Zann was surprised to see that a lot of the soldiers were women. They were all as tall as humans and had either blond or reddish-colored hair. The very undeniable fact they were elves could be seen by their pointy ears.

"Aunt Sasha, this is Zann Blackseed," she introduced him.

"Hello," said Zann with a nod, getting a scowl in return from the woman. She had graying hair piled atop her head. Her eyes were narrowed into slits and her mouth pursed. He could tell by her expression and the way the woman's fists were on her hips that she didn't like him or trust him in the least.

"My dear, do you really think it's wise to bring strangers into Glint right now?" asked the woman.

"I shot Zann with an arrow, so I had to bring him back to the castle to heal him," Lira explained. "He was just leaving when the portal opened again and that dark stranger tried to take Valindra."

"It was scary," said Valindra in a high little voice.

"This has got to stop," said the woman.

"I agree," Zann answered. "Queen Lira, can't you use your magic to protect your daughter? There must be something you can do."

The women looked at each other oddly, but didn't answer. Zann felt as if there was a secret he wasn't privy to knowing.

"Lira, a guard has just informed me that your father has returned," Sasha reported.

"Oh, good," said Zann. "I'm sure the king will be able to help you protect your daughter as well as the kingdom."

"My father isn't king," said Lira. "And this is a queendom, not a kingdom."

"What? He's not? It is? I don't understand."

"The elven queendom is ruled by women," Lira explained.

Zann chuckled, thinking she was jesting at first. After all, there was no such thing as a queendom. Was there? "Oh, you're serious," he said, noticing she wasn't smiling.

"Of course, she is serious," spat the woman named Sasha. "How can you not know this?"

"Sasha, you must realize that Zann is from the other side of the mountain," Lira explained. "Plus, we purposely live a life of seclusion, so it is understandable that he doesn't know about us and our ways."

"No one knows much about the elves where I come from," Zann admitted. "We only know of one, and that one, we'd rather forget. He is a rather pesky elf that shows up from time to time."

"Here, Sasha. Please take my daughter." Lira put the girl down and Sasha took her hand. "Guards, watch over my daughter until my return. Don't leave Valindra's side. I need to go talk to my father. Zann, will you please accompany me?"

"I don't know," said Zann, really not wanting to get involved. "King Grinwald is waiting for me to return. I really need to leave for Evandorm soon."

"Nightfall is already closing in. It will be dangerous traveling over the mountain in the dark. It would be best if you stayed the night in Glint and traveled in the morning instead. Please?" she asked, looking up at Zann with those big green eyes that held all the hope in the world. Something about this elf wench intrigued him and drew him in. He found himself not able to say no.

"All right, let's go talk to your father, but I am leaving right afterwards."

"Thank you. It's not a far trip to his home."

"His home? Doesn't he live in the castle?"

"Nay, that's not where he lives at all."

It sounded odd to Zann that the queen's father didn't live within the castle walls but he wasn't going to question it because he really didn't care. All he wanted to do was talk with the man to fulfill his commitment to Lira, and then get the hell out of here.

"All right, then. Let's go to his home," he agreed, looking back at the cottages dotting the area in front of the castle. They all looked quaint and inviting. Some were bigger than the others, but none of them looked elaborate enough to house the father of a queen. "Which one of them is your father's home?"

"Oh, none of those," she told him. "My father lives over there."

"Where?" Zann turned and his gaze followed her finger to where she pointed. His heart sank in his chest. There atop a pinnacle cliff next to the castle was a small house built into the rocks, way up high. It looked like a steep climb to get up there. It was evident now that this was not going to be a fast trip after all. "We have to climb all the way up there to talk to him? Really?" It was the most absurd thing he'd ever heard. Who in their right mind would live all alone up on top of a steep cliff like that?

"Yes," she said, leading the way. Zann followed. "How else do you suppose we'll get there?"

"Can't you just bring me with you and use your magic to transport us to the top of the cliff instead?"

"Nay, we'll walk. It's not that far of a climb."

With every step Zann took, his wound began to ache more and more. This was going to be one hell of a climb for someone who recently had an arrow in him. He didn't like the idea at all and already regretted saying he'd go with her.

Huffing and puffing, they finally made it to the top of the cliff. Before them was a small hanging wooden bridge that swayed in the wind and spanned a deep and frightening gorge. He held on to the hand ropes of the bridge and followed her, cursing himself inwardly for getting involved. Once they made it across the bridge without plunging to their deaths, Zann found himself standing in front of a little odd-looking hut made of wood. It was built right into the rock and had a bright blue roof.

"We're here," said Lira, stopping at the front door. She reached out for the doorknob, but hesitated.

"Well, let's go in," said Zann, needing to rest and desperately wanting a drink. "What are you waiting for?" The wind whipped his hair around. The temperature up here was much cooler than down below.

"I – I haven't been on the best terms with my father for quite a while now," she told him. He heard the nervousness in her voice. She didn't seem to want to enter the house.

"Well, I can see why you're not on good terms. If I had to climb up here every time I wanted to talk with him, I'd be on bad terms as well."

"Zann, I banished him here," she blurted out, surprising him. "It's my fault he lives atop a cliff instead of at the castle."

"You did what?" Zann couldn't begin to understand why she would do such a foolish thing. Especially to her own father. That is, not until the door swung open and he heard a familiar voice as well as some words he never wanted to hear again.

"Oh, surprise, surprise, it's the big oaf!"

Zann's head snapped up and he groaned. "What are you doing here, sage?" He just couldn't get away from this pesky little man. The elf seemed to show up everywhere Zann went. Now it seemed that Elric had a job as doorman or house servant to the father of the queen.

"Oh, you already know each other," said Lira. "That's nice."

"Unfortunately," Zann mumbled.

"Can we come inside?" asked Lira. "We need to speak with you, Father."

"Father?" Zann gasped. The last thing he ever expected was that the irritating, pesky elf was the father of the elven queen. This made things even worse.

"Come in, but don't touch anything, fool," spat the sage looking directly at Zann.

"You . . . live here," said Zann, stepping inside, taking a look around. It was a small house, but everything was as neat as a pin. It was clean and organized. Somehow this didn't surprise Zann in the least. He'd seen the magical touch of the sage when the elf fixed up Darium's house, meaning to make it his own recently.

There were crystals and gemstones decorating the place, and lots of scented beeswax candles burning everywhere, making the room smell sweet from cinnamon and spices. Cheery flower-print curtains hung over the windows. Elric even had decorative circles of interwoven ribbons and strips of leather hanging in the windows for some odd reason. He half-wondered if they were some kind of talismans to ward off evil spirits. Then he decided they weren't, since not even evil spirits would want to be around Elric purposely.

"Of course, I live here," scoffed the sage. "What did you think? I just come up here for fun because I have nothing else to do?"

"Nay, I wouldn't have thought that," remarked Zann, knowing how busy the little man kept himself on the wrong side of the mountain.

"Father, I'm sorry it's been so long since we've spoken," said Lira. "However, I need your wise counsel."

"Hah!" said Zann, biting his tongue afterwards. He supposed it wasn't polite to laugh at an elven sage, or to insult a queen's father. Still, when he heard the words wise counsel attached to the elf, it seemed ridiculous to him. He couldn't wait to tell his brothers about this.

"Sit down," snapped Elric, glaring at him.

"All right," said Zann, looking down to see the furniture was all tiny. It was the appropriate proportions for the little man, but much too small for someone Zann's size. If he sat on one of the chairs, his large body was sure to break it. "On further thought, I'll stand. I'm fine."

Lira sat down and made herself comfortable on one of the little chairs. The elf settled himself across from her. Zann walked over and stared out the open window. From this height atop the cliff, Zann could see the Isle of Denwop clearly. He noticed the volcano that sent up a thin trail of smoke from the island of the giants. The elves feared giants, since the big beasts loved to eat elves for a snack.

"Father, a portal opened and a warrior tried to grab Valindra," Lira told him, directly.

"Twice," Zann added.

"What?" The elf zipped over to Zann with his hands on his hips. "You had something to do with this, I know you did. Just admit it."

"Nay! I didn't," Zann protested. "If you were really such a wise sage, you would know that."

"Father, Zann actually saved your granddaughter from being abducted," Lira told him. "You should be thanking him instead of accusing him of anything."

"That's right," Zann answered a grin.

"Thank him? Thank the wolf?" asked Elric, cackling like an old hen. "I still say the big oaf caused it to happen somehow."

"I don't need to stay here and take this abuse. I'm leaving." Zann turned and headed to the door of the small house, but Elric ran over in a blur and blocked his path.

"If my daughter wants you to stay, then I'll let you," said Elric.

"No, thanks. I don't want to stay." Zann reached over the elf, trying to open the door. Before he knew it, he was knocked to the ground and the elf was standing atop his chest. "Mmmph," Zann moaned, feeling the pain in his ass more than ever now. This time, he couldn't say it was only from his wound.

"We need to figure out who is trying to capture Valindra," said Lira. "I was able to get this off her abductor." She pulled out the gauntlet and held it up.

"Let me see that." Elric rushed over and took the glove from her. He sniffed it and studied it, and then he did the oddest thing. He licked it. Damn, this elf was weird, thought Zann.

"There's dirt as well as ash on the gauntlet. Ash from a volcano," announced Elric.

"Volcano?" asked Lira.

"Of course. It's from the Isle of Denwop – the only volcano around." Zann stood up and brushed off his clothes. "It's obvious now that the abductor must be a giant."

"Nay, the man I saw wasn't a giant. You know that, Zann, since you saw him too. Mayhap the portal leads somewhere else. After all, the abductor wasn't any taller than the rest of us," said Lira.

"You mean, most of us," commented Zann, getting a nasty glare from Elric in return.

"You and Valindra are not safe in Glint," stated Elric. "You must leave here at once. The abductor knows where you are and will keep coming back until he gets what he's after."

"Leave?" Lira seemed horrified. "This is our home, Father. I am Queen of Glint. I cannot leave my castle or my people."

"You must. Just for a while," explained Elric. "At least until the big oaf and his brothers can figure out how to close the portal for good and stop it from opening again."

"Me? What? Nay," said Zann, shaking his head furiously. "I'm sorry but I am not getting involved. This doesn't concern me in the least. You and all your elven friends are on your own."

"You and Valindra will stay at Evandorm Castle where the wolf can keep an eye on you," instructed Elric.

"Ooooh, no. Nay, that is not going to happen," protested Zann, lifting up his hands to ward off the man's crazy suggestion. "I might live at Evandorm, but I'm only a huntsman. I don't even have a chamber in the castle. I sleep out in a small room attached to the kennels. Nope. Sorry, there is no room."

"I am King Grinwald's head cook now," boasted Elric. "The king has granted me a large room off the kitchen."

"He has?" Zann didn't like the sound of this at all. He wondered how the elf got Grinwald to do that. Zann had been trying to get a chamber inside the castle for years now and he'd never been given one. Zann was a huntsman, not just a blasted cook that was naught more than a servant! This wasn't fair at all.

"My daughter and granddaughter will stay in my chamber," continued the sage. "Besides, with all the soldiers around, they'll be well protected. Much safer than thinking this one would be of any help." Elric nodded sharply at Zann.

"Well protected at Evandorm?" spat Zann. "Are you forgetting the small fact that you are all elves? Magic has been banned in Mura. If the king finds out who you are, you'll all be killed immediately. This is a crazy idea and I cannot allow it."

"I agree with Zann, Father," said Lira. "It's much too dangerous. I can't let anything happen to Valindra."

"Then take your daughter to Kasculbough Castle instead," said Elric. "The big oaf's brother is king there. He won't care if you're an elf. After all, he is part fae himself. Plus, he's married to a witch. He doesn't ban magic."

"Oh, that's a good idea. It won't matter to them. I'll start packing immediately." Lira got up and headed for the door.

"Wait a minute! Don't I have a say in this?" asked Zann, feeling severely left out.

"You said you didn't want to get involved," Lira reminded him.

"Aye, but if you are coming to my side of the mountain and staying with my brother uninvited, then I am involved whether I like it or not. I should have a say in the situation."

"Nay. I don't think so," said the elf, biting at a hangnail, acting nonchalant.

"I'm sorry, but no one is going to Kasculbough," Zann told them. "I'm not letting my family get involved this time."

"I see," said the elf, rubbing his chin. "Well, I'd better get to sleep. I need to be back at Evandorm in the morning so I need to be well-rested." The sage stretched and yawned. "After all, I certainly wouldn't want to be so tired that I accidentally slip up and mention to King Grinwald that his huntsman is a wolf in lamb's clothing now, would I?"

"Damn you!" spat Zann, knowing that the elf would purposely do just that if Zann didn't agree to take the queen and her daughter to Kasculbough. He had enough trouble with King Grinwald from Evandorm as it was. Now that the elf was the king's head cook, this made matters even worse for Zann. "Fine," he agreed, having no other choice. "We'll go to Kasculbough immediately, and I'll explain everything to my brothers."

"We'll never be able to get there before night sets in.

We'll have to wait and leave in the morning," said Lira. "It would be too dangerous to travel through the mountains in the dark."

"Wait a minute," protested Zann. "I'm having second thoughts about staying in an elven castle for the night. Just forget it."

"Then stay with the fae folk," said Elric. "Or, you can stay right here with me. I don't mind. But you'll have to sleep on the floor."

Each option sounded worse and worse to Zann. He certainly didn't want to stay with the sage! And if he went to the Whispering Dale, he'd be forced to face his mother. Nay, he wasn't ready for that yet. Mayhap he'd just sleep in the forest, he decided. If he was in his wolf form, it wouldn't matter.

"Stay clear of the forests," said the sage, obviously knowing what he was thinking. "After all, if you've got an unhealed wound, the smell of blood will only attract every animal out there."

"I suppose you're right," said Zann, his hand going to his sore bottom.

"You'll stay at the castle and I won't hear another word about it," Lira insisted. "Now come. We'll go back to the great hall for something to eat."

"Great," Zann mumbled, following the queen out the door. He wasn't sure what elves ate, but something told him it was going to be even worse than the food of the fae folk. This was not something he was looking forward to at all.

Six

LIRA COULD TELL the occupants of the castle, especially her aunt, didn't like the idea of Zann staying there, even if it was only for a night. He was unwelcome, since he wasn't of the elven realm. She didn't care. The man had saved her daughter from being taken through the portal, and that is all that mattered to her. Valindra wanted Zann here, so Lira wouldn't disappoint her daughter.

"You'll sit here at the dais. Next to me," said Lira, leading the way up the three steps to the table on the raised platform. Valindra was already there, her seat being on the opposite side of her mother.

"Your kingdom doesn't seem much different than Evandorm really." Zann took in his surroundings as he headed to his seat.

"Queendom," she corrected him.

"What?" He looked up and his eyes darted back and forth. "Ah, yes. Of course. Queendom," he said with the sound of amusement in his voice.

"So . . . where is your king?" he asked. "Or husband, I should say. I'm not sure what his title would be in a queendom." Zann chuckled again and sat down. She noticed him wince a little because of his wound.

Lira sat as well. "My husband is dead. He was killed in our last battle with the giants."

"Oh," he said, becoming suddenly silent. "I'm sorry. I didn't mean to –"

"Enough said." She held up a halting hand.

"So your mother is dead then, I gather, since you are queen?" He reached out and broke off a piece of bread from the platter in front of him.

"She is."

"How long has she been gone?" He ripped off a hunk of bread with his teeth, reminding her of his wolf form with the way he ate.

"Four years now."

"What did she die from?" He kept firing questions at her, making Lira feel extremely uncomfortable.

"It's better if you ask less questions, and just eat. You need to regain your strength after your unfortunate accident."

"Accident? Is that what we're calling it now?" He chewed as he spoke.

"We need to talk about the portal." She put some food on her daughter's plate and helped herself to some wine.

"I don't know what you want me to say."

"How did you close those other two portals that you spoke of earlier?" she asked.

"This is different," he answered. His chewing slowed. "With those, we had . . . things coming through the portals and into Mura. Yours is going the opposite direction it seems. No one is trying to get in, but rather take someone out instead." His eyes fell on Valindra who was listening intently to their every word. "I think

I'll have some of that. What is it you're eating, Valindra?"

"It's my favorite," said the little girl, holding up a soggy piece of green. "Dandelion salad with candied acorns. Want to try it?" She started to hand the leaf to him.

"Nay, that's fine. I'll get my own, but thank you." He looked back at the bowl of greens on the dais and groaned.

Lira giggled inwardly, knowing that he was looking for meat.

"The cook will bring roasted roakan and perch when this course is finished," she informed him.

"Roakan? Oh, that thing that is like a deer. I didn't think elves ate meat since you stopped me from killing one earlier."

"Of course, we eat meat, although we limit the amount of animals killed for consumption. I only stopped you because you are a poacher."

His mood seemed to suddenly change. "All right, good. I'd like to taste that."

"I'll bet you would," she mumbled, wondering how much game he would have stolen from the forest of Glint if she hadn't stopped him with her arrow.

* * *

Zann was given Valindra's room for the night, since the little girl insisted on sleeping with her mother. He tossed and turned in the uncomfortable bed, feeling the pain in his backside more than ever. The weeds and spit the queen used to heal his wound and take away the pain, seemed to be wearing off. If his mother wasn't in the Whispering Dale, he might have considered going to the fae to see if they could heal him. But not wanting to confront his mother at this time, he decided to just stay here instead and continue back to Evandorm in the morning. He was sure his brother's wife, Talia, or some of her fae sisters or mother would be able to do something for him there.

After quite some time, he finally managed to drift off. Zann wasn't sure how long he'd been sleeping before he awoke with a start. The intense feeling of someone watching him made him shiver. He looked back over his shoulder to see that damned portal opening again, this time right next to the bed. Zann jumped to his feet, scooping up his sword from the bedside table. He spun around to see swirling colors of blue and red as well as a dark cloaked figure emerging from the center of the portal. It was that man again. The little girl's abductor. It had to be. He wasn't sure what to do or how to make it all go away. So, the best thing he could think of was to ask the intruder what he wanted.

"Who are you and what do you want?" Zann growled, holding his sword out with two hands in front of him as a dark cloaked figure stopped and stood there looking at him from just inside the portal.

"Help," he thought he heard the man whisper. "Lira . . . I'm . . . here."

This was odd indeed. It almost seemed as if the abductor was calling out for help, but that didn't make any sense at all to Zann. He curiously took a step closer to the bright opening of the portal, cocking his head trying to see more. Zann couldn't see the man's face, but when the figure looked up, he was sure he saw two bright green eyes that reminded him of Lira's.

The door to his chamber opened just then, taking his attention. Zann turned his head just for a moment, but when he looked back, the man and the portal were gone.

"Zann? Are you awake? Your mother is here," said Lira, poking her head inside the room.

"My mother?" Looking back to where he'd seen the portal, there was no trace of it or the dark cloaked man now. Zann slowly lowered his sword wondering if he had imagined the whole thing. After all, he was half-asleep when it happened. Hurriedly, he dressed, then quickly lit a candle. "Why is my mother bothering me in the middle of the night?" he complained, not wanting to see the woman. Especially not here, not now.

"Zann? I read your mind that you were hurt and staying here in Glint. I came to help you." His mother pushed the door wide open and brashly entered the room before she'd been invited.

"Really. Well, Mother, reading my mind is an invasion of my privacy and you have no right to do it," he snapped, sitting on the bed to don his boots.

Alai Na-Dae, or Alaina as everyone called her, hurried over to the bedside. His mother had a look of concern in her eyes. Zann didn't want to see it, because he refused to believe she really cared about him at all.

"I'm sorry, son, but when I realized you were so close, I just had to see you. How can I help you?" asked Alaina.

"You can help by leaving here, that's what you can do," he grunted. "You can also stop following me around."

"Zann! That is not respectful to speak to your mother that way," said Lira. "Plus, she is the Fae Queen and should be treated as such."

Zann didn't want to deal with any of this anymore. "I've changed my mind about helping you. I'm leaving now, and I am going back to Evandorm. Alone. By myself," he added the latter part just to stress his point.

Strapping on his weapon belt, he slid his sword into the scabbard and headed for the door.

"Son, wait, please," begged his mother.

"It was a mistake to come here, and now I am sorry that I did," he told them.

Zann left the women behind, hurrying out to the courtyard. To his surprise, it was already daybreak. He felt the fresh breeze against his face and stopped for a moment, looking out over at the Masked Sea that was just beyond the castle. The air on his face comforted him, making him feel less anxious for some reason. He closed his eyes and breathed it in, slowly letting out a deep breath. Then, he turned to go, bumping into his mother.

"Ah!" he shouted, her sudden appearance right in front of him, scaring him. "Don't do that!" His mother, being an elemental of the air, had the ability to dissipate and reappear somewhere else instantly, traveling on the air.

"I saw you just now, breathing in the air," said his mother. "That is the fae inside you, answering to the element. It'll comfort you if you just let it."

"I am not a fae, so stop saying that."

"It'll take you time, but you'll accept it eventually, just like your brothers have."

"Mother, what do you want?"

"I came to help you, son."

"Help me? Why do you even care? I don't need your help. When I needed you years ago, you were nowhere to be found. Now, I can't seem to shake you."

"Zann, we're ready," called out Lira, holding the hand of her daughter as they headed toward him. Zann groaned. It seemed he hadn't left quick enough. Lira had a large bag of her belongings thrown over one shoulder. "My father should be here by now. Have you seen him?" She looked around.

"I haven't, and neither do I want to," said Zann, feeling really agitated now.

"He is probably still up at his home on the cliff," said Lira.

"Then that is where he'll stay, because I'm leaving." Zann hurried off to the stable.

"I'll get him," he heard his mother say.

When he got to the stable, lo and behold, the stupid sage and his mother were both already there. He would never get used to these magical beings traveling so quickly and popping up where he didn't want them to be.

"Trying to leave without me?" asked Elric.

"What does it matter?" said Zann saddling his horse. "You have magic. You can just zip on over to Evandorm in the flash of an eye. So can my mother. I am guessing the elf queen and princess can do the same. So just go! You don't need to wait for me."

"My daughter can't do that," said Elric. "She lost her magic."

"What?" It surprised Zann to hear this.

"Father!" said Lira, entering the stable to overhear their conversation. "Did you have to tell him?" She didn't look happy about it at all.

"So, it seems the queen of the elven queendom doesn't have a lick of magic after all." Zann chuckled, being amused. "No wonder you wanted my help. What about her?" he asked, nodding to Valindra. "Does she have magic?"

"It's too soon to tell," said Lira. "Elven magic for a child doesn't exist. It will only start to emerge when she turns into an adult. Valindra is only four, so it will be some time yet."

"I see," said Zann, realizing just how vulnerable the woman and her daughter really were. "Well, what happened to your magic? Why and how did you lose it?"

"I – I'm not sure," she answered, looking down at the ground.

"Perhaps someone should tell the man in the portal you don't have magic," said Zann. "Then, at least, mayhap he wouldn't be calling for Lira and asking for her help." He pulled the strap tight on the saddle and climbed atop the horse.

"Who called out for me to help them?" asked Lira. "Are you saying you saw the man in the portal again?"

"Aye. I thought you and my mother saw him as well when you walked into my room. Didn't you?'"

"Mama, he was coming to get me. I'm scared." Valindra clung to her mother.

"I think my father is right in saying we should leave here. As soon as I have a horse saddled, we'll be ready to go," stated Lira.

"You don't need a horse. I'll give you all a lift back to the other side of the mountain," offered Alaina.

"Nay, Mother, don't do that," said Zann, but it was too late. The air started swirling around them. Before Zann knew what was happening, all of them – even his horse – were lifted up into the air, out of the stable, and traveling high above Glint Castle. "Naaaaaaay. Put me down," screamed Zann, holding on to his horse, as he and the others were lifted above the Picajord Mountains high up into the clouds.

His mother, being an Elemental of the Air, was able to control the weather. She could also use the element of air to her advantage to transport people. This felt terrifying to Zann. Darium had told him about his little flight in the air, but he never said it would be so frightening and awkward.

The whirlwind of air traveled over the tops of the mountains, setting them all down right inside the courtyard of Kasculbough Castle. When the wind stopped, Zann was still atop his horse. The women and the sage were standing on the ground next to him.

Soldiers of the castle ran up with their weapons drawn. Servants and villagers were frightened, running to hide in the shadows.

"Wait! Don't attack," Zann called out, jumping off his horse, holding his hands in the air. "I'm the king's brother. No one is going to hurt you."

"Zann? Mother? Is that you?" Zann's brother, Rhys ran down the steps of the keep followed by his wife, Medea. Rhys had their two-year-old daughter, Lily-Rae in his arms. Rhys was the youngest of the Blackseed brothers and also the largest. He was a big, sturdy man who had the power of great strength and the ability to heal himself. "How nice of you to visit, but next time warn me when you're coming. Put away your swords, it's just my family," Rhys told his guards. "Everyone, as you were."

"Aye, my king," shouted one of the knights, pulling the other soldiers back. They headed back to their posts.

"So who are these guests you bring with you?" asked his wife, Medea, walking over to join them. Medea had black hair and beautiful features. For a witch. Zann always thought witches were old and ugly, never having known one personally before meeting Medea and her sister, Rapunzel.

"I'm Queen Lira Pentstone of Glint, and this is my daughter, the Princess Valindra," Lira told them.

"Queen?" asked Rhys in surprise.

"Of the elven kingdom," Zann told them, seeing Lira glaring at him. "Queendom," he quickly corrected himself. "I meant queendom, even though it sounds ridiculous and I'm still not sure it is a real thing."

"Of course, it is. Welcome to Kasculbough," said Medea, stepping up to greet them. "I am Queen Medea and this is my husband, King Rhys. This is our daughter, Princess Lily-Rae," she said, reaching out and touching the child.

"Princess? Really, Rhys, is that what you're calling your daughter now?" scoffed Zann, thinking his brother was only flaunting his newfound title.

"Well, that's what she is," said Alaina, stepping up to Rhys and taking the baby from him. "Come here my little Lily-Rae and say hello to your grandmother."

"I'm out of here," complained the sage. With a wave of his hand, he disappeared in a blur.

"Wait! Father!" cried Lira, but it was too late. The pesky elf was gone.

"Father?" Rhys looked over at Zann. "Is the sage really her father?"

"Yep," said Zann. They both started to chuckle, but stopped and cleared their throats when they saw the nasty glares of the women.

"So, what are you doing here?" asked Rhys.

Rhys had long, brown hair down to his shoulders, while Zann's hair was light blond, almost white. Their eldest brother, Darium had long black hair with a white streak down the middle, but that was because he was a sin eater.

"Brother, can you house Lira and her daughter for a short while?" asked Zann. "Just until we can figure out why a portal keeps opening and a man keeps trying to kidnap her daughter."

"Another portal? Oh, nay," groaned Rhys.

"My feelings exactly," Zann agreed.

"Of course, we'd love to have you as our guests," said

Medea. Her disposition since becoming married and now pregnant for a second time had really seemed to change her. Instead of the dark witch she used to be, she was actually rather pleasant to be around now. Zann liked that. He didn't think women could change. He glanced over at his mother and started having doubts about that once again.

"Come inside, and we'll talk," suggested Rhys.

"Oh, I can't." Alaina handed the baby back to Rhys. "Since I'm now Fae Queen I am kept busy with my duties day and night. Actually, I planned a trip to Lornoon to see Portia-Maer, and then I'm headed back to the Whispering Dale. But if you need my help at all boys, just call for me on the wind and I'll hear you and come right away." Portia-Maer was another Elemental of the Air who had come to their aid just recently.

"Thank you, Mother," said Rhys. Zann remained quiet. Rhys looked over at Zann and gave him a look that could kill.

"Yes, thank you, Mother," said Zann. "Now, if you'll all excuse me, I need to go out and hunt."

"Now?" asked Lira. "But we just got here."

"I need to bring food back to King Grinwald. I will most likely be hunting well into the night, and then I'll retire at Evandorm, so don't wait up."

"Isn't that dangerous, hunting at night?" asked Lira.

"Queenie, I'm also a wolf, unless you've forgotten," said Zann, shaking his head. "Night is my favorite time."

"My name is Lira, not Queenie," she retorted with a stiff upper lip. "You can just call me Lady Lira if you want."

"Of course. Please forgive me, Lady Lira," he said, deciding not to sound crude anymore.

"How is your wound?" asked Lira.

"What happened?" Rhys wanted to know.

"It's nothing, really," said Zann. "It'll just take a little time to heal."

"If you had the power to heal yourself like I do, you'd already be fine," Rhys stated, saying it probably only to rub it in that Zann didn't have that power.

"Are you hurt?" asked Medea with concern in her voice. "Perhaps I can make up a healing potion."

"Nay, I'm fine," said Zann, his hand going to his bottom, not wanting to divulge to the others what really happened. After all, his ass wasn't wounded nearly as much as his pride.

Seven

LIRA FELT uncomfortable at Kasculbough without Zann there, even though Rhys and Medea were wonderful hosts. They were magical beings, and she liked that. Medea and her daughter were both witches. Lira hadn't known any witches before now and was eager to find out more. Rhys seemed to have extreme strength and also the power to heal himself, but that is all she really knew about him.

Lira was out of her realm here. She felt even more vulnerable than she had back at Castle Glint. Valindra, on the other hand, seemed to like it here. They ate earlier, and now all sat around in the solar where Valindra played with little Lily. The two girls got along nicely. It was good for Valindra to make new friends. Lira hoped it would take the little girl's mind off of that man in the portal. Lily waved her arms in the air, and all her toys lifted up off the ground, spinning in a circle.

"Lily, put those down, please," said Medea in a calm voice. "It's not nice to play that way around other children when they can't do that too."

The toys hit the ground with a loud clank, scattering across the floor.

"Lily is so young, and yet she has powers already?" asked Lira in astonishment.

"Yes," answered Medea. "I had powers that young as well."

"Is that a trait of being a witch?" Lira figured she might have asked the wrong thing when Medea and Rhys just looked at each other but neither of them answered.

"Yes, in a way, I suppose it is," Medea finally said, not offering to explain further.

"Is Zann coming back here to discuss the portal?" asked Lira, feeling as if they were reluctant to talk about witches, so she changed the subject.

"My brother is on the hunt. He won't return until morning," said Rhys. "I've sent a message for our other brother, Darium to join us in the morning as well. Don't worry, we'll figure out what's going on with the portal, I assure you."

"I found this," she said, pulling the gauntlet from her pocket and holding it up to show them. "It was worn by the man in the portal who tried to . . . to take my daughter."

Valindra stopped playing and looked up all of a sudden. Lira hoped she hadn't frightened her.

"Can I see that?" asked Rhys, reaching out for it. She gave it to him. "It looks like the gauntlet of a warrior or some kind of soldier."

"I agree," she responded. "My father said it has volcano dust on it. Zann believes the dust came from the volcano on the Isle of Denwop."

"Denwop?" Rhys looked up. "Let's hope not. I've recently had an encounter with King Sethor's giant when I came to Darium's aid. I don't fancy having to face any more of them."

"There's a giant here? On Mura?" Lira didn't like

the sound of this at all. It made her extremely frightened.

"Aye, there is. But just one. He's a mercenary and works for King Sethor at Macada Castle," Rhys explained.

"That's on the west coast, not far from here," added Medea, knowing that Lira was only familiar with the magical kingdoms north of the mountains.

"Well, I'm glad we're not there then. Giants and elves don't mix."

"So, I've heard," said Rhys with a yawn. "Well, I suggest we all get some shut-eye, and in the morning we will talk more about this portal."

"Time for bed, Valindra," Lira told her daughter.

"Nay! I don't want to sleep," Valindra said defiantly.

"She's too frightened to sleep, since the portal usually seems to open at nighttime," Lira explained.

"I think I can help," said Medea, picking up her daughter. "Valindra, would you like to sleep in the same room with Lily tonight? I'll put a magical protection ring around the room, so you don't have to worry about anything."

Valindra looked up at Lira in question.

"It's all right," Lira told her. "I'll stay there with you, too. We'll be safe. I promise."

Once the children were sleeping, Lira felt a little more at ease. She would stay here in the room with them the entire night. Feeling restless and much too anxious to sleep, she opened the window and peered out at the night sky. Thousands of stars twinkled back at her. The moon cast a bluish glow over the land. While there were trees and plants, this side of the mountain didn't look nearly as healthy or alive as Glint. It almost made her homesick, but just for a moment.

Then she heard the howl of a wolf, and looked out

toward the Goeften Forest. It was Zann. It had to be. She missed him for some reason, even though she'd just met him. Valindra felt safe in his presence, and for some reason, Lira did too.

At times like this, Lira wished she hadn't lost her magic. If she still had powers to protect herself, she would go out to the forest right now and look for Zann. She felt sorry for him and wondered more about his life. She couldn't even imagine what it must feel like to turn into an animal. The thought repulsed her yet at the same time intrigued her.

Closing the shutter, she headed back to bed, her head filled with questions about Zann that she wanted to ask the next time she saw him.

* * *

Zann raised his head and howled at the moon once more. In his shapeshifting form of a wolf, he stood on a cliff, looking down at Kasculbough Castle. He saw the elven queen staring out the window. The moonlight lit up her silken hair. Even from this distance, he could see her smooth skin and fine complexion. Why in the name of Zoroct was he attracted to an elf? Even in his animal form, he couldn't seem to stop thinking about her. Then again, mayhap his animal cravings were getting the best of him.

He ran on all fours through the Goeften Forest, no longer thinking about hunting. He hadn't made a single kill since he'd met Lira. Even now, he should be half done hunting for the night, but he hadn't been able to concentrate on the task at hand and had yet to start. Thoughts of her lodged in his brain, threatening to drive him mad. He could still see the hope in her eyes as well as the fear in her daughter's eyes when she had been so close to disappearing through the portal.

He didn't want to get involved. He just couldn't do it. Zann knew he was naught more than an oddity, the way he could shift from human form to animal form and back so quickly. He didn't know why he could do it, and neither did he know exactly how it worked. All he knew was that the second Blackseed son born was always a shapeshifter of one kind or another in his family line.

He didn't want this kind of magic.

All he wanted was to be like his strong brother, or have powers to move the air like his sin eating brother recently discovered. Instead, he was the freak of the family. If he didn't even like himself, how could he expect Lira to ever like him? He didn't think it mattered, but who was he fooling? Somehow, it really did.

He ran and ran until he could run no more. Then he made his way back to his horse, just outside the walls of Evandorm. Once he shifted back into the form of a man, he took his clothes from the travel bag and dressed. Finally, he headed back to the castle, with no kill at all, and no longer even caring. All he wanted was to go to his small room at the back of the kennel and get a good night's sleep. Zann hoped he wouldn't dream of the elf queen tonight. He didn't like elves, and didn't want to do something stupid . . . like fall for one of their kind.

* * *

"Get up, you big oaf, it's morning. The king is hungry and he's looking for food."

"Mmph," mumbled Zann, opening first one eye and then the other. The pain in his ass was back again, and this had nothing to do with his wound.

"Let's go!" Elric kicked at him. "Grinwald wants meat. What did you get on the hunt last night?"

"I didn't. Now go away and leave me alone. I'm trying to sleep." Zann rolled over on his pallet in his small room, only to see Elric on the other side of him now.

"You didn't hunt at all, did you? What were you doing all night?" asked the sage.

"None of your damned business. Now leave me alone." Zann turned back the other way. This time Elric was there with a serving spoon, hitting him over the head.

"Stop it!" he cried, pushing the elf away. Elric sailed through the air, smashing into the wall. His tall cook's hat fell off, revealing his pointy ears.

"Huntsman," called out a guard, banging at his door. "The king summons you anon."

"Great." Zann got up, brushing off his clothes since he hadn't bothered to change out of them last night. "I have nothing to give him, and he'll probably have my head."

"I can help you," offered the elf.

"I don't want your help, thank you." The last thing he wanted was anything from Elric.

"If you help my daughter, I'll go back to the kitchen and whip up a bunch of dishes, I promise. I'll tell the king you brought me the food early this morning."

"You can't do that," scoffed Zann, brushing straw off his clothes. "Can you?"

"You tell me." The elf stood up, pulled his hat back down over his ears and held out his empty hand. All of a sudden he was holding a chicken by the feet.

"Where did you get that?" asked Zann. "It better not be from the king's chicken coop. He counts on those eggs every morning. You can't be cooking up his prized hens."

"Oh, you are such a simpkin! I am trying to prove a point. How is this?" The chicken disappeared and the sage now held some kind of dead bird by the feet. Zann yawned and rubbed his eyes, his vision still blurry.

"If that's from the mews, the king will have your head."

"It's a partridge, you big oaf. You don't find that in the mews, do you?"

"It looks kind of like a falcon to me, but I'm half asleep, so I can't tell." Zann yawned again and stretched his arms over his head.

"So, are you going to agree to help my daughter? Or is the king going to chop off your head and have me serve that up since you neglected to bring anything back from the hunt?"

The guard continued to pound on the door.

"All right, all right, I will help her," Zann finally agreed. "Just get some food prepared for the king, and do it fast. Tell him it's from me."

"You'll do whatever I say, then?" The damned elf was the one to suggest this, and now he sounded like he was making some kind of other deal.

"Whatever you say? Huh?" Zann asked, not knowing exactly what he meant.

"Where's my huntsman?" came the growl of the king from outside the door.

"Damn. That's the king." Zann's head snapped around. "Go on to the kitchen. Hurry. Shoo," he said waving his hands at the elf, trying to make him go. "Make some food. Fast. Get chopping."

"Only if you agree to help Lira in whatever way I say."

"In what way?" he asked as the door started to open.

He wondered if the elf had some ideas about how to control portals, since Zann had none.

"You just go along with whatever I say in front of the king regarding my daughter. Got it?"

"Got it?" he repeated in question, but the sage took it as confirmation.

"Good enough." The elf zipped through the door when it opened and the guard and king walked in.

"What was that?" asked the guard, looking down at his feet. "Did you see something run past?"

"Just a rat," Zann mumbled, having a feeling he'd just agreed to something he was going to regret.

"All I see is an empty table," bellowed the king, pushing the guard to the side. "Blackseed, you'd better have food for me, and plenty of it. What did you get on the hunt?"

"I . . . I gave it to your new head cook. If you'll just ask him about it, he'll tell you everything he's made."

"It better be good, because I'm starving this morning."

The king was always starving, and this morning was no different than any other, but Zann didn't think he'd be smart to point that out.

"My king, your feast awaits you in the kitchen," said Elric from outside the door.

Zann breathed a sigh of relief. He followed the king and the guard out into the courtyard. Then, he stopped in his tracks when he saw Lira standing in the courtyard next to the elf. She was dressed in the gown of a noble, and thankfully wore a headpiece that covered her pointy ears.

"What is she doing here?" mumbled Zann, knowing this was going to prove to be nothing but trouble.

"Who is that?" asked the king.

"This, sire, is my lovely daughter . . . Lira," said Elric with a bow.

Lira looked as confused as Zann felt at the moment.

"Well, what is she doing here? What's going on?" asked the king. "I want my food."

"Sire, my daughter is marrying the huntsman this morning," Elric said, making Zann's jaw drop, hoping he hadn't really just said what Zann thought he said. "It is why I have prepared such a sumptuous feast like you've never seen before."

"What?" asked the king. "Nay. I don't know her. There will be no marriage and no celebration."

"That's what I say," mumbled Zann, hurrying over to the elves.

"If you will just allow my daughter to wed the big oaf – I mean your huntsman right now, right here in the courtyard, I promise you the feast will be on the tables right after we are done."

"Nay. I don't care about any wedding," snapped the king.

"Me either," mumbled Zann. He leaned over and whispered to Lira. "What is this all about? What is your father up to?"

"I don't know," she whispered back. "My father whisked me over here using his magic. I know just as little as you about what he's planned."

"Sire, the huntsman has been hunting all night for the wedding feast," said Elric. "He's even brought back with him a few roakans from the land of Glint." Elric looked over at Zann and flashed a smile.

"I did?" Zann groaned and looked at Lira. She shrugged.

"Roakans? That sounds intriguing I've never had one before," said the king, now interested since they'd mentioned an exotic food. "What does it taste like, huntsman?"

"Huh?" Zann looked up in surprise, knowing the king was expecting him to answer. "I – I suppose you could say it tastes sort of like venison," said Zann. "Then again, it is such an exotic taste, sire, that I am not really sure how to describe it."

"I think it tastes like chicken, only better," snapped the sage. "And as a special treat, I've prepared pazzleberry pies, my favorite," Elric continued, making Zann wonder if this was all true. He knew the elf could move fast, but could he really produce all these dishes in the blink of an eye?

"Ah, yes. Pazzleberries are my favorite too," said the king, licking his lips. Zann wouldn't be surprised if the man started drooling next.

"These aren't just any pazzleberries," continued Elric. "They have been collected by your huntsman from the Whispering Dale – the magical land of the fae." Zann shook his head, knowing the elf was probably lying, and not liking that he said Zann collected them. "The pies are made with fresh berries the size of your fist, Your Majesty." Elric made a grand show of bowing. When he did, his hat fell off. The elf moved so quickly replacing it, that Zann was pretty sure no one noticed his elven ears.

"Pazzleberry pies," repeated the king with a smile. His eyes lit up and his tongue shot out to lick his lips again.

"A feast worthy of a king, and prepared especially for the wedding of my daughter," added Elric.

"Fine, fine, they can get married if they want to, but I have no officiator to conduct the ceremony," the king told them.

"No need. I am skilled in performing weddings, and have done so many times," said Elric. "I would be happy to officiate the wedding, sire."

"You? A mere cook can do that?" asked the king in disbelief.

"I am also a sage, My King."

That got a laugh from the king, since it sounded so outrageous. The king probably figured Elric was only jesting, but didn't seem to care. "Then by all means, sage, get to it. I want some of that scrumptious-sounding food you mentioned. Blackseed, stand up here by me with the girl."

"Now, wait a minute," protested Zann. "I'm not going to –" He stopped in midsentence when he heard Elric clear his throat.

"I'm sure you'd like me to tell the king all about what else you caught on the hunt last night, don't you, huntsman?" asked Elric, threatening Zann to cooperate with him.

"Excuse me for a brief moment, sire." Zann turned his back on the king to talk to the elves in private. "Elric, what do you think you are doing?" he whispered. "I'm not marrying your daughter. What kind of a prank is this?"

"Yes, Father. What are you up to?" whispered Lira. "We don't appreciate it. This isn't funny."

"The big oaf promised to help you, Lira," spat Elric. "I am just carrying out the plan."

"The plan?" asked Zann. "We never had a plan, and I never said I'd marry her. I agreed to help with finding out something about the portal, that's all. This is crazy and makes no sense."

"I agree," said Lira. "Father, you can't force us to marry. There is no reason for this. Why would you do this to us?"

"Lira, I am a sage, and I know things," Elric whispered. He spoke to them but kept his eyes on the king. "You lost your powers when your husband died, and you need them back right now since your daughter's life is in danger. All you need to do to regain your magic is to marry again."

"Really? Are you sure about that?" Lira almost sounded like she believed him, but Zann knew what a trickster the sage was and he wasn't so easily fooled.

"Of course, I am sure."

"Well, I don't believe it," Zann whispered from the side of his mouth. He looked over to see the king impatiently tapping his foot on the ground.

"Zann, I don't believe my father would lie," said Lira. "But either way, it isn't for you to decide whom I marry," she said in a raspy whisper bending over to speak directly into Elric's ear.

Zann could tell that the girl didn't like this idea any more than he did. Still, he wasn't sure they had a choice now that Elric already got the king to agree.

"Oh, on the contrary, it is up to me and me alone," said Elric. "You see, Blackseed and I made a deal. If he goes back on his word, I'll tell the king the truth about him having nothing from his hunt."

Lira jerked upright and looked over at Zann. Her brows dipped. "You made a deal involving me? Without consulting me first?" She glared at Zann now.

"I said I'd help you, that's it. I thought he was talking about the portal, I swear. Your father agreed to whip up a feast for the king in exchange since I have nothing to offer King Grinwald from the hunt."

"With no food from the hunt last night, the king will kill him if he discovers the truth," added Elric.

"Nay," said Lira shaking her head. "He wouldn't kill you just for that."

"He would," Zann answered with a sigh.

"Father, you can't do this. It's not right," protested Lira.

"Try me," said Elric. "The fool promised to do whatever I said, and now he has to do it."

"You tricked me into it!" snapped Zann. "I didn't really agree to it. I'm not going to get married to anyone, and that's that. Figure out a way to tell the king the wedding is off."

"Nay." Elric stubbornly crossed his arms over his chest. "Instead, I'll tell the king the truth and you'll be dead." Elric laid down his ultimatum and it was evident that nothing Zann or Lira could do or say was going to change the little man's mind.

"Then go ahead and tell him. I don't really care," said Zann, throwing his hands up in the air, calling what he hoped was a bluff. "Now I can see why the gods warned us not to trust you."

"What's taking so long over there?" snapped the king. "Let's get this wedding underway."

"Go on, Elric. Tell him," said Zann, challenging the blasted elf, hoping he really wouldn't do something so rash in front of his daughter.

"Tell me what?" asked the king, stretching his neck and cocking an ear toward them in order to hear.

"Zann, wait," said Lira, resting her hand on his arm. She spoke in a soft voice so only he could hear her. "I don't want you to die. This isn't right. Mayhap we should just do as my father says for now."

"I agree it isn't right, Lira, but neither is your father's trickery. I said I'd help you, but not in this way. He needs to learn that he can't treat people this way."

"I understand that. And I agree it was wrong for him to do this to us. My father is less than honorable, and I know it better than anyone, I assure you. But mayhap we can trick him in return."

"What do you mean? How so?" Zann whispered, his eyes roaming over to Elric who busied himself brushing off his sleeve.

"We don't ever have to consummate the marriage. And if we don't, we can undo it, later. There is a way."

"There is?" he asked, contemplating the idea.

She nodded. "I think it might be in both of our best interests if we just go along with my father's plan for now. I don't want to give in to his crazy whims, but I also don't want to see you die."

"Well . . . if it'll help you get your powers back, mayhap. But I don't know. It doesn't feel right. Nay, I don't think . . . "

"Lira, do you take Zann to be your husband?" The sage was at their side.

"I . . . I think -" started Lira.

"You want to see him live, don't you?" said Elric, leaning in and whispering.

"Of course, I do," she answered.

"Good!" snapped the sage. "Now Zann, do you take Lira as your bride?"

"Now wait a minute," said Zann, realizing what just happened. The damned elf was using his tricks to control them once again. He was about to say I do not agree, but never got the words out. "I do -"

"Done. Married. Okay, kiss each other and let's eat," said the sage, rushing back to the kitchen, leaving Zann and Lira standing there with their mouths hanging open.

Once again, the trickster managed to get what he wanted.

"Congratulations, huntsman," said the king, slapping Zann hard on the back. "Well, go on, and kiss your bride. Make it a good one. We're all waiting and watching."

"I . . . I . . ." Zann looked over at Lira who seemed just as nervous about this as he felt. Then her eyes darted over to the king and back to Zann again. She nodded slightly. "Of course, sire," said Zann, knowing that to betray an order from the king wasn't a good idea.

Zann leaned over and pressed his mouth up against Lira's. He'd meant to just give her a quick peck to suffice the king, but once their lips touched, he felt a surge of warmth rapidly spreading through him. All the thoughts and fantasies he'd had about her last night seemed to be coming to life before his very eyes. Zann couldn't help getting caught up in the moment.

He slipped his arms around her waist, pulling her closer, never breaking the connection. Her hands rested on his chest, only adding to the tingling vibrations within him. He deepened the kiss, getting lost in the experience. He never thought he'd be kissing an elf, but now he was married to not just any elf, but the Queen of Glint. It was an exciting feeling in a way. Just as their lips parted, he decided he needed more.

Zann deepened the kiss, this time letting his tongue slip into Lira's mouth. So soft, so warm, so wet. So tantalizing and exciting! She smelled like sweet lippenbur lilies and freshly cut grass. Her lips tasted like honey mixed with pazzleberries and bilberry wine. Kissing the elf queen heightened his senses and made him heady. Mayhap it was his animal side making this such a sensuous experience, but even so, he didn't care. He didn't want it to stop. So lost in the moment, it was hard to remember that anyone else was even there.

"That's enough!" commanded the king, causing Zann to break the kiss and pull away from Lira. "Save some for the wedding night. Now, let's all head to the great hall and eat this feast you provided. If I like it well enough, I might even give you and your new bride a chamber in the castle. Mayhap I'll even give her a job as well."

"Great," mumbled Zann, looking over to Lira and letting out a deep sigh as the king and his entourage headed toward the keep. "I – I'm sorry," he apologized to Lira, his tongue darting out to taste her essence still lingering on his lips. Now, he would never get his fill.

"It had to be done," she said, her gaze dropping to her feet. If Zann wasn't mistaken, her cheeks were flushed. Just when he thought he might be mistaken, he saw her tongue dart out to run along her top lip. She was savoring his essence as well, it seemed. The slight action was alluring, making him stir beneath his belt.

"W- what just happened?" he asked her, his mind swarming with confusion. Whenever the sage was around, his actions were so fast that it made Zann's head spin. It wasn't unlike the way he felt from kissing the sage's beautiful daughter.

"I – I'm not sure. It all happened so quickly," she answered, wringing her hands together. "I. . . I think . . . I think we're really married, Zann."

"Yes. I believe so," Zann answered with a quick nod of his head. "May I escort you to the great hall, my lady?" He held out his arm. Lira gently reached up and rested her fingers atop it.

"Thank you," she said, her voice sounding shaky. When he looked over at her again, he saw her quickly wiping a tear from her eye.

It brought Zann back to his senses. This wasn't right and it never should have happened. Elric was playing with people's lives, and he never should have been allowed to wield such power. Because of him, Zann and Lira were now married, when they were two people who should never end up together. This was a bad situation they landed in, and it was all because of a crazy trickster.

All Zann could think about as they made their way

to the great hall, was that as soon as he got the sage alone
. . . he was going to kill the irritating little man.

...ght it, was discuss with a job to get the case alone...
...enough to kill the fascinating little man.

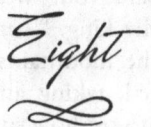

Eight

LIRA SAT NEXT to her new husband at the dais of the King of Evandorm, still wondering how she got into this situation. The king had been so excited about the meal her father promised, that he invited the newlyweds to sit up with the nobility – something that never usually happened unless you were of noble blood. Of course, Lira was a queen and used to it, even though no one here knew it. But Zann was only the king's huntsman so this was a great honor.

"I love this roakan, it is so tasty," said the king, taking a big bite of the meat. "You do need to tell me how hard it was to catch one of these, huntsman."

"Oh, it was much easier than you'd expect." Zann played with his food, not eating it. Lira could tell that their marriage really upset him. It upset her as well. She had no appetite either, and hadn't even taken a bite of food.

"I like the food of the elves so much, that I've decided I'm going to attack Castle Glint and its lands and seize it all for myself," continued King Grinwald with a low chuckle.

"What? Nay!" shouted Lira, starting to jump up out

of her seat. Zann's hand clamped around her wrist and he kept her from standing.

"Sit down," Zann warned her in a low voice.

"Knights, prepare your weapons right after the meal," called out the king. "Tomorrow, we'll start on our journey over the mountains to seize the castle of Glint." He chuckled, taking another big bite of the meat. "I can't wait to see how surprised those elves will be when my army shows up. We'll take them by surprise and they'll never know what hit them."

"I highly doubt you'd be able to do that," said Lira through her clenched teeth.

"Why not?" asked the king, looking over in question. "Is there something about the elves you know that I don't? Speak up, my dear. Tell me everything."

"She knows nothing about elves, I assure you, my good king." Zann interrupted, keeping Lira from answering. "I must say, sire, do you really think it is a good idea to move into the northern lands? After all, magic is a weapon that can be stronger than axes or swords, so you would be at a disadvantage."

"Hmmm," said the king in thought. He took a big gulp of wine and set down his goblet. "You're right, huntsman. Even though my army is strong, we are no match for magic."

"I agree," said Zann, leaning over to whisper to Lira. "I knew that would work."

"Therefore, I think I have no other choice."

"Than to withdraw the idea. I agree," said Zann. "Good decision, my king."

"Nay, that's not what I mean at all," said the king. "On the contrary, I think I'm going to have to team up with my enemy, King Leofric Sethor from Macada Castle. It's the only way we'll be able to overtake them. We'll have power and strength in numbers."

"What?" asked Zann, almost choking on his wine.

"Your words, huntsman, made me realize that I need backup. Sethor even has that mercenary giant. It'll come in handy since I hear giants like to eat elves."

"Good work," Lira whispered to Zann, ready to strangle him for even giving the king the suggestion whether he meant to or not. "You just made things worse! How could you?" She glared at Zann, despising him now.

"Blackseed, I want you and your new bride to join us in the surprise attack. Since it was you who brought me roakan and put the taste for the animal and the land in my mouth, I think it is only fair that you are there to witness me seizing the castle."

"We will not be there, and would never agree to witnessing such a horrific act like that!" Lira shot up out of her chair before Zann could stop her this time.

The king looked up in shock. "Blackseed, you'd better control that loose-tongued bride of yours before I cut her tongue out of her mouth myself. That is no way to talk to a king."

"Sire, that is my wife you are talking about." Zann jumped out of his chair now, looking just as angry and Lira felt. "Please, stop threatening her."

"You two are naught but my subjects. What gives you the right to speak in such a manner against me?" asked the king.

"I am not your subject and neither will I ever be." Lira's emotions got the best of her. Before she could think things through, she did something that she immediately regretted. She yanked off her headpiece and threw it atop the dais, exposing her elven ears. "I am Queen Lira Pentstone of the Queendom of Glint. I promise I will never allow you to harm a single one of my people."

"She's an elf!" yelled one of the knights.

"Seize her!" shouted the king. "Seize the huntsman and the cook as well. I've been deceived." On his command, his guards headed over with drawn weapons, surrounding the dais.

"Nice going," mumbled Zann, grabbing Lira's hand. "Well, it's a good time to start using your replenished magic about now. Take us away from here, and fast."

"I – I can't," said Lira, focusing and concentrating, but still her magic had not returned.

"What are you saying?" asked Zann. They stood at the dais, quickly surrounded by the king's soldiers. There seemed to be no way to escape their imminent fate now.

"I have no magic, Zann. I'm sorry." She looked over to him with tears in her eyes.

"Then I hope you are good at running. Let's go." Zann took off at a run, dragging her along with him, knocking over two of the guards along the way. He headed for the door of the great hall, but he was too late. It was no use. King Grinwald's guards appeared from the corridor now as well, surrounding them with their swords drawn. Zann yanked his sword from his weapon belt, holding it out, pushing Lira behind him.

"Shall we kill them, my king?" asked one of the men.

"Nay. Put them in the dungeon for now," the king answered, not bothering to even get out of his chair. He just continued eating. "I want them to watch while King Sethor and I annihilate the elven kingdom. With any luck, we'll take over the Whispering Dale as well."

"My king, the cook seems to have eluded us," reported a soldier, running in the from kitchen.

"Why am I not surprised?" mumbled Zann. "When there is trouble, Elric is the first to disappear."

"Grab them and lock them up, now!" screamed the king. "I'll deal with finding that wretched little cook later."

"Don't touch my wife," warned Zann, holding out his blade, moving it back and forth. "You'll have to kill me first to get to her."

"Zann, nay," pleaded Lira, gently placing her hand on his arm. "Please put down the sword. It's over."

"I will never surrender," Zann told her. "I will protect you, if I have to die doing it."

"That is noble of you, but it'll be all right. I promise. Just don't fight them right now, I beg you."

"How can it be all right?" asked Zann, thinking his new bride had become daft. "Your father just doomed us as well as your entire kingdom . . . queendom. Forever. How can you forgive that?"

"Please. Trust me," she said, looking deeply into his eyes. Zann looked back at her, seeming to consider the situation, but still he didn't lower his sword. "I am your wife now, Zann. We will deal with this together. But right now, it is best if you just put down the sword. Please. Do it. For me."

She tried to remain composed with her words as well as her actions. One thing she'd learned being the Queen of Glint was that losing control of one's emotions only made things worse. She had just proven that to herself and regretted reacting to the king. She had no idea how to get out of this horrid situation, but if they could get away from the others and just talk, she was sure she and Zann could come up with some kind of plan.

"Damn it," spat Zann, throwing down his sword. The metal blade hit the stone floor of the great hall, ringing out like a bell.

Before Lira knew what happened, they were

grabbed and dragged to the dungeon. The guards were forceful, throwing them both into a cell. The iron-barred door slammed closed behind them, locking them inside.

"Rot in there, you traitor and you stupid elf," growled one of the guards. Hatred filled his eyes.

"You're queen of the cesspool now," said another soldier, laughing and spitting at them through the bars.

"I'll kill you!" shouted Zann gripping the bars of the door with one hand and reaching out through them for the guard with the other.

"Stay back, you fool, unless you don't value that hand!" The first guard's sword came down toward him. Zann quickly pulled his hand back inside the cell. However, the blade nicked his hand and left a small cut that started bleeding.

"Damn you!" Zann ground out, holding his injured hand.

"Zann!" Lira ran to him as the laughing guards headed away. "Let me see your hand," said Lira, reaching out for him.

"It's fine. It's just a scratch." Zann pulled his hand away from her and started pacing back and forth inside the cell. "I'm going to kill that damned sage. I swear I will."

"It's no use letting my father upset you. It won't solve anything," she told him.

"No? Well, wait until I get my hands around that scrawny little neck of his. I'm going to –"

"To do what, you big oaf?"

Zann spun around to see the sage standing just outside the cell door.

"You!" screamed Zann running to the door, gripping the bars and shaking them wildly. He was so angry right now that it was probably a good thing he couldn't reach the elf because he couldn't control his emotions. If he touched him, he'd be apt to kill him.

"Father, how could you let this happen? This is all your fault," cried Lira.

"My fault?" The elf scowled at them. "Nay, that was you, daughter. You never should have foolishly revealed your identity. Everything was going as planned until you did that. How could you think it was a good idea? You are the one to blame for this situation, not me."

"You're right. I'm sorry," said Lira, looking like a scorned child.

Zann's heart went out to her. He knew she only reacted that way because she was trying to protect her people. He supposed if he was a king, he would have reacted the same way. "Never mind whose fault it is. Get us out of here right now, mage."

"Sage," the little man corrected him. "And what do you think I'm doing?" He held up a ring of keys. "I was able to pilfer these, but the sleeping potion I laced the food with won't last long so we have to move fast."

"You did what?" gasped Zann. "And how did you think that poisoning the king and his soldiers was a good idea? If they catch us now, we're as good as dead."

"Lira, use your magic," said Elric, trying the keys one after another in the lock, taking his sweet time.

"Father, I did and it didn't work. I married to restore my magic, but it has not returned."

"Ah, that's probably because you haven't consummated the marriage yet," said the elf. "Once you do, I'm sure it'll return." He continued to try the keys in the lock.

"Well, unless you think we're going to rut on the ground of this dirty cell like randy rats, I suggest we get out of here and think about that later. Give me those." Zann reached through the bars and snatched the keys away from Elric, easily finding the right one and shoving it into the lock. "I'm done listening to the nonsense that is spouted by a stupid sage," he grumbled, opening the door, wondering why the elf didn't just use his magic to release them.

"Well, if you feel that way, then mayhap you'd like to listen to a fool instead. That is . . . you!" snapped the elf, crossing his arms over his chest.

They heard the groan of a soldier from the guard room just outside the dungeon door.

"We've got to go. Now stop the fighting and let's get out of here while we still have a chance," said Lira, leading the way.

They stepped over the sleeping guards, making their way to the main door of the dungeon.

"Why weren't we affected by the sleeping potion in the same manner?" asked Zann curious as to why they were still wide awake.

"Did you eat the food?" asked Elric.

"Nay, I guess not. I was too upset to eat," said Zann.

"So was I," agreed Lira.

"Lira, you're an elf, so my magic sleeping potion wouldn't have affected you anyway," said Elric.

"And if I would have eaten the food?" asked Zann. "Would it have affected me?"

"Aye. If you had eaten it, you'd be passed out right now, too."

"Why in the name of Belcoum would you do such a thing?" asked Zann. Was there ever a purpose, a good reason, for Elric to act the way he did?

"Well, I suppose it was because I was having a hard time getting what I needed," explained the elf. "However, I knew it would be easy once everyone was passed out."

"What is it you needed, Father?" Lira stopped at the door and looked back over her shoulder.

"The king's hair." Elric proudly held up a braid of hair. "I already had hair from both the kings of Kasculbough and Macada, and now I have all three of them braided together." He swung the braid back and forth proudly showing it off.

"You are insane!" spat Zann. "You risked all of our lives for a stupid lock of hair?"

"It's for a very good purpose, I assure you." Elric stuck the braid into his pocket.

"I'd love to know the reason," said Zann. "However, right now I don't really care." He saw his sword by one of the guards, and bent down and retrieved it. "Lira, follow me. I've got a horse in the stables we can use and hopefully get away from here before they all awaken."

"What about my father?" asked Lira as Zann took her hand and hurried across the courtyard.

"With any luck, mayhap the sage will be caught and the king will decide to serve him for dinner."

"If I didn't know you were jesting, Zann, I'd think that was a very mean thing for you to say."

"Who said I'm jesting?" Zann mumbled under his breath, knowing this was all far from over between him and the irritable little elf.

Nine

"BROTHER, I'm sorry, but we didn't know where else to go so we came here." Zann and Lira had arrived at Kasculbough Castle ten minutes ago, and had already explained everything to Rhys. Zann didn't want to bring trouble to his brother's door, but needed protection for Lira and her daughter.

"Guards, watch for Evandorm's soldiers or even Sethor's. Close the gate if they come near," Rhys gave the order to his men.

"Aye, my lord," the guards answered.

"Mama, mama," cried Valindra, running from the keep and jumping into Lira's arms.

"Sweetheart, I'm glad you're safe."

Kasculbough was one of the three kingdoms this side of the mountain. It had been the darkest and scariest of the three until Rhys took over as king. The castle consisted of a huge keep made from black stone and red roofs. Cobblestone led from the keep over to a large pit in the ground. It was an oubliette used for prisoners, larger than any ever constructed. This one had even held a dragon recently. The walls surrounding the castle were quite thick and impenetrable, with at least three or more sturdy towers down each length of the walls. It wasn't on a cliff like Macada Castle, but was surrounded by a moat of water on four sides. It also sat close to the sea on the east side of Mura.

"We didn't know where you disappeared to, and were worried, Queen Lira." Medea walked out of the castle carrying little Lily.

"Please, just call me Lira. The queen part isn't necessary, Queen Medea."

"And Medea is fine for me as well." Medea smiled. Zann couldn't believe how much the woman changed since marrying Rhys.

"King Rhys, the sin eater and his wife approach," called out a man from the battlements.

"Good," said Rhys. "Let them in. And for Zoroct's sake, call him by his name. It's Darium. He doesn't even sin eat much anymore."

"What is a sin eater?" asked Lira, never having heard this term before.

"Our brother used to . . . sin eat," said Rhys, trying to explain it.

"Oh," said Lira. Zann could tell she didn't understand. Why would she?

"Darium would eat food, and drink ale off the chests of corpses," said Zann, only seeming to make matters worse.

"Oh my!" exclaimed Lira. "Whatever for?"

"Let me try to explain," said Medea. "The men are not good at things like this, Lira."

"Go right ahead, wife," said Rhys with an outstretched arm.

Medea tried to explain next. "When a person dies quickly, and has no chance to confess their sins, it is thought his or her soul will have no chance of getting to Heaven."

"Where?" asked Lira.

"The Haven," Zann interrupted. "Medea is not from Mura. Her gods and goddesses are different from ours."

"Actually, there is only one god and the devil, where I come from," said Medea.

"Really?" asked Lira.

"To make this long story short, my brother sin eats, thereby absorbing the sins so the dead one can move on," Zann interrupted.

"That sounds horrible," said Lira. "Why would he ever do that?"

"The firstborn son of a Blackseed is always a sin eater," explained Zann. "It's just how it is."

"Well, what happens to him after doing this?" asked Lira.

"Usually, a sin eater's soul is doomed to Hell – I mean, The Dark Abyss forever," explained Medea.

"Oh, no!" gasped Lira.

"Don't worry, we've seen to it that Darium's soul will be spared," Zann interrupted once again. "All right, so let's talk about the attack on Glint and also the portal. We've got to move this along." He paced back and forth impatiently like he always did when something was bothering him.

"Darium," Rhys called out with a wave of his hand, greeting their brother.

Darium and Talia rode over to them and dismounted.

"Something's amiss," said Darium. "I saw Grinwald's men conversing with Sethor's on the way over here. Whatever they are up to, I'm sure it's not good."

"Nay, it's not," said Zann. "They are teaming up to attack the elves and seize Glint."

"Damn," replied Darium.

"Darium and Talia, I'd like you to meet Lira, Queen of Glint, and her daughter, Princess Valindra," Zann introduced them.

"Oh, my. Hello," said Talia. "I met you long ago when I lived in the Whispering Dale but you might not remember me."

"Of course, I do. Hello, Talia-Glenn," answered Lira.

"Nice to meet you," said Darium with a nod. "How do you know my brother, Zann?"

"We're married," she said, causing Darium's jaw to drop.

"We were tricked into it by the stupid sage, but don't worry, we're not staying married," Zann tried to explain.

"I think there is a lot I've missed," said Darium.

"I'll explain it all to you later," Zann replied.

"By the way, Rhys and Medea," said Darium. "I'm not sure if Zann told you, but Talia's pregnant."

"Really?" squealed Medea. "That's wonderful, Talia. We'll be having babies together." Medea was pregnant right now with her second child.

Zann cleared his throat. "Excuse me, but we have some more important matters to discuss other than babies at the moment."

"Right," said Rhys. "Why don't the men come to my solar where we can discuss war while the women talk about other things."

"Nay, I'm coming with you," said Lira. "Medea, will you and Talia watch my daughter, please?" Lira put Valindra down.

"Of course," said Medea, holding out her hand. "How about we all go to the kitchen and get a piece of pie?"

"Speaking of pie," said Zann. "Has the sage showed up here yet today?"

"Nay," said Rhys. "Why?"

"Because this is all his fault. We were imprisoned and could have died because of him."

"Zann, that's not true," Lira corrected him. "It's my fault since I announced I was the elven queen right in front of the King of Evandorm."

Darium groaned. "You didn't."

"She did," said Zann. "And the sage laced the king's food with a sleeping potion, so things are about to get complicated."

"Why did he do that?" asked Darium.

"Because he wanted the king's hair," Zann told him with a shrug.

"Huh?" Darium looked very confused.

"Excuse me, but I think it's to our best interest to get to the solar right away and discuss how we are going to protect the people of Glint," interrupted Lira.

"Spoken like a true queen," mumbled Zann, impressed by his new wife's tenacity. "Now, if you'll somehow please call your father, Lira. I think he needs to be a part of this discussion, too. After all, he is supposedly the wise sage. Even though I still cannot figure out for the life of me how he got that title," he added under his breath.

"The sage is her father?" asked Darium, lifting his finger in the air.

"That's right," said Zann.

"I don't know where he is or how to call him." Lira shrugged.

"Can't you use your magic to do it?" asked Rhys.

"That's the trouble. I lost my magic, and it hasn't returned," she admitted.

"She was supposed to get it back once we married,

but obviously, that was just a lie made up by the mage," said Zann.

"Sage," Lira corrected him.

"I said you need to consummate the marriage first, and you haven't done that yet, have you?" came a voice from behind them.

Zann turned to see the sage standing there, probably having overheard the entire conversation. He wondered if the man could somehow turn invisible as well as move so fast that no one ever saw him.

"Of course, we haven't consummated the marriage, Father. We've just been married," Lira told him.

"And we're not going to, either. It's what we've decided," added Zann, getting an odd look from Lira. He had a feeling that mayhap he shouldn't have divulged that information to Elric.

"If you don't, you'll never have your magic returned and we are all doomed. Doomed, I tell you," ranted the elf, waving his fists in the air dramatically. "You cannot rule Glint with no magic, daughter. You just can't," he all but shouted.

"Excuse me," interrupted Darium, still holding a finger in the air. "I just wanted to clarify that the sage is Lira's father?"

"Yep," said Zann. "I could hardly believe it myself."

"So, then, the sage is now your . . . father-by-marriage, Zann?" Darium couldn't hold back his chuckle.

"Let's continue this conversation in the privacy of the solar," said Zann, noticing too many people inside the walls of Kasculbough watching them with interest.

"I agree," said Lira, leading the way.

Rhys and Darium hung back, coming over to speak with Zann as they walked.

"So you're really not going to consummate the marriage, brother?" Rhys asked.

"The elf is beautiful. It's not like you to pass up sleeping with a pretty wench," added Darium. "By the way, I still can't believe you're married to an elf and the sage is your new father."

"Stop it, Darium. This is hard enough without you reminding me about it constantly," snapped Zann.

"You're married to the girl now," Rhys reminded Zann.

"And you really don't plan on bedding her?" asked Darium, not seeming to hear anything that Zann said today.

"You heard me, Darium, so quit asking," snapped Zann.

"I don't get it," said Darium. "Usually we can't keep you out of a pretty wench's bed. Now, you're married to a beautiful girl and you won't even touch her? What is going on with you, brother? Not to even mention the fact that she is a queen and you're turning that down."

Zann watched Lira from behind as she talked with her father on the way to the keep. The women all decided to join them, and followed along as well. Lira took a minute to bend down and scoop up her daughter, making Zann's heart about break.

Lira truly was a beautiful woman, and seemed to be a loving, caring mother as well. If he stayed married to her, he'd be an instant father to little Valindra. This frightened him. He wasn't even sure how to be a father to a child and wasn't sure he wanted to be one. Or at least, not so soon.

He didn't know Lira well, but he'd been thinking about her since they met. He had never felt this way before about any of the women he'd been with. This was all strangely different. Kissing Lira made him feel alive and happy and as if he wanted to change his ways. It was as if there was some sort of connection between them that he couldn't deny. He was enchanted by her . . . or perhaps beguiled by her charms. Now she was his wife, and he still couldn't believe it. Zann wanted more than anything to consummate the marriage, but he had promised Lira that they would end the marriage as soon as they could. Damn, why did he have to make that deal, when all he wanted to do right now was to break it?

"I made a deal that I cannot go back on," said Zann. "I promised Lira that we'd end the marriage soon, so I don't see how I can consummate it now."

"Is that what you really want, Zann?" asked Rhys. "I see the way you look at the girl. I don't believe you want to end it."

"I have to admit, I was tricked into marrying Lira," Zann told his brothers. "But when we kissed, I really felt something between us. It was a connection that I've never felt with anyone before."

"It's called lust," said Rhys. Both he and Darium chuckled.

"Nay, it's more than that," said Zann. "I can't explain it, and I don't believe I'm saying this, but I actually don't think I'd mind staying married to Lira."

"Really," said Darium. "Well, if Lira should change her mind about the deal, you wouldn't have to stay away from her after all, would you?"

"Nay, I suppose not," said Zann. "But she won't change her mind. Lira is a very stubborn and opinionated woman who knows what she wants."

"And you, brother, are a man who usually doesn't back down from a challenge once he knows what he wants," Darium added.

"But is it really what I want?" asked Zann, feeling confused.

"I agree with Darium," said Rhys. "Zann, just convince Lira that she doesn't want to end the marriage after all."

"How do I do that?" asked Zann. "I don't think she even likes me."

"Notice he asked how and not why?" Darium chuckled again. "I think you answered your own question about what you really want, Zann."

"We see right through you, brother," added Rhys.

"Mayhap I do want this after all," admitted Zann. "But do you really think I should try to get Lira to agree to break our deal? She's an elven queen and I'm only a huntsman . . . or used to be one. I'm not sure what I am anymore."

"What do you think you should do?" Rhys asked. Both he and Darium smiled at Zann without saying another word. Then they turned and walked to the keep.

"Mayhap they're right," mumbled Zann, running a weary hand through his hair. It wouldn't be so bad staying married to the elven queen, would it? But would she really even consider staying married to him? Perhaps he should try to change her opinion after all.

Zann wondered what would make Lira want to couple with him and continue to be his wife. Then he smiled, realizing exactly what would do it. It was the promise of something she wanted more than anything else. Getting back her powers. He knew now what to say to her, and in the end, they would both get what they wanted. But then again, could he really go through with it and keep a clear conscience?

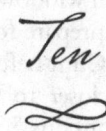

Ten

"**WE HAVE GOT** to stop the kings from attacking Glint," said Lira, pacing the floor of the solar now the same way that Zann was doing. It was a large room with a bed on one side and a table and chairs on the other. Trunks lined walls that were covered with hanging tapestries depicting fighting men, and oddly enough, even a dragon. Lira paced one direction and Zann the other. They kept meeting in the middle on their way back across the room and had to side-step each other.

"Why did you have to tell the king who you really are?" asked Zann, sidestepping her once again and continuing to pace.

"I didn't mean to," said Lira, feeling really bad about this now. "It is in my blood I guess. I only wanted to protect my people."

"Protect them?" snapped Zann. "All you did was put them in harm's way. You should have stayed quiet."

"Arguing isn't going to help us figure out what to do." Darium poured himself a tankard of ale. Talia, Medea, and the children were at the opposite side of the room. Rhys sat at the table next to Darium.

"I agree," said Rhys, reaching for the pitcher and pouring himself a drink as well.

Lira's father leaned against the wall with his arms crossed, over by the open window.

"I'll have my army prepare for battle," stated Rhys. "Mayhap we can get to Glint before the other two kings, since Kasculbough is closer to the coast and it is an easier path over the mountains."

"Mayhap Mother can help us," suggested Darium. "She can use her powers of the air to transport us there quickly."

"Nay! Don't involve Mother," snapped Zann. "I don't want her help."

Lira stopped pacing, looking over at Zann. "What is your issue with your mother?" she asked. "You rejected her offer to help you at Glint, and you're doing the same thing again now."

"I don't want to talk about it," said Zann. "Now, can't you elves use your magic to somehow protect Glint from the attack?"

"I still don't have magic," Lira reminded him, feeling more than frustrated to have lost her powers. "I wish I did."

"That can be arranged," said Zann in a low voice. Their eyes met, and she found herself not able to look away. Was he suggesting what she thought he was? If so, she wasn't sure how she felt about it.

"Lira, you need to couple with the huntsman," blurted out her father. "Do it, and your powers will return."

"I – I don't know," she said, looking down and playing with her belt rather than to look at Zann right now.

Zann's hand covered hers. She looked up to find herself once again lost within the depths of his orange-toned eyes.

"It might be the only way, Lira," he told her in a soft voice. "After all, we are married now."

"But it's not even a real marriage." She pulled her hand away from him and walked over to stare out the window. "I need to get back to Glint. I never should have left my people."

"Excuse me for asking," said Rhys. "But what can you really do to protect them since you don't even have magic?"

"I am their queen!" she retorted. "I have an army, and I need to lead it. Glint needs to be prepared for the attack. I need to protect them, don't you understand?"

"Of course we understand." Medea was the one to speak up now. She hurried over to Lira. "I can use my magic to help your queendom," she told her.

"Nay, Medea," Rhys protested. "It might only trigger the darkness inside of you if you do. I don't want that to ever happen again. Especially not now, when you're pregnant."

"I am not going to just leave her defenseless, husband," said Medea. "I need and want to help."

"Me, too," said Talia, leaving the children playing on the floor and running over to join them. "I am fae. I'm also an Elemental of the Earth. I can use my powers to call forth the animals and plants and all of nature to come to our aid."

"But you are pregnant too," said Lira.

"I know, but it doesn't matter. My husband now has fae powers as well," said Talia, looking over at Darium. "Powers of the air."

"I don't exactly know how to use them yet, but I'll try," Darium answered.

"And I have my strength on my side," added Rhys. "I still think if we ask Mother and the other fae to help, they would. They are our allies."

"I said, no," snapped Zann. "Besides, I don't think the women should get involved. It's too dangerous."

"We are all in this together," Medea told him.

"I agree," said Talia. "We are all family now. I'm sure my mother and sisters would help us as well if I asked them. All of us working together will make a powerful team."

"But is it enough to defend ourselves from two different kingdoms?" asked Lira, still worried about what was about to transpire.

"I think it is," said Rhys with a satisfied nod. "Too bad we don't have Medea's dragon to help us out right now."

"It's not my dragon," Medea corrected him. "It is my brother-by-marriage's, and he has two of them. Mayhap I should go through the portal back to England and ask Marco for his help."

"Nay, we don't need to involve so many people," protested Zann. "Besides, they are not even from Mura. This is our problem and we will solve it. If I can't deter the women from helping, then so be it, but no one else. Rhys, can your army be ready to march over the mountain by first light?"

"I think so," said Rhys. "Of course, I'll have to leave some soldiers behind to defend Kasculbough. I wouldn't put it past Sethor or Grinwald to use this as an opportunity to attack Kasculbough as well, if we're all gone."

"What do you have to say about all this, Father?" asked Lira, realizing he had been so quiet this entire time.

"I don't think we should forget about the portal, Lira," Elric answered. "That is a great concern, and yet you all seem to have pushed it aside. Your daughter is in grave danger, unless you've forgotten."

"I think the planned attack on Glint needs to be addressed first," said Zann. "After all, the portal hasn't opened since we've been on this side of the mountain. Perhaps it won't happen again."

"You are a fool if you believe that," snapped Elric. "Of course, it is going to happen. You can count on it. We need to be prepared."

"Father? Have you had some sort of premonition? Do you know this for sure?" asked Lira.

"Daughter, I am a sage, not a mind reader," grunted Elric. "Besides, you are the one who has the premonitions, so you tell me."

"I don't know," said Lira in thought. Her gaze traveled over to her daughter. Little Lily and Valindra were playing together on the floor. They looked so happy. "I haven't had any more premonitions since we left Glint," Lira explained. "Perhaps Zann is right. Mayhap if Valindra stays here on this side of the mountain, she'll be safe."

"I can stay back at Kasculbough and protect her, as well as protect the castle," Medea offered.

"I don't like the idea of that," said Rhys, worrying about his wife, even though it seemed Medea had more power at her fingertips than all of them put together.

"Then I'll stay with Medea and the children, if it'll make the men feel better," offered Talia.

"I think that's probably a good idea," said Darium. "I know it would put my mind more at ease, not having to watch out for the women while we're fighting Grinwald and Sethor."

"So be it," said Rhys, gulping down the rest of his ale and getting to his feet. "I'll get my troops together and we'll leave at first light."

"Thank you," said Lira, feeling very grateful for all the help these people were giving her, although she'd only just met them. They were naught more than strangers to her, yet they acted more like family.

"You're making a mistake," warned Elric.

"Nay, Father, I'm sure this is the right answer," Lira told him. "Can you pop back to Glint and warn them? Tell Sasha what's happening. She'll ready the troops and make sure our defenses are in place."

"I can transport and take you there with me," said Medea. "I can get you there tonight so you can handle this yourself if you want. Then, I can return to Kascul-baugh to watch the children."

"Well . . . I . . . " Lira looked over to her daughter, and then back at Zann. Something made her want to stay with them tonight instead of leaving. She couldn't explain it, but she didn't feel right leaving them right now. "I think I'd like to travel with the rest, first thing in the morning, but thank you."

"I'm outta here," said Elric with a scowl. Her father disappeared in a flash.

Lira still hadn't really made amends with her father, and realized that she and Zann had something in common after all. Neither of them trusted the only parent they had left.

"I suggest we all get prepared and then try to get some shut-eye," said Zann. "Tomorrow is going to be a harrowing day."

"Aye," said Lira, feeling anxious, thinking about spending the night with Zann.

"Brother, do you have a room for Lira and me?" asked Zann.

"Of course," said Rhys. "Darium, I have a chamber for you and Talia, too," Rhys told their brother. "And one for the children."

"Nay, that won't be needed. My daughter will stay

with us," said Lira. That caused more than a few surprised looks from the others.

"Wife, I think mayhap it would be better if Valindra stayed with Lily for the night. Don't you?" asked Zann. His eyes drank her in. She was sure she felt lust in his gaze. Mayhap it should have repulsed her, but instead it sent a delicious shiver through her body.

Lira wasn't sure what to do or say. As much as she trusted that Valindra would be safe here, it still made her very nervous to be away from her daughter. But on the other hand, the portal hadn't appeared on this side of the mountain yet, so perhaps her worry was for nothing. She wanted to spend the night with Zann – her husband – alone.

"I'll watch the children overnight. I'll even stay in the bedchamber with them," offered Medea. Lira had heard that Medea had a dark side, even though she didn't know the girl at all. Medea had been nothing but kind to her since she arrived, but Lira was still leery of her. It was her protective nature as a mother, she supposed. Then again, Medea was a mother too, so she was sure she would never hurt Valindra. This was a hard decision.

"I – I'm not sure," she answered. "I think perhaps it would be best if my daughter stayed with us tonight."

"Whatever you want," said Medea with a shrug.

When Lira glanced back over at Zann, he was no longer looking at her like he wanted to eat her. Instead, he had an expression on his face that told her he was severely disappointed in her decision. She didn't care, she told herself. Even if they were married, it wasn't going to be for long. She and Zann were from different sides of the mountain, they weren't meant for each other. When they returned to Glint, she would dissolve this farce of a marriage. Then, she would do the proper thing and find an elven man to marry.

"Come along, Valindra," she said, holding her hand out for her daughter. "We will spend the rest of the day together, and tonight you will sleep with me."

"I don't want you to leave without me, Mother," said the little girl. "Can't I go home with you tomorrow?"

Home. The word lodged in Lira's chest. While Glint truly was their home, it hadn't felt like it, ever since the deaths of her husband, and her mother. And when her brothers never returned from battle, she realized they had died as well. It put such a weight on her shoulders and a damper to her spirit that she wasn't sure she could ever feel the same way about Glint as she had when she grew up there as a child.

"You'll stay at Kasculbough until I can secure Glint from the attack," she told her daughter.

"But I'm the Princess of Glint," said Valindra with sad eyes. "You said I needed to stay strong. I want to be with you. I want to return to Glint and help fight off the bad men."

"You'll have your turn someday, sweetheart, but not now." Lira brushed back her daughter's downy locks of hair. Then she hunkered down and pulled Valindra to her chest and squeezed her tightly.

Emotions welled-up inside her. Lira wanted nothing more than safety for her daughter, as well as her people. Being queen wasn't easy. It made it extra challenging since she didn't have any powers to defend herself or her family and loyal subjects anymore. She always thought she'd be able to rely on those powers as queen, but now it wasn't so.

She looked up over the head of her daughter to see Zann staring at her from the opposite side of the room.

He looked so handsome. It was hard for her to comprehend that this man was her husband now. She'd been without a husband, or even a man since Laeroth's death. She had refrained from being with any man because she felt as if she needed to keep his memory alive. Lira hadn't allowed herself to have feelings for anyone else. But what she felt today when Zann kissed her, made her wonder if she'd only been deceiving herself by trying to remain loyal to the memory of a man who was long gone.

"Everything is going to be all right, sweetheart," she told her daughter, wondering if this was only a lie as well.

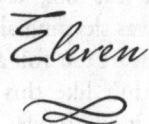

Eleven

BY THE TIME Zann had helped his brothers in preparing for battle, and the trip over the mountain they would take in the morning, it was late and most everyone was already in bed.

Feeling tired and worried, he opened the door to the chamber that he and Lira would be sharing along with her daughter. The last thing he wanted to do on his wedding night was to sleep alone. And that was exactly the way it would be since Valindra was sleeping with them. Even if the opportunity arose now, he wouldn't make love to her. He wasn't the kind of man to claim a woman with her child right there in the room, asleep or not.

The nighttime candle flickered in the darkness next to the bed, enabling him to see Lira's silhouette under the covers. It should be him in the bed with her tonight, but instead he wouldn't get close enough to even touch her. It was too tempting. Zann didn't trust himself close to her. Nay. He would try not to think about how badly he wanted Lira. Instead, he would sleep on the floor and forget they were even in the same room.

Too tired to even keep his eyes open any longer,

Zann headed to the other side of the room. He quickly removed his weapon belt, and his boots and clothes followed. Clad only in his braies now, he yawned and stretched, taking one last look at the bump under the bedcovers. His wife was sleeping alongside her daughter instead of him. His heart felt full and also empty at the same time. Zann didn't like this feeling and did not want to think about it any longer. He lay down on the cold floor to sleep, with no blanket. His body was hot for his wife and he desperately needed to cool down.

He had already started to drift off to sleep when the voice of an angel awoke him.

"Zann? What are you doing on the floor?"

"Huh?" He sat up, taking a moment to gather his bearings. Lira hunkered down next to him, smiling sweetly.

The flame from the candle in her hand lit up her face, and almost seemed to make her strawberry-blond hair glow. Her long, loose locks cascaded over her shoulders, only adding to her beauty, making her look like a goddess.

Lira was clad only in her bedclothes and had no other covering. The thin nightdress entailed a low V at the neck, exposing the tops of her perfectly rounded breasts. Zann's eyes settled there for a moment and then he forced himself to look away. Egads, didn't she know how hard this was for him just to look at her and not be able to reach out and touch her? The wench was going to drive him mad.

"Lira," he whispered. Merely saying her name aloud was torture. This beautiful elven queen was his wife now, but still, he could not touch her. The kiss they'd shared had been too quick, but so tantalizing that it left him wanting more. He wasn't getting more, he reminded himself. Not tonight, and probably never.

Soon, he wouldn't even be married to her any longer. This whole thing didn't sit right with him at all.

He felt an overpowering urge to pull Lira into his arms and kiss her . . . but he couldn't. He wouldn't. Not with her daughter in the room. Besides, she was off-limits now, and he had to remind himself that this marriage was not even real. It was naught but a prank pulled on them by that stupid, irritating sage. Why had Zann ever allowed it? He should have just let the sage tell the king he had nothing from the hunt. The king's punishment for him could never have hurt as much as this did right now. Then, he remembered it was Lira who talked him into going through with the wedding. The woman was like a siren of the sea, luring men in with her words. He did it because he found that he could not turn her down.

"Please, don't sleep like a dog on the floor," she told him. "I don't like it."

"Why not?" he grumbled. "I'm used to it, having done so many times in my wolf form." He wondered why she even cared.

"You're not a wolf tonight, Zann," she reminded him. "Tonight, you are a man . . . and my husband. I think we need to act like husband and wife, don't you?"

"Lira, what are you saying?" he asked, feeling confused by her words. "If you expect me to sleep in bed with you and not touch you, I cannot do it."

"You are my husband, Zann. I am your wife. We need to fulfill what is required of us."

"I'm confused. It sounds like you are saying we should make love." Zann wondered if he was dreaming, since she was the one who had made it clear they would not partake in consummating the marriage.

"Isn't that what married people do?" she asked him with a smile.

"But we're not married. Not really." Zann shook his head. Mayhap he could clear this vision he was having since he knew it couldn't be real. "Stop taunting me, please. Lira, you have reminded me of it more than once now."

"I know," she said, her smile disappearing. She released a deep breath and continued. "Zann, I think . . . I think I've changed my mind about not consummating the marriage."

"Why?" he asked, becoming immediately suspicious. "Because you need your powers and this is the only way to get them back, according to you father?"

"Well . . . I have to admit that thought did cross my mind. Tell me, would it bother you if I said that was the reason?"

Zann let out a sigh. "Yes, it would. But I suppose I can't blame you, Lira. If I had powers and lost them all and had a chance to regain them, I'm sure I would take any measure to make sure it happened. You know, I often wish I did have powers. Real powers I mean, not just this curse of shifting into a wolf. If I did, I would feel immortal, I swear. It must be a good feeling, I suppose."

"Zann, how do you feel about making love with me?"

"Well, I have to admit something to you that I am not proud of, Lira. I had every intention of using the excuse of you regaining your powers to try to lure you into bed with me tonight. It was wrong of me, but I was going to do it not only for that reason, but solely for my own wants and needs. I am sorry." Zann hadn't planned on revealing that fact to her, but he didn't want to lie to her either. She deserved better.

"Then, why won't you?" she asked, surprising him since this wasn't what he thought she'd say at all. He thought she would respond in a way similar to what she had done with anything else involving him lately.

"I don't want to make love with you if we're only going to break off the marriage afterwards," he told her. "I've decided if we make love, I want to stay married to you. But then, I suppose it doesn't even matter anymore. Your daughter is in the room, and I would never get intimate with a woman when a child is present."

"Valindra's not here, Zann."

"What?"

"See for yourself." She smiled and nodded to the bed.

"All right, I will." Zann stood up and took the candle from Lira. He walked over to the bed with Lira right behind him. Patting the covers, he glanced around the room, realizing that what the elven queen said was true. "Where is she, Lira? Did she take a walk to the garderobe? You know, it's not safe for her to be out around the castle alone. Especially not at night. There might be drunken soldiers that will give her trouble. I will go after her right away." He took a step, but she stopped him. She reached out and retrieved the candle from him and stuck it back into the tall, iron holder next to the bed.

"Lira?" he asked in question, wondering what she was doing and why she didn't seem concerned.

"Stop worrying," she told him. "My daughter is fine. She is not out wandering the corridors alone, I assure you. I would never allow that."

"Then where is she?"

"She is spending the night with her new friend, Lily-Rae. She adores the girl, and they love being together. I have never seen Valindra smile more. Medea and Talia are watching over the children."

"I don't understand. I heard you tell Valindra that she would be sleeping with you tonight."

"I did. However, I changed my mind. I thought we should spend our wedding night alone. Together, that is. Just the two of us, with no one else around."

"Really?" A flash of hope surged through him. Could she possibly have changed her mind about breaking off the marriage too? Did she truly want to be intimate with him? Did she really want to be his wife? He reminded himself it was only because she wanted to regain her powers so she could defeat the kings' attack that she wanted to do this. Part of him couldn't blame her, but it still hurt. Zann struggled with his decision. He really wasn't sure this was a good enough reason for them to couple. Especially, if they were going to annul the marriage later.

"I-I don't know, Lira. I'm not sure we should go through with this."

"You mean, you don't want to couple with me?" Her smiled faded quickly. "Oh. I understand."

"Nay, that's not what I mean. Yes, I want to make love with you, but not like this. Not for the reason you have in mind."

"And what do you think my reason is?" She looked at him from the corners of her eyes.

"I know you only want to do it because your father said that is the way to regain your lost powers. You basically admitted to me a moment ago that it was the case."

"Nay, I did no such thing. I asked what you would think if it had been my real reason, because I wanted to know how you felt, Zann. However, I assure you it is not the case at all. We are husband and wife now, and this is what we're supposed to do. I understand that, and don't want to brush it off as not being important."

"Sit down, Lira," said Zann with a sigh, sitting on the edge of the bed, patting the spot right next to him.

She hesitated. Zann thought for a moment that she wasn't going to do it. Then, ever so slowly, she lowered her bottom to the bed.

"What is it?" she asked. "You seem as if you want to talk about something important."

"In a way, I do. I just want to get to know my wife first, before coupling with her."

"Interesting."

"How so?"

"From what I've heard, you don't usually mind how well you know a woman before you bed her." She grinned slightly, but it wasn't a happy smile at all.

He didn't like to hear this piece of gossip springing from her lips, especially when it was true. "I see you've been listening to loose tongues around the castle."

"Well, is it? Just gossip, I mean? Or is it true?"

Now it was his turn to hesitate before he answered. "Nay," he admitted, shaking his head and looking the other way. He dragged a hand through his hair, feeling like naught more than a skirt-chaser now. "Aye," he added. "Lira, I'm sorry to have to tell you that you've been tricked into marrying probably the biggest philanderer in all of Mura. Everything you've heard about me, I'm sorry to say, is true."

"I see." She was quiet for a moment before she answered. "It doesn't matter," she finally replied, once again surprising him. "I see now that the act of marriage is something you hold sacred. If not, you would have already bedded me, and not hesitated in the least. I like that about you, Zann." She reached out and gently laid her hand on his arm, her warmth encompassing him fully.

"I like you," he said. "I find myself attracted to you . . . very much."

"But?" she asked, waiting for him to finish.

"This is all happening so fast."

"I agree."

"I feel as if we were tricked into the marriage."

"We were."

"I also know that all we need to do for you to regain your powers as the mighty Queen of Glint, is for us to couple. No matter how absurd that sounds to me, I suppose it is true," he added under his breath.

"I am not thinking about being a queen right now, husband. All I want to do is to get to know you better. I haven't had a man since my husband's death. I am nervous about making love, I cannot lie."

"Really?" His head turned in utter astonishment. "So, you mean to tell me that you haven't coupled since you lost your husband? It's been that long?"

"That's right," she said with a nod, swallowing forcefully. "It has been four years now."

"Wow," he said, not even able to comprehend not coupling for that amount of time. "Well, why didn't you?"

"I guess I felt guilty and just couldn't do that to Laeroth."

"I don't understand. He's dead and you're alive, sweetheart. What is there to feel guilty about?"

"I received the title of queen at my mother's death, one month after my eighteenth birthday," she explained. "I had also just birthed a baby. The giants on the Isle of Denwop attacked a few weeks later and I was required to give commands. I didn't really know what to do. I had to act quickly. I gave the order for the elves to fight back. It was what my mother would have done. She was ruthless when it came to defending the queendom. It was also what my aunt, Sasha, advised me to do."

"Yes, of course. You did the right thing."

"Did I?"

"I didn't know about the giant's attack," said Zann, feeling stupid about the entire situation.

"Of course not. You were on the other side of the mountain. The land of magic and the land of the humans are separate and this didn't affect you. How could you have known?"

"So . . . what happened?" he asked. "Did the giant's invade Glint?"

"Nay. We cut them off at the coast. The fae helped us. They never got further than the shore."

"Well, that's good."

"Laeroth was killed in the battle, Zann. He and my twin brothers, Korack and Keevan, were the only ones who actually got across the water and to the Isle of Denwop. I . . . I watched from the boat as a giant scooped up my husband and . . ." She whimpered and held her hands over her face. "I'll never forget the sounds of his cries for help."

"Don't," said Zann, reaching out and taking her hands in his, knowing that giants often ate elves, and that this is what happened. This couldn't be easy for her. "I don't want you to have to relive it." His heart went out to her. How could anyone endure seeing their loved one eaten by a damned giant?

"I could have tried to save him, but I didn't. I was too frightened to even use my magic," she continued. "I froze. I just stood there and watched as the giant took my husband. Another giant went after my brothers, and they ran inland. Korack and Keevan never returned. I knew then that they had died as well because of my fear. It was all so horrible, that I try not to think about it." A tear dripped down her cheek. "Their deaths are all my fault."

"Nay, it wasn't you fault, Lira. Don't say that."

"It was my fault!" she shouted, tears flowing freely

from her eyes now. "The fae were the ones who used their powers and were able to send the giants back to the Isle of Denwop. If it wasn't for them, we all would have died. My family needed me, Zann. They needed me, and I didn't help them."

"I thought elves have powers," he said. "Why didn't your husband and brothers use them?"

"Elves only come into their powers when they reach adulthood," said Lira. "I had just received my powers having just turned eighteen years of age, and I wasn't even sure how to use them. My brothers were only sixteen, and never had a chance."

"Didn't your husband have powers?" asked Zann.

"Nay. He was a year younger than me. I should have stopped him from fighting, but instead I ordered everyone to help defend Glint. Now, I wish that I wouldn't have let anyone without powers risk their lives. But I didn't. It's all my fault."

"What about your father?" asked Zann. "What did he do to help the situation?"

"My father . . . my father is crazy, and I think you know that. I never had a strong relationship with him. Mayhap he would have taught me how to use my powers eventually, but there wasn't time. Sasha was going to teach me but said since I'd just birthed a baby and lost my mother she said I needed to wait a little to regain my strength."

"So you don't even know how it feels to have powers?"

"Not really. I mean, a few things happened but they frightened me so much that I didn't try to do more. I felt worthless and so alone."

"No one instructed me about shapeshifting either, so I know how you feel. Sometimes we need to figure things out for ourselves and in our own way and time.

Still, you can't put the blame on yourself for the deaths of your family members."

"I do," she said, starting to cry. "If I hadn't ordered the attack, and if I had stopped them from going, they'd still be alive today."

"Stop it, Lira. It's not your fault. The giants were attacking and needed to be stopped. I am only sorry I didn't know about it, or my brothers and I could have come to help you."

"We don't expect humans from the other side of the mountains to assist us. Once the fae helped. When the battle was over, I went back to Glint feeling like a failure. I let my people down, Zann. I did nothing to help them. I even forbade any of the elves from going to the Isle of Denwop to collect the bones of my husband and brothers, because it was too risky. I couldn't let any more elves die. I just couldn't face the fact I had lost the people I loved. I guess by not finding closure, I somehow didn't have to face the fact that my husband and brothers were never coming back."

"I'm so sorry, Lira." Zann put his arm around her shoulders and pulled her closer. "I don't know what to say to take your pain away."

"I deserve everything I got," she spat through gritted teeth, now sounding angry with herself instead of sad. "It was my own cowardice that caused me to lose my powers, even if I couldn't control them."

"So you could really do magic?"

"I threw fire from my hand and it scared me. I didn't want to even try anything else. It was after the day of the battle that I realized I'd lost what little power I had. It never happened again. I don't deserve to ever get it back, either."

"Now, that's not true," he said, putting his arm around her shoulders. He continued to hold her other hand in his. "Everyone has times in battle when they are frightened. Even me."

"You?" She shook her head, not believing it. A tear dripped from her eye, making a trail down her cheek. "I can't believe that. You are the bravest man I've ever met, Zann."

"Sweetheart, I get the feeling that you don't really want your powers to return, do you?"

"I – I don't know." She bit at her bottom lip, seeming to try to hold back her emotions. "I do know that I don't feel that I deserve to have them returned. And even if they do come back . . . I no longer think I want to use them."

"Of course you do. Now, that's just silly talk."

"Is it?"

"Having powers is a good thing," he tried to convince her.

"I heard that your brother's wife, Medea, had powers that almost destroyed her. I don't want that to happen to me. I never want that to happen to Valindra when it is time for her to come into her powers, either."

"That's different," said Zann. "Medea isn't an elf. She is a witch who was born with dark magic."

"I don't care. I don't think I want powers anymore."

"But you're Queen of Glint. It is important that you have powers so you can rule and protect your realm. Right now, you need to remain strong. You are about to lead your people into battle once again."

"Nay. I don't think I want to be queen anymore," she said softly. Her words were so quiet that at first Zann thought he'd misheard her. "I don't want to command anyone to fight. I can't go through it again. I just want to be a good mother to Valindra, that's all. And a good wife."

"That is admirable that you want to be a devoted

wife and mother," he told her. "However, you need to mourn the loss of Laeroth and your brothers. Only then will you be able to move on."

"I can't help but feel that I have made a horrible mistake."

"Regrets only make a person weak. You made a choice, and as queen, you need to stand behind your decisions."

"It's so hard, Zann. I never knew being queen would feel like this."

"I can feel your pain, Lira. I'm sorry."

"I abandoned my family," she continued. "I left them to die when I froze and didn't help them. I didn't even collect their remains so they could have a proper burial. I am a bad person."

"Nay, you're not. You made that decision to protect the others," he reminded her. "You kept any more elves from dying that day, by insisting they didn't cross the waters and go to the Isle of Denwop to look for your family's remains. You thought of the other elves and their families. It was a noble thing to do."

"I guess so," she finally agreed, sniffling, seeming to consider his words. "They all had families and children. I just . . . I had to make the choice. I did what I had to do, in order to save the masses. Even if in doing so, I had to abandon those I loved."

Abandon. That word rang out like an alarm in Zann's ears. Lira's story only reminded him of what his mother told him, of why she had abandoned Zann and his brothers when they were naught but children.

"My mother made a similar choice to yours when I was a child," he told her. "She abandoned me and my brothers, leaving us to be raised by my father who was a Sin Eater. We were told she was dead."

"You were? Why?" asked Lira with a sniffle.

"It was my parents' decision to deceive us. They fought a lot when I was growing up. They were so different from each other and had no right ever getting married. My mother didn't want her children growing up in and atmosphere like that. But she is fae and cannot lie. That, she said, was the reason she could never return. If so, she would have to tell us the truth about how she gave us up to our father."

"That sounds so harsh," said Lira, wiping away a tear with the back of her hand. "I'm sure your mother thought it was the best thing for her children. For you and your brothers, Zann. If not, she wouldn't have done it."

"I suppose so, but she didn't even fight for us!" His emotions swelled and rose to the surface now. Lira's experience and emotions about her situation only brought his out as well. "How can I forgive a woman who didn't care about me as a child? A mother who thought of herself over us?"

"Is that what you think she did? I don't know all the details, but I don't see it that way at all. She is your mother, Zann. A mother does what she feels is best for her children."

"Nay. She was horrible to do that to us," he growled.

"I did something similar by abandoning my husband and my brothers. Does that make me a horrible person, too? Because I often think it does."

Lira's words were soft but powerful, making Zann think about his own situation a little deeper. "Nay. That is different, Lira. You were thinking about your realm, not yourself. I don't blame you in the least and neither should you be so hard on yourself."

"The way I see it, we have this in common, Zann. I also believe your mother did what she had to, for the good of you and your brothers, even if you can't see that right now."

Zann didn't want to talk about himself anymore, so he changed the subject. "Why did you banish your father from the castle?" he asked her.

"It happened right after the battle. I did it, because he never gave up hope of finding my brothers. He was convinced they were still alive and he told me I was wrong. He wanted me to send troops back to the Isle of Denwop to look for them. But I didn't. Instead, I just sent him away so I wouldn't continually be faced with what already happened and what I could not change."

"Why didn't Elric just go himself to look for them if he was that adamant about it? He has a lot of magic."

"He wanted to go. He probably would have if the gods hadn't stopped him."

"The gods? What are you saying? What do they have to do with any of this? I don't understand."

"My father is not only a sage but a messenger of the gods," she explained.

"You've got to be jesting!" Zann found this hard to believe. Is there nowhere that that irritating little elf didn't go?"

"It's true. He said the gods told him that this was my lesson in life and that he couldn't interfere. They threatened to take away all his powers if he ever even attempted to go to the Isle of Denwop himself."

"Wow. I had no idea," said Zann. "I guess it isn't a good thing to disregard the gods and goddesses and their wishes. They can get nasty."

"I am sorry to admit that I blamed him for everything when nothing was really his fault. I blamed him for the death of my mother too, since he couldn't cure her illness. She had a weak heart, and that's what took her life in the end. I blamed him for my loneliness of not having a husband, and for me being a single mother to my child."

"Surely, that wasn't his fault."

"I know that now. But I asked him for guidance as to what to do about the war before I ever gave the order. He told me I needed to act like a queen and defend my people. That was the deciding factor for me in sending all those brave elves to battle."

"This is a lot to put on your shoulders, I know. But surely, each of those warriors knew their chances of being killed before they ever even agreed to fight."

"Perhaps. After I saw my husband die and my brothers run, I couldn't watch anymore."

"Then how do you know your brothers really died? Mayhap your father is right in thinking they survived."

"How could they? And it's been so long. Even if they had escaped at first, they're long gone by now. If not, they would have found a way to come home."

"I see." Zann let out a deep breath.

"I admit I was horrible to my father. I sent him atop the cliff to live and told him to never return. I also said I never wanted to see or talk to him again. He was never allowed to even see Valindra grow up."

"I suppose that is why the sage is kind of . . . crazy?"

That got a smile out of her. "Well, I can't really take the blame for that one," she said, wiping at her eye. "He was always odd. My father might be a sage, and supposedly very wise, but honestly, I get the impression it was a courtesy title only. Elric has always been a little on the eccentric side."

"How in the world did he ever get the position of being messenger to the gods?" asked Zann with a chuckle. "That one is hard to digest."

"I'm not sure about that. You see, my father is a lot older than you think."

"How old?"

"I don't know for certain since he won't talk about it. But my aunt, Sasha told me once that my mother said he is hundreds of years old."

"Elves live that long?" asked Zann in surprise.

"I can't say I've ever heard of any elves being that old," she answered.

"Now I see why he's not of stable mind, and also so ornery." Zann faked a shiver. "I can't imagine anyone would really want to live that long. And just think of all the poor people he aggravated over that amount of time."

They both laughed at that, and it broke the tension.

"Lira, would it be so bad if we stayed married after this is all over?" he asked her.

"I don't know. I'm an elf and you're a . . . I'm not exactly sure what you are."

"I'm part fae. I've discovered that lately, although I have no magic regarding it. My only magic is being a shapeshifter, and that is from my father's side of the family."

"Why?" she asked.

"Why what?"

"Why do you shapeshift, and not your brothers?"

"I can't answer that. All I can tell you is that it is the way it's always been. Only males have been born to the Blackseed family for generations."

"But Rhys and Medea have a girl."

"Yes," he said in thought. "Mayhap things are changing after all. You see, the first son born to a Blackseed has always been a Sin Eater."

"Like your brother, Darium," she said with a nod.

"Yes. And the second son takes on the trait of being a shifter. That's me."

"But your father wasn't a shifter?"

"Nay. He was a first son, and a Sin Eater. But my grandfather was a bear shifter. I don't remember him much, but he taught me a little bit about shifting when I was very young."

"Oh," she said, sounding confused. "And Rhys is the youngest?"

"He is. Rhys inherited the power of extreme strength. My great grandfather had it, too, I've been told, although we never knew him either. Rhys always had the power to heal himself as well."

"Is that a Blackseed trait?"

"Nay. That came from the fae side of the family, although we didn't know it until recently."

"Zann, how does it feel to . . . to turn into a wolf?"

"I can't explain it. It feels . . . weird sometimes. At other times it feels . . . good actually. Freeing, I guess you can say. Then again, sometimes it just feels as if I'm cursed. I always wanted real powers, but don't consider shapeshifting into a wolf one of them."

"I still don't understand why it happens to you."

"It's in my blood, I suppose." He shrugged. "There are some things involving magic that have no explanation. I don't understand how your father can move so fast, and chop up food in a matter of seconds either."

"I know," she said with a giggle. "I don't understand either. I suppose he keeps getting faster with age. I don't think I inherited that power, so it has never happened to me."

"What kind of powers did you have? Before you lost them, I mean."

"Well, just the normal ones of high elves, I suppose. I'm not really sure since I had just started receiving them when they stopped."

"High elves?"

"Nobles. We tend to have more powers than normal elves."

"Oh. You said you threw fire from your hand. Were you able to do anything else?"

"I moved things without touching them, once or twice," she explained. "And I think I started to turn invisible, but I'm not exactly sure. I might have had more powers later on, but I didn't have them long enough to find out."

"Invisible? Really?" This interested Zann. "I often wish I could do that."

Lira continued. "The only power that seems to have stayed with me is the power of premonition, but that might not even be a power at all. It comes and goes, but it happens only when I'm sleeping, it seems."

"I think you deserve to have your powers returned to you," Zann told her.

"What are you saying?" She looked at him as if with caution.

"I'm saying, I will make love with you, just so you can get your powers back. Even if you want to end the marriage afterwards, I understand. Even though, let me make it clear, I don't agree with ending it. However, I want to help you in any way I can, and so I will."

"Thank you, Zann." Her cheeks blushed and she grinned. "It has been such a long time."

"Then, you'll wait no longer." Zann reached over and tilted her chin upward with his fingertips. Pressing his lips gently against hers, he kissed her.

Her arms wrapped around him and she returned the kiss, making Zann feel heady. Something about this elf stirred things inside him that had never been awakened before.

. . .

Lira surrendered to the feelings inside her that had been dormant for so long. Recently, they had been brought back to life by Zann. His lips touching hers caused a wave of emotion to go coursing through her body. She felt protected and safe in his arms. It also felt right to be with him.

Even though Lira didn't know Zann well, it didn't concern her. If he was a bad person, she was sure she'd have been able to tell by now.

Zann ran his hands slowly down her back, stopping and shifting to her front, to caress her breasts next, right through her thin shift. He was gentle, and that surprised her. Since she knew he was often in his animal form, she had expected him to be rough, like a beast.

When his hand dipped below her bodice, she didn't stop him. It excited her to no end when his fingers rolled her nipple, causing it to go taut. Then he removed his hand and pushed up her nightdress little by little, running his hands along her thighs.

She whimpered, feeling anxiety as well as anticipation coursing through her. The higher his hands went, the more excited she became. All she could think about was the ecstasy she was about to feel when they made love.

Eagerly, she helped him to remove her nightdress. He was already nearly naked, so she didn't need to do the same to him. Lira hadn't been able to stop looking at his chest since he'd undressed, with the intention of going to sleep earlier. He had thought she was sleeping, but she wasn't. She was waiting for him and too excited to sleep.

"Husband," she said, running her hands down his sturdy chest, watching as his nipples hardened under her touch. She couldn't help but squeeze the muscles in his upper arms. So hard. So solid. So amazing.

"Wife," he said, laying her back on the bed, lowering his head to her chest. His mouth closed over one nipple, causing her to moan in a sultry manner. He made magic with his mouth and tongue, bringing a dormant part of her to life once again. It was like the thaw of spring after a long, cold winter. She had been feeling dead, but now, because of Zann, she came to life once again.

The spiral of heat coiled in her belly, slowing climbing until she felt the tingling of excitement encompass her entire body from her head down to her toes. Then, he caressed her ears, about driving her mad with want.

"I've never made love to an elf before," he whispered in a deep voice. "Your ears are intriguing. They are so pointy at the tips, yet so soft." He slowly traced the tip of her ear with his finger. A tingling sensation ran down her ear all the way to her groin.

"An elf's ears are an erogenous zone," she explained.

"Really?" His hand stilled and his mouth took its place now. He nibbled on her ear, and blew a gentle breath inside it. Her body jerked and her back arched. And when he used the tip of his tongue to trace the outline of her ear next, she felt her head about exploding with sensuous pleasure. Lira could no longer hold back her cries of desire.

"Aaaaaah, ooooooh," she moaned, squirming beneath him, feeling each touch of his tongue as if he were licking her most private part.

"You like this, my little elf?" he whispered, causing a throbbing pulse to strengthen between her thighs. She had started to climb, and didn't want to descend. This feeling was welcome and long overdue.

"Y-you don't know what you're doing to me, Zann," she said through a ragged whisper.

"Oh, I think I know exactly what I'm doing." This

time, he slipped his hand under the band of her braies and cupped her womanhood at the same time he nibbled her ear. And when his tongue dipped into the ear canal, he slid one finger inside her, causing her to jerk and squeeze his arm between her knees. She felt a wetness between her thighs that she hadn't felt in a long time now.

Zann continued to flick his tongue and fingers in unison, bringing her to a height of titillating arousal. She didn't know how much longer she could hold back before she burst with pleasure.

"Please, Zann," she begged. "I want to feel you inside me. Now. All of you. I need to feel you right now."

"Are you sure about this?" he whispered into her ear.

"I am more sure about this than anything in my life right now."

She didn't have to ask him again. In a flash, he'd removed his braies as well as hers, and straddled her.

She looked down to see his engorged form. She moaned again with want. Reaching out, she boldly wrapped her fingers around his hardened shaft. "Mmmmm," she purred. "I want this!"

"I do, too," he said, seeming to be as excited as her.

"Elves can be very promiscuous when it comes to sex," she told him. "We like it a lot. Too much, sometimes."

"I hear from my brother that the fae are like that too," he answered.

"Aye, elves and fae are similar. Are you sure you're ready to experience this?"

"I think I'm the one who should be asking if you are ready for the likes of me."

"I am," she said. "I want you, Zann. I want you now more than I've wanted anything in life." Desire coursed through her, mingling with lust and life. She had to feel him inside her, and she needed it now.

"I can't wait any longer, sweetheart," he mumbled.

"Neither can I, Zann. If I wait any longer, I swear I am going to burst."

He pushed her legs apart with his knee, sliding his hardened shaft into her slowly, guided by her own liquid lust.

"Ooooooh," she moaned, throwing back her head and arching her back. And when he had entered her completely, she raised up her legs and hooked them around his waist, meeting his thrusts with the motion of her hips. They did the dance of love, both climbing higher and higher to the crest of extreme pleasure and delight. It didn't take long before they both surrendered to their desires, and the release was simultaneous for them both.

"Aaaaaaah," he moaned, followed by a sound that mimicked a growl and then a slight howl. It almost made her laugh since he sounded like a wolf. And when they parted, breathing heavily, holding each other tightly, she realized that they had just consummated their marriage. Now, they were truly man and wife.

"That was . . . fantastic, Zann," she said, lying on her back and staring up at the ceiling.

"Aye," he answered, his breathing labored as well. "I never expected making love with an elf would be so satisfying."

"Are you sorry you did it?" she asked.

"Nay. Are you?"

"Not at all."

"Lira, did it work?" he asked.

She chuckled. "I'd think the sounds of our love-making would have answered that question, Husband."

"Nay, I don't mean that. I know we were both fully

sated. I meant the magic. Has your magic returned like your father said it would?"

"Oh. I don't know."

"Try something. Anything. See if it returned."

"Well, all right." She sat up in bed and waved her hand through the air, trying to knock over a chair. Nothing happened. "It's not working. I can't move things, Zann."

"Try throwing fire."

"What? Nay. Not in here."

"The window is open. Throw a fire bolt out the window."

"I'll try." She did as he asked, but once again, nothing happened. "Nay," she said. "I can't do it."

"Try turning invisible then. Mayhap the magic comes back a little at a time."

"Good idea." She focused on becoming invisible, not feeling the tingle she felt when this happened to her in the past. "Can you still see me?" she asked.

"Yes," he said, pulling her into his arms. She lay her head atop his chest, feeling sad and defeated. Zann kissed her and gently brushed back her hair.

"It didn't work, Zann. I'm still powerless, and about to go to battle once again. I don't know what to do."

"Don't worry about it tonight, sweetheart." He wrapped his arms around her, letting out a sigh. "Let's just embrace what we have right now, tonight, and not worry about tomorrow."

"Aye," she agreed, cherishing each moment that she spent with Zann. "I won't let it worry me." She said the words, but didn't mean them. While she coupled with Zann because she wanted to be his wife, she realized that mayhap a small part of her did hope it would return her powers. She had told him she didn't want her powers anymore, nor to be queen. She meant it at the time. But now that she was feeling better, she wondered if she only felt that way so she wouldn't be disappointed if her powers didn't return. If she was going to lead her realm into battle, it certainly would be better if she had powers she supposed. She felt torn inside, and decided she wasn't sure about anything anymore.

Lira heard Zann's breathing change and realized he had already fallen asleep. As tired as she was and as much as she wanted to sleep, Lira couldn't relax.

Tomorrow, she would be faced with the duties of a queen. Once again she would have to lead the elven realm into battle. She didn't know if she could do that. She didn't really want to. All she wanted was to stay here feeling safe in Zann's arms and to be a family with him and Valindra. Unfortunately, she couldn't do that either. She was the ruler of Glint, and had duties to perform. There were responsibilities that fell on her shoulders alone. It was all so overwhelming! Lira was about to lead her people in a battle, and she had no powers to protect herself or to protect the others. It left her feeling even more vulnerable than ever before.

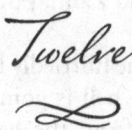

Twelve

"ZANN? Lira? We're ready to go," came Rhys' voice from outside their room early the next morning.

"Aye. We'll be right there." Zann hopped out of bed and started to dress. "Lira, sweetheart, wake up," he told her. "We need to leave now."

"Mmmm?" Lira opened one sleepy eye and then the other. She smiled at Zann, looking so inviting that he had to lean over and kiss her.

"Damn, I wish we weren't going to battle. I'd love nothing more than to spend the day in bed with you, wife."

"Me, too." Lira sat up and yawned. She had just stood up, naked, when the door swung open.

"Zann, we're all waiting," said Rhys, about to enter the room.

"Nay!" Lira spun around and held out her hand. The door slammed into Rhys and closed on its own, as if someone had actually pushed it.

"Ow!" Zann heard his brother mumble from the corridor.

"Lira? I think you just used your magic," said Zann excitedly.

"Aye," she said, looking at her hand in astonishment. "I guess I did. I didn't mean to do it. I just didn't want your brother to see me naked."

"This is great," said Zann, putting on the rest of his clothes.

"I – I guess so." She hurriedly began to dress.

"Zann? What the hell is going on in there?" came Rhys' grumpy voice from the hallway. "And why did you slam the door in my face?"

"We'll meet you in the great hall, brother. We'll be there momentarily," Zann called out.

Lira was quiet while she dressed. Too quiet, in Zann's opinion.

"What is it, sweetheart?" he asked, pulling on his boots and standing to don his weapon belt. "Are you bothered by the fact we made love last night?"

Her head snapped upward and her eyes opened wide. "Nay. Never, Zann. I will cherish that for the rest of my life."

"Then what is troubling you?"

"Nothing," she said, not looking at him when she answered. She hurriedly ran a brush through her hair and used her nimble fingers to braid her long locks.

"It's nice that you have your powers back. Try something else," he said, anxious to see what else she could do.

"Nay. Not now," she told him, almost sounding perturbed. This was when he realized that she wasn't excited about having regained her powers after all.

"Lira? Look at me."

"What for?" She finished braiding her hair, and then laced her bodice.

"Sweetheart." He walked up behind her and wrapped his arms around her waist, kissing her on the ear from behind.

"Don't, Zann," she said, with her eyes closed.

"You don't like that?" he asked.

"I do. Too much. But it isn't the time for that now."

"I understand." He released her and she turned to face him.

"Please, don't take this the wrong way. I'm happy to be with you. I just don't want it to end. I don't want to lead the elves into battle, and I don't want anyone else to die."

"It'll be all right, Lira. I'll be there with you. So will my brothers and an entire army. Besides, you have your powers back now so you have nothing to worry about. Kings Sethor and Grinwald might have armies and a giant on their side, but they don't have powers to aid them like the elves do. Therefore, they are at a disadvantage. Go ahead. Try some more magic. See if you can throw flames. Or mayhap turn yourself invisible. I can't wait to see what you can do." He was more excited about this than she was for some reason.

"Nay. Not now. We've got to go." She headed for the door.

"You're afraid to use your powers to help your people, aren't you?" he asked, causing her to stop with her hand on the door latch. She answered without turning around.

"Forget what you saw, Zann. I don't really have my powers back. It was just a fluke. I'm sure it won't happen again."

With that, she opened the door and left the room, leaving Zann standing there feeling even more confused than ever.

* * *

"Mama," cried Valindra as soon as Lira walked into the great hall of Kasculbough Castle.

"Baby, come here," said Lira with a smile, hunkering down and holding out her arms. Her daughter ran to her. Lira picked up the little girl, giving her a tight squeeze.

"I want to come with you," said Valindra, causing Lira's heart to ache. The last thing she wanted was to leave her daughter behind. Especially since she didn't know if she'd ever see her again.

"It's not safe for you to come with me, Valindra. You need to stay here with our new friends. I'll come back for you soon."

"Do you promise?" asked Valindra. "Do you promise you won't die?"

This was going to be hard to answer. Lira didn't want to lie to her daughter, yet she also didn't want the little girl to be scared. She honestly didn't know if she'd return at all.

"I will do my best," she said, kissing her daughter. Inside, she felt like she wanted to cry. Outside, she kept her emotions at bay and tried not to let anyone see how upset she really was.

"Lira. It's time to leave." Zann came up and put his hand on her shoulder.

"Don't leave." Valindra grabbed Zann around the legs tightly, almost causing him to fall. "I want my mother and father to stay with me."

"Father?" Zann looked over to Lira, not sure how to react. "I'm not your father, sweetheart," he told her. "I mean . . . not really."

"She never knew her father and has never had one until now," Lira explained.

"Oh," Zann answered, at a loss for words.

When Valindra referred to Zann as her father, it

made Lira realize that they could truly be a family now. She married Zann and they had consummated the marriage. Valindra never knew Laeroth since she had been a baby when he died. However, she seemed to easily accept Zann as the man to take his place. It made Lira feel that this was right and not wrong. She only hoped that Zann would return from battle, too. If anything happened to either of them, she wasn't sure that Valindra could survive. She also didn't want her child to end up being an orphan.

"Now, now," said Zann, picking up the little girl and giving her a kiss on the head. "We'll be back before you know it. Just be sure to listen to Medea and Talia while we are gone. Can you do that for me?"

"Uh huh," said the little girl with a nod, staring into Zann's eyes.

"I want to see you smile before I go." When she didn't smile, Zann tickled her. Valindra giggled.

"Come on, Valindra," said Talia, taking her from Zann. "Lily-Rae wants to show you how she can levitate her toys again."

"Nay!" Lira jolted. "No magic. Please," she said.

Talia looked at her and then her eyes roamed over to Zann. "All right," she said softly. "If that is what you want, I will try to make sure we all respect your wishes."

"It's better for now if there is no magic," Zann told her, trying to stick up for his new wife even if he didn't understand her request.

"Of course." Talia smiled and headed away with Valindra in her arms.

"Thank you, Zann," said Lira, once she had gone.

"Sweetheart, what is the matter?" asked Zann, starting to become concerned. "Medea's child has magic. Even though I backed you up just now, it is really not your place to tell her not to use it."

"I would rather Valindra not be exposed to a lot of magic. Not now. Not yet."

"I get the feeling magic is suddenly making you uncomfortable."

"I have to admit, I'm having second thoughts about getting my powers back and I'm not sure I like it," she told him.

"But, why not? Now that your powers have returned, you can use them to your advantage to rule and protect Glint."

"I don't want them! They only cause trouble. We are all better off without them."

Zann could see that there was much more to this than she was letting on. There was something she wasn't telling him and he wanted to know what it was. However, he wasn't sure this was the time to press her for information. They were about to go to battle and needed to keep their heads clear.

"All right," Zann said. "We can talk about this later. The traveling party is ready to go. We need to get a head start so we'll be ready to defend Glint when Kings Sethor and Grinwald and their armies show up."

"I know," she said, letting out a sigh. "I am ready to do my duty as queen. Let's return to Glint."

* * *

Zann rode his horse alongside his brothers, as Rhys' army headed over the Picajord Mountains. Darium's raven flew high overhead, circling around and keeping a lookout for trouble.

The sun rose on the horizon causing the sky to brighten in beautiful hues of orange and pink. Birds chirped happily. The many trees swayed in the gentle breeze bringing life to the mountain. Everything seemed so serene and beautiful that it was hard to believe a battle would soon take place.

"Has anyone seen Grinwald's army yet?" asked Zann.

"My raven saw them heading to Macada Castle to team up with King Sethor earlier this morning," reported Darium. "Talia was able to get the information from the bird before we left."

"Well, they won't risk having to ride around Kasculbough to cross the mountains here," said Rhys. "They'll more than likely cross on the west side."

"That's steeper and further away," said Zann.

"Good. It'll take them longer," remarked Darium.

"Yes, but they'll come out closer to Glint than we will after they cross, so hopefully we will beat them there," Zann answered.

"Brother, why did you slam the door in my face this morning?" asked Rhys.

"I didn't. That was Lira," Zann explained.

"Really?" asked Darium with a chuckle. "She is feistier than I thought."

"We made love last night, and she was naked and she didn't want Rhys to see her," said Zann.

"You consummated the marriage," Darium said with a nod of approval. "I'm glad to see someone is interrupting you in the marriage bed the way you two kept doing to me."

"Does she have her powers back now?" asked Rhys.

"How do you think she slammed the door on you from across the room?" Zann asked him.

"You don't sound excited about it," Rhys continued.

"I am, but I'm not so sure about Lira."

"What does that mean?" Darium looked back over

his shoulder at his brothers as he led the way through a steep pass.

"It means, I don't think she really wants her powers back, but for the life of me I can't understand why," said Zann. "Honestly, I'm not even sure she really wants to be queen anymore."

"What happened to make her feel that way?" Rhys wondered.

"She lost her husband as well as two brothers in the last battle against the giants. She has been blaming herself for their deaths for years now."

"I'm sure she's not to blame," said Darium. "I'd be more apt to believe the sage is responsible for anything that went wrong. By the way, where is that irritable little man? Shouldn't he be here?"

"Aye," said Rhys. "He's so pesky, I thought he'd be here doing whatever he could to bother us by now."

"I'd appreciate it if you three would refrain from talking about my father behind his back."

Zann turned his head to see Lira on her horse right behind him. He groaned. "How long have you been there, Lira?"

"Long enough to know that all this gossip is only slowing us down. We have a castle and people to defend. Now pick up the pace." She kicked her heels into the sides of her horse and sped past them.

"Lira, slow down. It's dangerous," Zann called out.

"I guess we should have been a little more discreet with our conversation," said Darium.

"Nay, it wouldn't have mattered," Zann told them. "Right now, I don't think it matters what we do or say. Lira is going to find something to be angry about, because she's obviously not happy with herself and that isn't something anyone can easily fix."

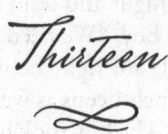

Thirteen

LIRA RODE LIKE THE WIND, leaving the rest of the travelling party behind. She needed to get away from everyone and ponder things by herself. With the wind in her face and the lush green land of Glint all around her, she already felt better.

She was the first one to the castle. Riding in though the open gates, she slid off her horse and handed the reins to her stable boy, Morthil.

"My queen. You've returned," said the boy with a bow, taking the reins from her.

"Where is Lady Sasha?" asked Lira, trying to keep her mind on business. If she didn't, she'd only start worrying about Valindra again, or thinking about making love with Zann. Right now, she didn't want to think about anything other than securing Glint from the two kingdoms coming to attack them.

"She's inside the castle with the sage," said the boy.

"My father is here?" Hearing that made Lira feel anxious. She knew Elric was going to ask about her powers. She also knew it wasn't going to be easy to lie to him about how she was feeling. He wouldn't be happy with the truth.

"Aye," said the stable boy. "The sage told us about the attack about to take place on Glint. He is discussing the plans with Lady Sasha."

"Find my head knight and send her to see me immediately," she told the boy. "We need to prepare. The soldiers of Kasculbough are right behind me and coming to help us, so see to their needs as well."

"Yes, my queen." The boy took her horse and ran off.

Lira made her way across the courtyard, hesitating before she entered the keep. Taking a deep breath, she slowly released it and went inside. Sure enough, her aunt and father were at the dais talking.

"Daughter," said Elric, looking up from his tankard of ale. "Have you brought the rest of those big oafs to help you fight off the kings coming to attack us?"

"Zann, and his brothers, and the soldiers of Kasculbough are right behind me," she stated.

"Lira, is it wise to ask for their help?" asked Sasha. "We don't need them. They're not from our side of the mountain."

"Yes, Sasha, we do. And since our attackers are from the their side of the mountain, it is even more important that Zann and the others are here. We have strength in numbers."

"We are elves with magic. They don't have powers, so what good are they?" complained Sasha.

"After the last battle with the giants, I will not risk any more elven lives. We will accept any help we can get," Lira told her.

"I see," said Sasha, pursing her lips and looking down to the cup in her hands. Sasha was a lot like Lira's late mother with her way of thinking. They both believed in being strong and fighting and never asking for help from outside kingdoms.

"So, daughter, did you consummate the marriage?" asked her father, getting right to the point.

"I did. We did," said Lira with a stiff upper lip. She saw Zann enter the great hall and make his way over to them.

"Then you have your powers back, don't you?" asked Elric.

Zann stopped next to her, not saying a word.

"No. Yes. Well, I might. I'm not exactly sure," she answered.

"For goodness sake, try it," said Sasha. "It is more important now than ever. You'll need your powers as soon as the battle starts."

"There is no time for this now," said Lira. "We need to prepare our defenses and get our army ready."

"I'm here, my queen," said her head knight, Veara. The knight was a strong woman who was good with a sword. Veara was a big woman with broad shoulders. She was a good ten years older than Lira and experienced in warfare.

"I am here as well," said her steward, Gilma, another woman whom she trusted and could always count on. Gilma was tall with red hair and good with a bow and arrows.

"Veara, get the warriors armed and in position," commanded Lira. "Place the archers atop the battlements facing the mountain since that is the direction from which our attackers will come. Gilma, you are in charge of the archers. Veara will lead the soldiers on the ground. Has word been sent to the elves of the countryside to come into the castle's walls for their own protection?"

"Aye," answered Veara. "Most of them are already here."

"Good," said Lira with a nod. "Once everyone is inside, we will close the gate."

"We sent word to the villagers as soon as the sage told us about the battle," said Lady Sasha. "I gave the order myself."

"Thank you," Lira said. "Then, as soon as the soldiers of Kasculbough are inside, have the gates closed and bar the door."

"Aye, my lady." Gilma nodded and ran off to do as told.

"My brother and his men will be of better use to Glint outside the castle walls," said Zann. "I am sure that is where Rhys will want his army to be."

"We'll start inside," Lira ordered. "We can try picking them all off from within the protection of our own walls."

"My queen, I have to agree with Zann," said Sasha. "We need an army outside the gate for hand-to-hand combat."

"Nay," Lira protested. "We're doing it this way. I am trying to protect as many of our people and Kasculbough's soldiers as I can."

"Lira, they're soldiers," Zann said softly. "They need to be in the midst of the battle."

"I've given my orders," snapped Lira, not wanting Zann's family to die in this attack.

"Will we be using the hot oil, my queen?" asked the head knight.

"We'll start with the archers on the battlements," said Lira.

"I think we should throw fireballs at them as well," said Sasha.

"We don't have many elves left who can do that," Lira pointed out.

"Then we'll use the hot oil dropped on our enemy as suggested," said Sasha.

"Mayhap. But first we'll start with arrows to

frighten them away," Lira instructed. "I'm not looking to kill off the enemy, just to scare them away."

"Of course, my queen." Veara ran off to do as told.

Zann stood watching, impressed by Lira's ability to act like a leader, but also a little confused as to why she said she didn't want to hurt anyone. He could see the confusion on Sasha's face and her father's as well. This was war! The enemy's feelings shouldn't be taken into consideration. Lira needed to do whatever she had to in order to protect her queendom.

As soon as the others left, Sasha confronted Lira.

"What is the matter with you?" she snapped. "You seem as if you are not fit to lead this battle. If you will not give the orders to kill our attackers to save our people, then I will."

"It's not that. Of course, we will do whatever is needed," explained Lira. "I am just . . . so tired of so many needless deaths, that's all."

"Where is Princess Valindra?" asked Sasha.

"My daughter is safe at Kasculbough," Lira answered.

"Safe? With humans?" sniffed the woman.

"She is with my sisters-by-marriage," interrupted Zann. "One is fae, the other a witch, and both are quite capable of protecting the girl, I assure you."

"Lira, you need to use your powers," said Elric. "Try them now. They should work if you've consummated the marriage. Unless you're lying to us?"

"Nay, she is not lying. I can vouch for that." Zann's eyes met Lira's and interlocked for a moment. Her cheeks turned a rosy shade before she quickly looked the other way.

"Father, I don't think I have powers," she answered.

"They didn't return?" he asked in confusion. "Well, why not?"

"Lira," said Zann softly, looking over to her, not wanting her to lie.

She seemed frustrated or upset. Then, she nodded slowly. "I did have a burst of power and was able to close a door, but that is all," she admitted.

"Well, try it now," Sasha commanded. "It is as good a time as any. We need to know if we can count on you to defend Glint as soon as the attack starts."

"I – I suppose I can try."

"It's all right, sweetheart. It's for the good of your people," Zann told her. "Try it."

Lira slowly raised her hands. "I'll try to knock over that goblet." She looked as if she were really focusing but nothing happened.

"Try fire," commanded Sasha. "Fire is our strongest weapon. If you have that, nothing else matters."

"All right." Lira tried again, waving her hands in the air, but no fire emerged.

"Can you turn invisible?" asked her father. "Try that now, daughter. Concentrate. Focus."

"I'm trying," she said in frustration. When the look of failure washed over her face and nothing happened, Zann realized that it wasn't her powers that Lira had lost, but her confidence. "I – I'm sorry, but I don't have powers. I can't do anything." Emotion seemed to well up in her and she rushed off before Zann could stop her.

"Lady Lira, come back here." Sasha ran off after her, leaving Zann standing there with the damned elf.

"Well, I suppose I should go help my brothers prepare for battle." Zann was in a hurry to get away from the crazy man. He turned and started away, but in a blur Elric zoomed in front of him and then stopped. Zann stopped, too, or he would have crashed into him. "Do you really have to do that?" he complained.

"Did you two really consummate the marriage? I need to know the truth." Elric crossed his arms over his chest and raised an eyebrow.

"We told you we did. Did you want details? Nay. Don't answer that. You know I'd never give them."

"All these years I have been waiting for Lira to marry again so she could regain her powers."

"Is it common for an elf to lose her powers just because her husband died?" asked Zann.

"Nay. But in her case, something very traumatic happened to cause it."

"I know. Seeing her husband eaten by a giant will do it I suppose."

"Is that what she told you?" Elric made a face, making Zann feel as if he'd been a fool.

"Well, I thought that's what she said. Mayhap I just assumed it. Isn't that what happened?"

"Why don't you ask Lira?"

"Are you saying my wife lied to me?"

"I'm only saying trauma can cause a person to do things or even say things they don't mean. It's a big part of why Lira banished me, you know."

"Tell me more."

"I'll tell you nothing, fool."

"if you're not going to tell me a thing, why are you still standing here?" asked Zann.

"I think I've chosen badly."

"What does that mean?"

"I needed to find her a husband, but I must have made a mistake choosing you for her. You must be the problem. You are not magical enough to trigger her powers after all."

"*You've* chosen her husband?" asked Zann. He let

out a breath of frustration when he realized that what the elf said was true. "Yes, this was all your doing, wasn't it? Well, why did you choose me for her if I'm not good enough? You don't even like me or my brothers."

"You three don't like me is more the way it really is," said the elf with a sniff.

"Whatever. Please move so I can go help fight this battle."

"Nay. Without strong powers, the elves will not win against the two kingdoms of Mura," warned Elric.

"There are three kingdoms of Mura if I must re-mind you," Zann answered. "And my brother's soldiers are here so we'll have a strong enough army."

"Nay. That's not good enough! If Lira isn't going to use her powers, then the elves have no chance of winning."

"What do you mean? You make it sound like she's purposely not using them." Zann was growing tired of Elric's riddles.

"That's exactly right. She is blocking her powers, and I don't like it. It doesn't befit an elven queen to act this way at all."

"Well, there's nothing you can do about it, so just let it be," Zann told him, wanting nothing more than to get away.

"Nay. There is something I can do." Elric grinned. "I have a task I need you to carry out. Come with me, wolf."

"Now, wait a minute. I'm not going anywhere right now, and especially not with you."

"Shut up and give me your hand."

"What? Nay," Zann protested, backing away from the elf.

Against Zann's will, Elric grabbed on to him and sped away, taking Zann with him. Everything around him turned into naught but a blur. It was so fast that it made Zann's head spin. When they stopped moving, they were in the elf's house atop the high pinnacle cliff. Zann felt like retching.

"W-what did you do to me?" Zann put out his hand to steady himself against the table so he would not fall.

"I couldn't wait for you to mosey up here, so I gave you a little boost, that's all," said Elric with a chuckle. "Time is of the essence, you know. We've got to move fast if we're going to get the attackers out of Glint and back to the other side of the mountains where they belong."

"I've got to sit down for a moment." Zann truly felt like he was about to vomit. His head ached and he couldn't see straight. He had no idea how the elf could always move this fast and not get sick.

"You get used to it after a while," said the elf, obviously reading his mind.

Zann went to sit on the tiny chair and missed it completely, staggering and falling to the floor.

"I've got something I made for Lira," said Elric. "Since I had a feeling she was going to need a little help regaining her powers, I was proactive." The elf opened a box and pulled out what looked like some kind of circular headpiece. Then he walked over and kicked Zann. "Get up, you big oaf. You are wasting precious time. I need you to convince Lira to wear this, and do it fast."

"Wear that? Why?" Zann pushed up to a sitting position, staring at the object in the sage's hand. It was the oddest thing he'd ever seen. Woven around the metal circlet was some kind of braided substance enhanced by colorful ribbons. "What the hell is that?"

"It's the crown of ultimate power, of course."

"Huh?" Zann reached over and took it from the elf to inspect it, thinking it was naught but a jest. "It's braided hair," he said, seeing all different colors of braided hair woven into bright ribbons and then attached to the circle of metal. "This isn't anything of power. It's just . . . junk."

"It is powerful, I tell you," snapped the elf, snatching it back out of Zann's hands. "This is made from hair I've collected from some of the most powerful beings ever."

"Wait a minute. Is that my hair?" he asked suspiciously, seeing the bright blond braid that almost looked white. He recently had to give some of his hair to the elf as payment at his brother's wedding. "And is that also the hair of my brothers and their wives?" Zann got to his feet and started laughing. "This is why you wanted locks of our hair? To make this phony crown of power to trick your daughter into thinking her powers really returned?" This was the funniest and most absurd thing he'd heard in a long time. And of course, it came from the most irritable, craziest man in all of Mura.

"Shut up, you fool," snapped the elf, zipping up to top of the table, holding the crown out to him. "If Lira wears this, she'll have all the powers of everyone who paid me in hair to do them a favor."

"Paid you? Didn't you steal the king's hair?"

"Never mind how I got it. It's none of your concern. Just do it."

"This just proves that you truly are out of your mind."

"I'm not!" The elf became so angry that he stomped his foot atop the table, making the dishes that were there rattle. "I have interwoven hair from that witch and her sister, as well as the fae. Whoever wears this will have their powers, as well as the strength of your brother, Rhys, and the newfound powers of your brother, Darium, too."

"So, then, since you also have my hair, I suppose whoever wears this will be able to shapeshift into a wolf like me, too?" Zann chuckled, but stopped laughing when the elf put the crown of hair on his head and immediately turned into a wolf. He snarled and snapped at Zann, causing Zann to jump back and out of the way.

Then the wolf shook its head and the crown fell off. The elf turned back into himself.

"See? I'm not lying. It really works," said Elric.

Zann's heart lodged in his throat. He hadn't been expecting that to happen. "H-how do I know you didn't already have the power to shapeshift before you even put that crown on your head?" asked Zann, thinking the elf was only tricking him once again. "After all, you have a lot of magic on your own."

"Stop being a dolt!" snapped the elf. "Have you ever seen me turn into a wolf before? Have you? Huh?"

"Well . . .nay, I guess not. But that doesn't prove a thing."

"All right, then. I didn't want to have to do this, but it seems there is no other way to get it through that thick skull of yours that I am not lying. Put it on," he demanded, waving the crown in front of Zann's nose.

"What?" Zann pushed his hand away. "No way. I'm not going to wear someone else's hair. That is disgusting and just . . . weird."

"You are such a fool."

Before Zann knew what had happened, the elf zipped around the room and returned to the top of the table. Zann felt something odd and reached up to discover the crown was on his head.

"Well? Nothing's happening," said Zann with a shrug. "I knew this wasn't real. This just proves it."

"Pick up my fire pit," commanded the elf, nodding to something across the room.

"That?" Zann looked over to see a huge, heavy fixture nearly as tall as him. It had four legs and was made of iron. A grated door opened in front to allow one to make a fire within it. On a metal ledge above the grate, the elf had a few pots sitting there. Zann was sure Elric used this heating device to cook food atop it as well as inside. For such a little man, Zann had no idea why the fire pit was so big. "That's made of iron," he said to the elf. "It looks heavy. I'm sure it would take at least two men to lift it."

"Do it!" snapped the elf.

"Fine. I'll prove to you this is ridiculous. I don't have any newfound strength, I assure you." Zann walked over to the fire pit and started to reach out for it with both hands.

"Just use one hand," instructed Elric.

"One hand?" Zann looked at Elric and chuckled, shaking his head. "Sure. Why not?" He bent down and wrapped his fingers around the leg of the iron fire pit and tried to lift it. "See? I told you. Nothing happens." He gasped aloud when he lifted the heavy piece in one hand and without even really trying. "Amazing," he said, putting it back down. "It must just look heavier than it really is."

"Oh, you are as stubborn as my daughter! Try something else. Control the air, the way your brother does," said the elf in a hurried voice, waving his hands around wildly. He rushed over and opened the shutter covering the window. "Go on, you big oaf. Try it."

"All right, I will," said Zann, just having fun and wanting to antagonize the elf. He walked over to the window and looked up at the sky. It was getting really cloudy and dark. "I'll just move all those clouds aside and let the sun shine through. How does that sound?" he asked in a sarcastic tone.

"It sounds perfect. Do it!" commanded Elric.

Zann wondered why they were wasting all this time. Especially after the elf was the one to point out that time was of the essence. He didn't want to do this because he felt like a fool. Still, he figured if he did it and proved his point, he'd be done with this and be able to go help his brothers fight. He lifted his hands up to the sky. "Go away, clouds," he said, waving his hands wildly like the elf had, just to be funny. To his surprise, the damned clouds actually parted and disappeared. The sun broke through, shining brightly. "Well, what do you know?" mumbled Zann staring at his hands, surprised that it worked.

"How does it feel?" asked Elric.

"Mayhap it was just a coincidence. I'm sure the wind picked up and blew the clouds away on its own."

"Nay, that's not what happened. You did it!" The elf stomped his foot again, having some sort of fit.

"If so, I guess mayhap my fae power is emerging, finally." He gave a satisfied nod.

"It's not your power that is emerging! You are using the power of your fae brother. Don't you understand?"

"This is all just coincidence, Elric and nothing more. No one can make a crown of power and there is nothing you can do to make me believe it."

"I can, and I did so make it. I tell you that it really works. Now, if you need more proof, try something that you know you can't do and that a fae of the air cannot do either."

"Like what?" asked Zann, still not convinced this wasn't just a stupid game made up by the elf because he was bored.

"Throw fire from your hands."

"What? Hah!" That really made Zann laugh. "I'm wasting too much time up here. I need to get back to help my brothers." He didn't take two steps before the damned elf was in front of him again making more of his silly demands.

"Do it," snapped Elric. "It is one of the tricks of that powerful witch, Medea. "Do it, now. It'll prove to you that I am telling the truth. You will be using her power, entrapped in the lock of her hair that is woven into the crown."

"Even if I wanted to, I don't know how to throw fire."

"You don't need to know how to do it. Just think of making it happen, and it will."

"Oh, sure. Like I'd just raise my hands like this and say, FIRE, and – whoa!" All of a sudden, flames shot out of Zann's hands and caught the curtains on fire. He stumbled backward, catching himself by laying a hand on the wall.

"Don't burn my favorite curtains, you fool!" In a split second, the elf had doused the flames with a pitcher of water. He moved so fast that Zann barely saw him do it.

"It – it really does work," said Zann, staring at his hands in amazement. "I think I rather like this. After all, I always wanted to have some real powers, and now I do."

"It's not for you." Elric snatched the crown off of Zann's head and shoved it into his hands. "And it doesn't work unless the person has it on their head. Now, this was made especially for Lira, so only she should wear it. If anyone who doesn't have a lot of real magic, like you, wears it, it could lead to great disaster."

"Disaster? Nay, I don't think that's possible," said Zann, inspecting the multi-colored crown. "This crown holds some great power, and I am going to have a lot of fun with it."

"It's for Lira, not you!" Once again came the stomp of his foot.

"Right," said Zann, trying not to anger the elf more. "That's what I meant." The last thing he wanted now was for Elric to take this away from him.

"The crown also holds the power of the three kings of Mura."

"The kings of Mura?" asked Zann.

"Aye. Kings Grinwald, Sethor, and the late King Osric."

"But they don't have magic," said Zann, not understanding this part at all. "Why did you add their hair to the crown?"

"I did it because I knew someday they might cause a threat to the elven queendom. But with this crown on, Lira can ward off the kings because she'll know what they know, holding their power – their plans and all their thoughts, in her head."

"Now that is really amazing, and could prove to be quite helpful." Zann studied the crown once again.

"Take it to her, Zann. Explain to my daughter that she has to wear it," said Elric. "I would do it myself, but she and I are still not on good terms. I don't think she'd listen to me."

"I don't think she'll want to wear it," said Zann. "Lira doesn't seem to want magic for some reason. Besides, she won't listen to me, either."

"You are her husband. She'll listen to you."

"Nay, I don't think so. Perhaps I should just leave this here." Zann really wanted to keep the crown, but felt it would be best left with the sage instead. Otherwise, it would be too tempting for him to want to use it.

"She will need it, I tell you."

"Nay. I'm sure we have the strength to defeat the kings, even without this," Zann protested.

"Zann, you need to convince her to start using her powers again. It is crucial. This war with the kings is nothing compared to what else is in store for her."

"What do you mean?" asked Zann. "What could be worse than a war with two kingdoms?"

"War with the giants," said Elric, causing a shiver to run through Zann's body.

"Why would you even say that? Did you see that happening? Did you have a premonition?" asked Zann, firing his questions at the man quickly, wanting answers.

"I didn't need a premonition to know it. It is evident that the giants will invade our land soon."

"Nay. They did that once before, so that must be what you're picking up."

"Nay. They will do it again."

"You can't be certain."

"I am. Now go." Elric picked up the crown and shoved it back into Zann's hands. "Give this to Lira."

"Well, if a battle with the giants does happen, then you can use your magic to fight them off," said Zann.

"Nay. I can't. It is something Lira is going to have to face alone if she is ever going to overcome the reasons that are holding her back from using her powers. Besides, I couldn't help her even if I wanted to. The gods forbade me from going to Denwop or fighting the giants."

"Mayhap you're wrong about this whole thing," said Zann. "The giants have left everyone alone for a long time now, right? Why would they return?"

"They'll return, mark my words. But this time, things will be different."

"Different? How so?" asked Zann.

"This time, they won't be attacking just to take over our land. This time, they will be running for their lives."

"What does that mean? That makes no sense," said Zann.

The elf's head snapped up and his eyes opened wide. "They're here!"

"Who's here? The giants?"

"The kings and their armies have arrived from the other side of the mountain. You need to get that crown to Lira, and do it fast. If she is to win this war for the elven queendom, she needs to use powers. The powers in this crown will allow her to do just that."

"Now, wait a minute, Elric. What if –"

Zann never got to finish his sentence. The elf grabbed him and shoved him outside, slamming the door behind him.

Zann looked down the cliff from the elf's house to see that what he said was true. Kings Sethor and Grinwald were storming the castle with their troops. The battle had begun.

It was going to take too long to walk down this cliff. Zann wanted to get back to the castle quickly. He needed to give this crown to Lira. He looked down at the crown in his hands, thinking about what the elf had told him. If this crown truly possessed all the powers of those whose hair was entwined, then he should be able to transport, like Medea and her sister, Rapunzel. It certainly would be faster than hiking down this cliff. With a shrug, Zann put the crown back on his head and thought about transporting to Castle Glint. He felt a rush of air against his face and once again everything blurred. Then he felt himself slam into something, and the air was knocked from his lungs.

"Brother, get up," said Darium, looking down at Zann. "What are you doing on the floor? The battle has begun."

"I – I'm really here?" Zann jumped to his feet and looked around to find himself in the great hall of Castle

Glint. "Yes!" he exclaimed, excited that he had actually just transported.

"I don't know what you're babbling about, but I'm going up to the battlements to see if I can use my elemental power from there to help in any way. We need you, Zann."

Zann removed the crown and stared at it with awe.

"What are you doing?"

"I – I need to find Lira," said Zann. "I have to give this to her."

"Zann, what in the world is that?" asked Darium, pulling it away from him and glancing at it and then shoving it back at Zann again.

"It's a crown of hair that the sage made."

"I know it's hair. And I also know you are starting to sound as addlepated as that pesky elf."

"It's a crown of power, Darium. It's going to help us win this war against the kings," said Zann, hearing Darium's laughter before he even finished speaking.

"Brother, I hope you're drunk. Because if not, I'd think you are as crazy as that stupid sage. And that is something I'd never wish on anyone, I assure you."

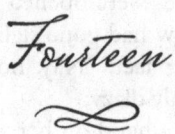

Fourteen

"CLOSE THE DOOR and lower the gate. Quickly," commanded Lira, strapping on a weapon belt as she hurried across the courtyard with Sasha at her side.

"Here they come," shouted her head knight, Veara.

The rattling sound of the gate being lowered filled the air, mixing with the shouts from their attackers as they stormed the castle. Several elves closed the large wooden doors and barred it as well. In times like this, Lira wished the castle had a moat, or at least a drawbridge. It certainly would help. Then again, the elven queendom and the lands surrounding it were normally peaceful. They had never had a need until today. Moats and drawbridges would be beneficial fighting humans. However, if it was a giant attack, their tall walls were the best defense.

"Ready the archers," yelled Sasha, looking up to the battlements. She headed up the stairs to the wall walk to join them.

"Our attackers have grappling hooks and ropes, my queen. They also have an entire regiment of archers," yelled one of her warriors from atop the battlements. To

Lira's horror, the man was struck by an arrow and fell to his death, landing right at her feet.

"Nay!" she screamed, bending down to check the man's pulse. His eyes were opened wide and he wasn't breathing. The arrow had gone right through his head. Blood pooled at her feet. "Nay, no more deaths," she cried, feeling suddenly dizzy.

"Lira?" She felt a hand on her shoulder and turned to see Zann standing there.

"Zann. I'm glad you're here." She stood up and reached out and laid her hand on his chest, feeling a surge of emotions flood her. All she could think about was her late husband and her brothers. The thought of how they'd died made her feel panicked and shaky. Her stomach lurched and bile rose in her throat.

"Your father wanted me to give this to you." He handed her an odd-looking crown with braids of hair woven into it.

"What is this?" she asked. "Zann, we don't have time for this nonsense. We are at war, in case you haven't noticed."

"They are using the grappling hooks and ropes to scale the walls," yelled one of her warriors. "Can we drop the hot oil on them, my queen?"

"Nay," she shouted. "Not yet."

"Lira, you can end this war right now. Just put on this crown of power," Zann told her. "It contains all the powers of everyone who ever gave a snippet of their hair to your father."

"Lira, we need you," shouted Sasha from the battlements. Lira looked up to see her aunt throwing fire balls at the kings and their men down below.

"In a minute," she said, looking back at Zann. "What are you talking about?"

"It's the crown of ultimate power," he told her once

again. "You've got to try it. It really works. I tried it and I was able to throw fire, control the weather, and even transport." He chuckled. "You'll even be able to shapeshift into a wolf like me now. You'll have the power of the fae and witches, and so much more."

"Nay," she said, shoving the crown back at him, frightened by the thought of all that power. All that magic.

"Nay?" He looked up at her in question as the battle continued. Men and women shouted, and the their attackers started to appear atop the walls now. "Zann, I've got to go. They need my help." She took a few steps and he rushed in front of her to stop her.

"Nay, Lira. Your father said you will not win this war unless you use your powers."

"I don't have any powers!" she screamed above the noise, angry, frightened, and starting to feel hopeless.

"If you wear this, you will. Just take it. Here, I'll put it on your head for you." When Zann reached out to do so, she pushed him away.

"I said, no, Zann. Now stop it! Leave me alone." She left him standing there, and hurried off to join the elves to fight this needless war.

"Brother, are you going to join us today or not?" asked Rhys from atop his large gray warhorse that had a speckling of white spots that looked like snowflakes. He had his army of soldiers behind him. "We are going out the postern door and sneaking around the castle to confront Grinwald and Sethor."

For the life of him, Zann didn't know why Lira wouldn't wear the crown. It would be so simple to stop this war before too many died from either side. Still, she refused to do it.

"I'll be there," Zann told his brother, looking down at the crown. If she wouldn't wear it to help the cause, then Zann decided he would do it for her. He put the crown on his head and looked up and smiled at his brother. "I'll take care of everything, Rhys. You don't need to risk your life or the lives of your men."

"What in the name of Belcoum are you talking about?" snapped Rhys, drawing his sword and waving his men over to the postern gate at the back of the castle.

"I have powers now. I'll stop this war on my own."

"Zann, shifting into a wolf isn't going to do a thing to stop this battle," said his brother.

"Nay, mayhap not. But how about this?" he asked, raising his hand in the air and shooting a fire ball over the wall. Screams were heard from the other side as well as more shouting from their attackers.

"Zoroct's eyes!" spat Rhys, his jaw dropping in surprise. "How did you do that, brother?"

"It's this nifty little crown that the sage made for his daughter. It holds all the powers in it of every one of us who have ever given the elf a snippet of our hair." All of a sudden, Zann could hear the thoughts of Sethor and Grinwald in his head. "Rhys, don't use the postern gate! Sethor knows you're going to do it. He and his men are waiting there for you along with his giant."

"How do you know that?"

"I know what the kings know now that I have this crown. It has snippets of their hair woven into it as well."

"Hold up, men!" Rhys shouted from atop his horse. "We'll open the main gate and storm them from the front instead," Rhys commanded. "Open the gate!" he shouted.

"Nay, don't do that either," warned Zann.

"Why not?" asked Rhys.

"Grinwald is holding back. He knows we'll try to come for them. Our best bet is to surprise them from behind. They won't be expecting that."

"From behind?" asked Rhys. "Zann, we are inside the castle in case you haven't noticed.

"I'll give you a little help. I'll transport you and your men one at a time to the forest behind them."

"Egads! You are talking nonsense."

"Shut up and hold on. I'm not sure if I can take the horse too, but we are about to find out." Zann mounted the horse behind his brother, wrapping his legs tightly around the steed and his arms around his brother. "Get ready for the ride of your life."

* * *

Lira used her bow and arrows from atop the battlements, fighting off the kings of Mura and their men. Every time one of them climbed up a rope and popped their head over the wall, they were pushed back down by the elves, but it was becoming exhausting. There were so many of them, and so few elves. Rhys and his soldiers had wanted to meet the attackers outside the castle, but Lira had purposely ordered the gate closed before they'd had the chance to do so. The last thing she wanted was for Zann to lose his family, the way she had hers.

Her aunt was angry with her about it, but Lira didn't care. She didn't want to see Zann's brother die trying to protect her queendom. She didn't want to see anyone die. This battle was already taking a toll on her and the rest of the elves. It was her nightmare coming to fruition once again.

"They're climbing over the walls too fast," yelled Sasha. "Lira, you need to send troops out to fight them. There are too many to ward them off from here."

"Not yet," she said, but her aunt didn't agree.

"You are not fit to be queen of Glint," snarled Sasha. "Your mother would be appalled at the way you are acting." Sasha turned and looked over toward the guards standing on the wall walk near the entrance. "Drop the hot oil," she commanded.

"My lady?" asked one of the soldiers, looking over at Lira.

"Do it now!" continued Sasha.

"Nay!" cried Lira, but it was too late. She heard the screams of the soldiers from the other side of the wall, and could only imagine what horrible deaths they were experiencing right now. Her eyes closed and she wavered, holding on to the merlon so she wouldn't fall.

"Ah, good, Rhys is out there with his men. Now we're getting somewhere," said Darium.

"What?" Lira's eyes popped open. "Nay, they can't be. They were inside the castle walls."

"Zann is down there, too," reported Darium, peering over the wall.

"He is?" gasped Lira, hoping he was mistaken.

"I'll give them a little help if I can." Darium lifted his hands and created only a small whirlwind that swept down and knocked some of the soldiers off the wall and to the ground. "If I could only figure out how to do it like my mother, I'd send them all back to the other side of the mountain." Darium stood there staring at his hands, shaking his head, still not skilled in using his newfound fae powers.

"Zann really is down there." Lira peeked out from a crenel, an opening in the battlements for shooting arrows, seeing that what Darium said was true. Zann as well as Rhys and his men on horseback were attacking the kings' armies from behind, taking them by surprise. Zann had his sword drawn and was fighting a man on foot. "How did they all get out there with the gate closed? And with the horses, too?"

"Don't ask me," said Darium. "I'm just glad they did. I think I'll join them." He ran from the battlements, making his way down the stairs.

"Nay! This is wrong," said Lira, looking out once more to realize that Zann was wearing the crown of power that he'd been trying to get her to put on her head. "Oh, no," she said, seeing Zann lift Sethor's giant with one hand, hurling him high into the air. Then he shot fire in the opposite direction, taking down even more soldiers.

"How did your lover do that?" asked Sasha, walking up to her, looking over the wall. "He doesn't have the power of throwing fire, does he? I thought he was a mere human."

"He didn't before, but has it now," said Lira. "Zann is wearing the crown of power that Father made for me."

"What? Nay, that's not good," said Sasha with wide eyes. "If he doesn't usually have powers, he will be obsessed with them and they will take control of his actions."

"Well, he does have the power to shapeshift," said Lira.

"That's not enough," answered Sasha. "He'll never be able to control all that power. This isn't going to end well for him. My queen, you've got to get that crown back from him before he gets himself killed. You are Queen of Glint, so don't let your people, or your husband down."

"I – I can't," she said, feeling frozen to the spot. Her limbs felt heavy and she was unable to move, frightened so badly that she was frozen to the spot. All she could think about was Laeroth and how she watched him die. How it was all her fault.

"If you don't help him, you might as well kiss your husband goodbye right now. Now he's using a power of a fae, and I'm sure he doesn't know how to control it."

Lira looked down to see Zann waving his arms over his head. A large tornado could be seen starting to emerge from the clouds.

"Nay. This isn't good," said Lira. "Sasha, he has too much power, you are right. He also has the powers of the witch, Medea."

"Well, let's hope for the best," said Sasha, throwing another fire ball over the wall at their enemies. "If he can control it, he might just help us win this war after all."

"You don't understand," said Lira. "When I was at Kasculbough, I found out that Medea was born from dark magic. She has been doing a good job controlling it, but it also means dark magic is interwoven into that crown from her hair."

"This isn't good, Lira. Dark magic will fight the light magic of our kind. It'll possess him and make him go mad," Sasha explained. "You've got to warn him. He won't be able to control himself. You've got to stop him before it's too late."

"I will," said Lira. "I'll sneak out there and stop him myself."

"Sneak out there? Lira, there is no getting through that horde of soldiers trying to knock down our front door."

"I know a way." Lira sighed, releasing a deep breath and pushing her fear aside. She'd been doing all she could to hold back and keep her powers from coming through. But with Zann in so much danger, she pushed past her inhibitions, calling upon her power of invisibility, hoping this was going to work. With her eyes closed, she concentrated and continued to breathe deeply. A familiar tingling sensation rushed through her body and suddenly she felt as light as a feather. "Can you see me, aunt?"

"Nay," said Sasha, her smile lighting up her face. "Your power of invisibility has returned, Lira. Now use it for the good of the queendom."

"I will," Lira answered. "But first, I must stop Zann before he is overtaken by the powers of dark magic."

"I'm sorry for speaking to you so brashly, My queen," said Sasha. "But I had to do what needed to be done. I hope you understand."

"I do," said Lira, feeling glad her aunt spoke to her that way. She needed the reminder that she hadn't been acting like a queen, leading her people into battle. "I understand, and now I will do what I feel needs to be done as well."

Fifteen

ZANN FELT INVINCIBLE, indestructible, and almost like he imagined a god would feel right about now. He finally had more powers than just turning into a wolf, and he liked it! With this crown of extreme power on his head, no one or nothing could stop him now. All the magic within the crown was flowing through him at the same time. And while it was great to feel so almighty and powerful, it was a little over-whelming at the same time.

His head felt like it was going to burst since he was able to hear the thoughts of both kings at once. Still, this enabled him to keep one step ahead of them at all times. He pushed through the massive confusion swarming his brain, knowing that it didn't matter. All that mattered was that he stopped this war. He already used the power of throwing fire, and lifting heavy objects. Now, he was creating a whirlwind from above to whisk away all the soldiers that came from the other side of the mountain, and both kings as well. He alone was going to be responsible for ending this war, and it made him feel proud and good. Damned good. It was a feeling he could get used to, never having experienced this before.

"Zann, what are you doing?" called out Darium, now on the battlefield fighting with them. Zann figured he must have come through the postern gate since King Sethor moved his men to the front of the castle once Rhys and his army appeared. He looked up at the sky. "There is a tornado forming."

"Aye. Nice, huh?" Zann asked with pride. He had a weird feeling deep inside him that was growing stronger and stronger. He didn't understand it, but he suddenly had the urge to do away with everyone and everything, and control the entire world now. Much like Medea had when her dark magic had controlled her. He was sure this wasn't a normal feeling and that it had come from Medea's dark magic. But dark or not, there was nothing he could do to stop it, and neither did he want to.

"Stop it, Brother." Darium was almost blown over. Things went flying through the air. Soldiers went flying by, trying to hold on to anything they could as they were lifted up into the air. Trees were uprooted and the sound of cracking branches filled the air. "We're all going to get blown away." None of the soldiers from either side could manage to fight anymore. They could barely stay on their feet because of the strong wind Zann created.

Suddenly, Zann remembered he also had the power of an elemental of the earth. He was anxious to try it.

"I'll call the vines to hold you in place, Darium. You won't blow away, don't worry."

He thought in his mind about calling out to nature. Then vines crept along the ground, winding around the feet of many. Animals attacked from the forest, and birds dipped down from the sky, ready to peck out the eyes of any man in their path.

"Zann, stop it," yelled Rhys, riding his horse over and shouting to be heard since the tornado was getting closer and closer, threatening to destroy everything in its path.

"I don't know what's got into him, but he's gone crazy," yelled Darium, using his sword to cut the vines that had a mind of their own and were winding all the way up his body now.

"I know what it is," said someone from behind him. Zann turned to see Lira materializing from thin air.

"Yes! Your powers are working," said Zann excitedly. "You were invisible, Lira. You did it! That's great. I wonder if I have that power as well. We can take over the world together."

"Take over the world?" Rhys fought a soldier from atop his horse. "What is the matter with you, Brother? Why are you talking this way?"

"He's using the crown of extreme power that my father made, and it is too much for him to handle. He's not used to having so much power," Lira told them. The tornado swept through the sky, getting closer and closer to the castle. Black dirt swirled up in the air and into the funnel. Clouds darkened the sky, making it look like night. The air turned frigid as the tornado roared, sounding louder than any beast. The sky opened and rain and hail pelted down from above. Lightning flashed constantly, followed by a continuous deep rumble of thunder. "It looks like he's also using Medea's dark power. He can't help himself. The darkness is controlling him. It's got to stop."

Lira reached out, snatching the crown from Zann's head.

"Hey, nay!" Zann shouted, gripping the other end of it, trying to get it back. She used her power of telekinesis to flip the crown up in the air, out of Zann's hands and far away from him.

Unfortunately, it fell on the ground right between King Grinwald and King Sethor.

"What's this?" asked Grinwald, picking up the crown.

"That's my crown of power. It is what I used to do all this," shouted Zann, splaying out his arms. "Give it back to me, right now."

"Crown of power?" asked the greedy King Sethor, his eyes lighting up. "I want it, Grinwald. Hand it over to me."

"Nay," said Grinwald, reaching up to put it on his head. But before he could do so, Sethor ran his blade right through the man's side. Grinwald sputtered, clutched his body, and fell to the ground as Sethor pulled his blade back and smiled.

Lira watched in horror as everything unfolded right before her eyes. Too much power, as well as the dark powers of the crown had made Zann act irrationally. Now, the power of greed was affecting others and a king was severely wounded over it. Not to mention, the tornado moved closer and closer as the battle continued. The animals and plants that Zann had called forth were now also out of control, running or flying in circles, acting vicious to anyone who got in their way.

"We've got to do something," yelled Rhys. "This can't continue."

"I'll stop the damned funnel," Darium called out, finally getting untangled from the vines, planning to use his newfound powers of the air to slow it down. However, before he could, a large tree was uprooted and it came hurling right toward Zann.

"Brother!" yelled Rhys, jumping off the horse, catching the trunk before it hit Zann. He used his power of extreme strength to toss the tree the other way.

"King Grinwald is severely wounded and close to death. King Sethor did it," called out one of Grinwald's soldiers. Now, the two sides started to fight each other instead of fighting the elves. Rhys' men and the elven army stopped and watched, confused as to what was happening.

"King Sethor, they are gaining on us. What do we do?" called out a soldier from Macada Castle.

"I've got the crown of power. We don't need to worry. Let's seize Castle Glint." Sethor put the crown on his head and mounted a horse. With a war cry, he waved to the others to attack the castle.

"Nay! I've got to stop him. I've got to get that crown," said Lira, finally ready to use her magic again.

"Let me do it," said Zann, starting to pull off his clothes. "I'll go in wolf form and get it back to you."

"Don't bother," she said, using a blast of fire to knock Sethor off his horse. The man looked up from the ground. He was injured but not dead. "Now the crown," said Lira, holding out her hand. The crown flew from Sethor's head and landed in her hand. Sethor rolled on the ground to put out the flames on his clothes. The soldiers didn't even seem to notice, still fighting each other and trying to keep from being pulled up into the air by the funnel.

"I think I've just about got the tornado under control," shouted Darium. "Now, if we could only get someone to control these damned plants and animals." He shook his leg, trying to get the vine to stop entangling him since it was only slowing him down.

"Can you do that, Lira?" asked Zann.

"Nay," she said. "Only a fae can."

"But you've got the crown," he shouted, putting his clothes back in place since he no longer needed to shapeshift.

"Never mind. I've brought the fae to help," came a woman's voice on the wind.

Lira looked over to see Alaina, the fae queen, Zann's mother. "My queen," she said, dropping down to one knee.

"Get up, Lira," growled Zann. "It's only my mother."

"She is the fae queen, Zann," answered Lira.

"And you are the elf queen, so you don't need to bow to her," he reminded her.

"I saw the tornado from the Whispering Dale and knew something was wrong," said Alaina. "We came right away to help." Two of the fae were with her, and they immediately stopped the attack of plants and animals.

"King Sethor is injured and cannot fight," shouted a soldier from Macada Castle.

King Grinwald is injured and needs to be protected," shouted one of Evandorm's men. They started dragging him across the battlefield.

"Get me back home," shouted King Sethor. His mercenary giant picked up him up in his arms and headed toward the mountain.

"Our king is nearly dead," yelled a soldier from Evandorm as two of them put the king over a horse. "Retreat. Retreat!" he shouted.

The two armies from across the mountains ran from Glint, heading back home. The winds subsided. With the animals and plants under control, all was becoming calm once again.

"Zoroct's eyes," gasped Zann, looking down at all the dead bodies littering the ground. "This is a horrific sight."

"The battle is over," Lira shouted to her army. "Put down your weapons and help retrieve our dead."

"What about Grinwald and Sethor's dead soldiers?" asked Darium. "What will we do with them?"

"I can handle that," said Zann's mother. She used her powers of the air to lift up the dead soldiers that were from across the mountain. "I will return them all to their proper castles." Then, in a flash, the bodies were transported over the mountain and gone from sight.

Zann's head throbbed and every muscle in his body ached. He felt a sharp pain between his eyes and figured it had something to do with the abrupt absence of all the power he'd been wielding. He felt empty now, and a stab of grief that made his heart ache. Zann felt terrible for the way he'd acted, and went over to apologize to his wife.

"Lira, I'm sorry I took the crown," he told her. "But your father said you needed to use it to stop the battle. When you wouldn't wear it, I took it upon myself to do just that in order to help. I don't know what happened. I am not sure what went wrong. I didn't mean for things to get so out of control."

"This is what happens when magic is misused, although it wasn't entirely your fault, Zann. My father wove the dark magic of your brother's wife into the crown as well. You are not used to having powers so strong. You couldn't have controlled it. None of us could."

"Egads, that was my wife's dark magic that did that?" asked Rhys. "I thought we'd seen the last of it."

"We have," said Lira, throwing down the crown. She used her powers, throwing a fireball at it, and the crown ignited and started to burn. "Let us collect our dead and see to the injuries. Thank you, Fae Queen for your help, and also for the help of the fae folk. My husband is lucky to have such a wonderful mother."

"Zann?" asked Alaina. "Did you want to tell me something?"

"I think by now you've figured out that I am married to Queen Lira, Mother," said Zann. "Excuse me, I need to help bury the dead elves."

Zann stormed off, feeling like exploding. It wasn't just the withdrawal of power this time. This time, it was his immense feelings of still despising his mother that filled his head instead.

"Brother, wait," said Rhys running after him. "What is your problem?"

"Well, let me see," said Zann putting his hand to his chin. "Could it be that I was possessed by dark magic and almost killed everyone when all I was trying to do was help, because I, brother, don't possess any real powers of my own beyond shapeshifting? Or could it be that the mother who abandoned us as children had to show up to fix my mistakes and make me look like more of a fool than I really am?"

"You're talking nonsense, Zann. Mother was only here to help."

"I finally didn't feel worthless around the rest of you, but look what it got me," snapped Zann. "Everyone will hate me now."

"Everyone will be grateful to you," said Rhys as they walked. "I understand it was Medea's darkness that caused that, and in time everyone else will know that too."

"Mayhap, but how am I going to explain that to the rest of Glint?"

"They'll understand."

"Will they?" Zann stopped in his tracks and looked around. "Tell that to the families of the dead, Rhys."

"Stop it, Zann! This is not done by your hand."

"How do you know that?"

"I know it, because I saw with my own eyes, Grinwald and Sethor taking down elf after elf. This was war, brother. You cannot expect anything less."

"Mayhap," said Zann looking back to see his mother and Lira talking as they walked back to the castle. The small fire burning the crown was behind them now. "But tell me, did mother really have to show up?"

"She saved the day, in case you didn't notice."

"Nay, she didn't. All she did was make me look like a fool."

"Zann, Mother would never do that. She only wanted to help," said Rhys.

"And so did I, brother," said Zann, shaking his head. "So did I."

Sixteen

"WHY DID you let Zann wear the crown of power, Father?" It had been a long day, and Lira was tired and wanted to sleep. Feeling exhausted physically, mentally, and emotionally from the battle, the happenings of the day took a toll on her. She'd never meant to use her powers, but when Zann's life was in jeopardy and so many were being killed, she realized she had to try. She didn't like what that crown of power did to her husband, and she wasn't happy with her father for giving it to Zann in the first place.

The sun had long gone down. The dead elves were tended to, and Zann's mother sent the dead enemies back to their homes using her power of the wind to do it. Zann's brothers stayed to help clean up, although the army of Kasculbough had left on their journey back over the mountain. Things hadn't gone the way Lira had hoped today. Then again, with war, they never do.

"I didn't know the big oaf was going to actually use the crown during the battle," said her father, pacing back and forth in Lira's bedchamber. The day was at an end, and everyone felt sad and sullen. It was out of respect for the dead elves that everyone in Glint retired to their homes or chambers to mourn. "However, I was watching, and he didn't do bad . . . for a wolf."

The statement shocked Lira. "If you were watching, why didn't you help defend Glint? We could have used your powers, Father."

"I couldn't, Lira. The gods warned me I can't get involved in any type of war anymore, not just with the giants. I couldn't disobey them."

"Father, I know you only meant to help me, but when you do things like this, don't you see that it only causes trouble?"

"The only trouble I see was that you refused to use your elven powers, my dear. If you hadn't done that to begin with, I never would have had a reason to bring out the crown."

"I didn't want war! I didn't want anyone else to die." Lira's emotions rose to the surface, making her body tremble.

"Sometimes, we can't help it, my dear."

"And sometimes . . . we can."

There was a knock at the door. Zann poked his head inside the room. "Lira? I hope you don't mind if my brothers stay the night and leave for home first thing in the morning."

"Of course not," she answered. "They are more than welcome."

"What about me?" asked Zann, stepping into the room, but then stopping when Lira glared at him. "Am I . . . welcome as well?"

"Well, gotta go," said Elric, zipping off before Lira could even stop him.

Lira let out a deep breath. "Of course, you are, Zann. We're married now. Please, come in."

He quietly entered and closed the door. He stood there for a moment, as if he wasn't sure what to do.

"Zann, you look like a deer in the torchlight," she said with a giggle. "Why are you still standing there?"

"I . . . I wasn't sure if you'd still want me. After today, I mean." He looked so uncomfortable, shifting from foot to foot.

"Come here, husband." She held out her hand. He slowly walked over to her where she sat, and she stood up and gave him a hug.

"What was that for?"

"It was for your help today."

"My help?" He pulled back and looked at her oddly. "Lira, I was power-crazed today. I'm sorry, I don't know what happened. I was truly out of control, and I'm not proud of it."

"I admit I'm not happy with your decision to wear a crown that was not meant for you. You caused a lot of havoc today."

"I know." Zann lowered his head. "You have every right to hate me."

"I could never hate you." She reached over and kissed him on the cheek.

"No?" A quick smile lifted the corners of his mouth but lowered just as fast.

"Zann, I know exactly what happened today. When I refused to use my powers to help win the war, you stepped in as the queen's husband to do the job that was required of me. Thank you, Zann."

"I'm confused," he said, dragging a hand through his hair. "I could have brought about the deaths of multiple kingdoms – or queendoms, today with my greed for power. Yet, you're thanking me?"

"You didn't do that. You helped Rhys and his men attack from behind. That alone saved many elven lives. Now, come, have some wine with me." Lira led him over to the bed. She poured wine from a bottle into a goblet and handed it to him. Then she sat down on the bed and patted the mattress next to her. Slowly, he sat, and took a quick swig of wine, handing the cup back to her.

"Can I be honest with you, Lira? Without you getting upset at me, I mean." Zann fidgeted on the bed.

"Of course," she said. "Speak freely."

"I initially did what I did because I felt you were being selfish."

"Really?" She raised a brow and took a sip of wine.

"I felt as if you didn't want to use your powers to help anyone else. That is why you lied to your father when he asked if you'd regained them."

"I told him the truth," she said.

"Only because I forced you to."

"Zann, I'm tired. Do we really need to talk about this any longer?" She slid the goblet on to a bedside table.

"I'm sorry, sweetheart." He pulled her into his arms. "I never should have said that. I'm the one who was selfish, wanting to have powers like my brothers. I am glad you burned the crown because I don't ever want to feel that way again. It was as if I couldn't get enough power. I wanted to take over the world, not caring who I hurt or killed to do it. It was actually pretty frightening."

"Nay, Zann, you were right in a way, trying to help us." She looked up at him, not able to keep from crying.

"What's the matter, Lira?" He gently brushed away her tears. "I'm the one who should be crying since my mother had to come to our rescue, making me feel worthless."

She chuckled at that. "I see your manly pride is getting in the way again. Your mother is a good woman and someday you will realize that."

"We were talking about you, not my mother," he reminded her.

"You're right. I want to tell you what really happened the day my husband died."

"Oh," he said, his hand sliding off her shoulders. "Your father hinted that there was something more, but he refused to tell me what it was."

"Good," she said. "Because if he had, I think I would have had to kill him."

They both chuckled at that.

"The day my husband died, he didn't get eaten by a giant like I let you believe."

"Then what did happen to him, Lira?"

"I was there with him. On the Isle of Denwop. I took several boats to the island with some of my soldiers, my husband, and my twin brothers."

"Were they all killed, then?"

"Nay. I told my soldiers to retreat as soon as I realized we couldn't fight off the giants on their own land. They left, however, my husband and brothers didn't listen. They had managed to chase some of the giants back to Denwop, and they wanted to make sure they were going to stay there before they left."

"I have a feeling it was a mistake. A mistake that cost them their lives."

"Zann, my husband, Laeroth was picked up by a giant, that part is true. It looked like he was about to be eaten, so I tried to stop it."

"That's good. Right?"

"Yes and no. I used my powers to make part of a mountain fall on the giant. The only thing is, I didn't know how to work my powers yet and it was too much. You see, my husband was crushed beneath the stones as well. I stood there motionless when I realized what I had done and that I was unable to help him."

"But you could have moved the stones off of him. With your powers, right?"

"Perhaps. But it was too late. I saw my husband lying there, and I could tell he was dead, his neck broken. It was such a horrible sight. I – I couldn't even move." She closed her eyes and shuddered just thinking about it. "I froze, feeling like my life was over. I caused his death, not the giant. It was all my fault."

"I'm sorry, Lira." Zann put his arm back around her. "You tried to help him when his life was threatened. You did a good thing. You didn't know how it was going to end."

"The giants were angry with me for killing one of their own. My brothers tried to stop them from coming after me while I just stood there, waiting to be killed. Korack and Keevan threw rocks at them, and the giants ended up chasing them instead."

"So . . . did the giants kill your brothers?"

"Well, if they didn't, I am sure I did with my next actions."

"What did you do?"

"I was frightened, and angry, and sad that my husband was dead. I started throwing fireballs everywhere. My powers made a landslide happen. The giants chasing my brothers fell, and they were buried by all the dirt and stone."

"And your brothers? They were under the rubble too? Or were they under the giants?"

"I don't know," she said, starting to bawl now. Zann held her closer. "They were gone, along with the giants. With the amount of dirt, rocks, and debris that fell, there was no way they could have survived. I frightened myself since I couldn't control my powers. My anger along with my powers cost the lives of my husband and then my brothers who were doing naught but trying to help me."

"So you left the island?"

"I did. I was so frightened that I ran. I took the boat back over the water, and didn't stop until I returned to Castle Glint. I am so ashamed of myself. I did a horrible thing. I don't deserve to be queen."

"Ah, I see now," said Zann. "And since you were sure you killed your brothers, along with your husband by using your powers, you didn't want your father to go looking for them. Because then he would find out the truth."

"I couldn't face him. I couldn't face the truth, and so I told no one," cried Lira. The damned-up emotions she had held inside her for so long burst forth and she wept bitterly, clinging to Zann.

"Do you think your father knows?"

"I think he might have seen from the shore but he didn't say anything. I don't know."

"It's over. Let it go."

"Valindra was only a month old at the time, and my emotions were out of control from birthing a baby. I felt so alone, and worthless. Like a murderer and a traitor. I blamed everyone for their deaths. I blamed my father and even banished him to the top of a cliff rather than to have to ever face him again."

"Shhhh," said Zann, stroking her hair. "It's all right, Lira. You didn't deliberately mean to hurt anyone. You were only trying to help."

"I am a horrible person and a terrible queen, Zann. I don't even want to be queen. I never did."

"Don't say that. Being queen is a privilege and you should honor that."

"It is a curse and a tremendous responsibility. I don't want to do it anymore."

"Lira, you might not want to be queen, but think

about your daughter. She is Princess of Glint. If you give up the position, you will be determining her future for her as well."

"Valindra," she whispered, missing her daughter. She sniffled and wiped her eyes. "Zann, I want to go to her. I miss her. I need her here with me."

"We'll go back to Kasculbough. Tomorrow, Lira."

"I'm so glad she is safe and wasn't here today to see all this. How can I shelter her from death and war?"

"You can't. If she is to be queen someday, she'll need to face it. So do you."

"Mayhap you're right." Zann handed her a hand cloth and she blew her nose and wiped her tears. "I'm just glad my daughter is safe."

"Why don't we get some sleep? It's been a long day." Zann stood up and started undressing. Lira did the same.

When she was naked and about to slip her night-dress over her head, she glanced over to see Zann staring at her.

"What's the matter?" she asked.

"Nothing," he said, flashing a smile. "I'm just looking at my beautiful wife and thinking how lucky I am to be married to her."

"Oh." Her eyes traveled downward and settled on his hardened manhood. "Oooooh," she said. "I understand."

Getting under the covers naked, she held out her arms. "Come to me, husband. I have a duty I'd like to perform."

"A duty as queen?" he asked, climbing onto the bed and straddling her.

"Nay. My duty as a wife."

"I won't stop you from that, even though I don't

like it when you call it a duty." Zann used his hands to hold himself away from her. Then he leaned over and kissed her, his long hair falling around the both of them.

"Zann, I was so frightened today," she whispered, kissing his face and then his chest.

"It's all right to be scared sometimes. It's not easy being in your position as queen."

"Nay. I mean, I saw you down in the midst of the battle, and I was afraid that I was going to lose you, too. That is what jolted my powers back into place. I regained them because I knew I needed to use them to save your life. You didn't know how to use the powers any more than I did when I used mine on Denwop."

"And thank you for that."

"I realize we don't even know each other well, but I have strong feelings for you."

"And I have strong feelings for you as well, Lira." He kissed her neck and collarbone, and then her breasts.

"My daughter never knew her father at all. Still, I heard her call you father. When she did, it frightened me at first, but now I am glad."

"Me, too," he said, laying on his side, running his finger up and down her torso.

"Zann, I think . . . I think I am falling in love with you."

"Really?" That seemed to surprise him. "Are you sure? Are you sure you want to love someone like me?"

"Well . . . yes. I do."

"Good," he said with a deep chuckle, leaning over and kissing her on the nose. "Because I like you, Lira. A lot. I like your strength and that you are determined, and everything about you from your pointy little ears down to the tips of your toes." He ran his finger along the edge of her ear, making her feel randy.

"Like? You like me?" she asked.

"Yes."

"Oh. I guess I was hoping for a little more."

"I have never been in love before, and I'm not sure how it feels," he explained. "However, I do think this strong feeling of liking you I have, is already turning into something more."

"Something more? How much more?"

"Well, I'm not sure but . . . I think I love you, too."

"Thank you for that." She smiled and reached up and tapped him on the nose. "Even if you didn't really mean it, it was exactly what I needed to hear right now."

"I did mean it, sweetheart. I have never felt this way about any other woman in my life"

"It's all right, Zann."

"You don't believe me. Do you?"

"I didn't say that."

"I guess I'm just going to have to show you exactly how much I do love you. Starting with this." His mouth was on her ear again and so was his tongue.

"That's lust," she said through a heady whisper. She started to feel the tension releasing and her body relaxing.

"It might start out as lust, but it's so much more than that my little elf queen." He rolled her on top of him and it made her giggle.

"Are we going to couple or not?" she asked.

"Nay. We're not going to couple, we are going to make love. Like a husband and wife who are extremely powerful together."

"I don't think this is the time to talk about the power of magic, husband."

"I'm not. I am talking about so much more, Lira. I am talking about the power of love."

They made love like husband and wife, more than

once that night. And as they slept in each other's arms, Lira felt for the first time in her life that she had done something right. That is, that she had married a wonderful man who she never wanted to lose – Zann Blackseed.

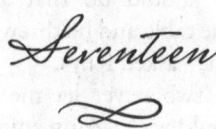

Seventeen

IT RAINED THE NEXT MORNING, and with the rain came problems. It seemed that some of the homes of Glint were damaged in the battle, and the roofs were leaking from the high winds and rain and hail from the storm. While the dead elves had only added up to about a dozen, it was still a mournful time for Glint. The castle didn't have too much damage, but the land of Glint and the cottages suffered greatly.

"Zann?" said Lira as they finished their morning meal. "I know we were planning on going back to Kasculbough today, but would you mind if we stayed another day or two so we can help my people repair their homes and support them through these hard times?"

"I am so glad to hear you say that, sweetheart." Zann pulled her to him right there at the dais and kissed her passionately. "I think it's a good idea."

"I think it would be a good idea if you two kissed like that behind closed doors, instead of in front of me when I am trying to eat," complained Rhys.

Zann's brothers as well as Sasha were sitting at the dais with them. Zann's mother had returned to the Whispering Dale last night. Lira's father stayed at his home on the cliffs and hadn't even stopped by for a visit this morning.

"Now, now," said Darium, adding his opinion. "I don't think they should do that at all." His raven hopped around the table and he threw it a few crumbs.

"No? Why not?" asked Rhys.

"Because you two never let me enjoy my honeymoon, so why should we let Zann enjoy his?"

"Now, brothers, you know I can be happy anywhere, as long as I am with my beautiful wife. Not just behind closed doors, but anywhere at all," Zann told them.

"Anywhere?" asked Lira with a smile. Zann thought she was being playful so he went along with it.

"That's what I said. Where would you like me to be happy next? The stables, or perhaps in the woods?" Zann smiled proudly until he heard what Lira said next.

"Good. I'm glad to hear you say that. Because I think I'd like you to accompany me to visit your mother today in the Whispering Dale."

"What?" Zann's smile faded and his head snapped up. "Now, wait a minute." His wife tricked him, not unlike what her father did to him and his brothers constantly. He started wondering if this was a trait of all elves.

"You said you could be happy with me anywhere, husband. So prove it," said Lira with a giggle. "Accompany me to see your mother."

"Lira, this isn't fair, and you know it."

"You did say that you could be happy anywhere," Darium intervened. "I heard it."

"Me, too," agreed Rhys. "And mayhap you two can stop by and see Lira's father on the way back." Rhys and Darium both chuckled at that. "After all, the sage is your father-by-marriage now, brother."

"Don't remind me," grumbled Zann.

"If that doesn't turn a person sour, I don't know what will," Darium whispered to Rhys.

"Actually, I think that's a good idea," said Zann, watching Lira squirm now just like he had when she tricked him into visiting his mother. He was sure her father wasn't someone she really wanted to visit. At least, not for a long while, since the episode with the crown of power.

"Nay. We'll see him on a different day," said Lira, picking up her goblet and chugging down some wine.

"Nay, we won't," Zann answered. "If we're going to visit my mother, then I think it's only right we visit your father, too."

"I can't believe our brother just said that," Darium whispered to Rhys. "It sounds like two punishments for Zann today."

"And he inflicted one of them upon himself," said Rhys.

"We have already agreed to stay and help the villagers thatch their roofs and replant the crops that were ruined in the battle," said Lira, trying her best to get out of it. "It will waste too much time to visit my father, too."

"I'm sure, since my brothers are so eager for us to visit both of our parents, that they'd be more than happy to stay another day or two in Glint and help us out. Wouldn't you, brothers?" asked Zann with a big smile. He watched as his brothers both stopped laughing and their smiles disappeared. Now it was their turn to squirm.

"Well, I'm not sure that's possible. You see, I was planning on leaving today. I miss Talia," said Darium.

"And I miss Medea and my little, Lily-Rae," said Rhys.

"Well, I miss my daughter, too," said Lira. "Mayhap we should cancel these plans after all. Then we can all travel back to Kasculbough together today instead."

"Now wait a minute. Brothers?" asked Zann under his breath. "What do you say?"

"Rhys made a face and threw his hands up. "Fine, I'll stay."

"Darium?" asked Zann.

Darium was drinking. He slowly pulled the goblet away, looking back and forth from one brother to the other. "Damn it, I give up on spending any time with my new bride, because it is never going to happen. Sure, I'll stay and help out as well. I'll send Murk with a message to Kasculbough so our wives won't be worried."

"You can do that?" asked Lira, sounding impressed. "I thought you had fae powers of the air, not of the earth."

"That's true. But I figured it's time I learn to talk to animals. I'll just tell the bird the message and Talia will be more than capable of communicating with Murk, even if I don't know what transpires."

"My queen, the rain has stopped and the sun is starting to shine," said a messenger approaching the dais.

"I wonder if mother was listening to us," mumbled Zann, since his mother had the power to control the weather as well as to read minds.

"The weather did seem to clear up quickly once we decided to stay," said Rhys.

"It doesn't matter. This will make the trip to the Whispering Dale nicer now. It'll be easier to help the villagers as well." Lira stood, and so did all the people eating in the great hall. "Everyone, just sit down and finish eating. Please, take your time," said Lira, holding out her arms, smiling at the knights, servants, and castle's occupants. "Lady Sasha will be in charge until my return from the Whispering Dale."

"Really?" Sasha looked up and a slow smile spread across her face. "Thank you, niece. That was nice of you to announce that."

"Aunt Sasha, I have every confidence in you. I am putting you in charge of the men who are going to be helping in the village as well."

Zann heard his brothers groan and knew they weren't happy about having to answer to a woman. "This is a queendom, not a kingdom," he said softly to his brothers. "I know it's a lot for you two to accept, but try your best to be good while we are gone, will you?"

A half hour later, Lira and Zann were riding their horses toward the land of the fae. Zann felt a knot in his stomach the size of a melon. He was doing this for Lira, but really didn't want to have to confront his mother at all. He still hadn't forgiven her for abandoning him and his brothers when they were children.

"What's the matter, Zann?" asked Lira, looking ever so vibrant today. It did them both a world of good to spend the night making love and snuggling in each other's arms. "Are you worried about seeing your mother?"

"What do you think?"

"I think you need to let go of things from the past and instead, get on with your life."

"Look who is talking," he mumbled, seeing the scowl from Lira. "I'm sorry," he apologized. "I didn't mean it. I'm just anxious about seeing Mother. I have not had a real conversation with her since she returned into our lives."

"It's all right, Zann. I know you are right. I have been trying to let go of my guilt for what happened to

Laeroth and my brothers. It is going to be a long process, so I just hope that you will support me and be by my side as I try to get on with my life as well."

"You know I will, sweetheart. I cannot even imagine losing a spouse, let alone two brothers. I don't know what I'd do if I lost you, or Rhys and Darium."

"I also know I need to make amends with my father and hope you will help me with that as well."

"I'll try, but honestly, I don't have a very good relationship with the sage either."

She giggled. "Then we will do it together."

* * *

The scent of lippenbur lilies filled the air as Zann entered the Whispering Dale atop his horse with Lira following on her horse, right behind him. Lippenbur lilies were the flowers of the fae. Zann recently found out from his brothers that the flowers were also an aphrodisiac. He stopped, looking at an entire field of the white with pink flowers atop their tall stalks that were spread out in front of him. His brother Rhys had told him that he and Medea made love there. Now he could see why. It was enchanting and beautiful and smelled amazing.

"Why did you stop?" asked Lira, bringing her horse to a halt next to him.

"I was just admiring the flowers."

"You realize if we stay here any longer we're going to want to make love. The scent is already affecting me."

"And would that be so bad?" He turned to look at his wife, and smiled mischievously.

"Zann, that's not the reason we are here and you know it. You are just stalling. Now, you need to make amends with your mother, because that is what's important."

The Whispering Dale, home of the fae folk was a very enchanting place. Little cottages of wattle and daub lined the hills and valleys. Some of the homes were also constructed of wood. A few were even made of stone. Each cottage was neat and well-kept. Looking out across the dale, the sun lit up the many roofs that were more than colorful in vibrant tones of orange and blue. On the outskirts of the dale was terraced land that the fae farmed. It faced the Whispering Dale, but on the other side of it were cliffs that led to the sea. This area also sat adjacent to the high pinnacle cliff where Elric lived.

Birds chirped noisily and the colorful flowers seemed to be dancing in the breeze. Butterflies the size of his hand flitted over his head. There was a stream running through the valley with two curved stone bridges leading over them. Many of the homes were surrounded by colorful blooming trees. Campfires burned at some of their front doors.

"I love coming here," said Lira, looking around and taking a deep breath. "It always smells so sweet." A butterfly in the colors of yellow and blue floated by. Lira reached up, letting it land on her hand. Several dragonflies buzzed around Zann's head playfully, darting over to the water and then back again.

Everything seemed perfect here. It was such a happy atmosphere, that if Zann hadn't been coming here to confront his mother, he might have taken the time to actually enjoy it.

"Zann? Is that you?" Across the stream, Zann saw his mother emerge from a cottage, waving her arm above her head in a greeting.

"It's time," said Lira, gently blowing on the butterfly, sending it back up into the sky. The sky was bright now that it had stopped raining. Big, puffy white clouds hung lazily on a background of bright blue. A rainbow curved through the sky, ending right at the Whispering Dale.

Zann wanted to smile, but instead he groaned.

"What was that for?" asked Lira.

"I was just thinking that this is a perfect place to live."

"Well, you are part fae. Mayhap someday you'd want to live here."

"Oh nay, not me. I meant for sprites or faeries or even elves like you. This is all too perfect for me. I'm happy back home. I'm not leaving my side of the mountain again."

"You're not?" When she looked over at him with a concerned look on her face, he realized why. They were married now. They had never discussed where they were going to live. "Zann, you can't go back to Evandorm to live. With the king severely wounded and after you were helping the elves fight, you're now his enemy. You'll be blamed for their misfortune."

"Oh, I suppose you're right." Zann hadn't really thought about that until now. But Lira was correct. While Zann had been huntsman to King Grinwald and lived within the walls of Evandorm, that wasn't going to be possible anymore.

"We are husband and wife now," she told him. "I thought you'd be living at Castle Glint with me."

Zann didn't know what to say and so he didn't answer. He had always been close to his brothers and would rather live where he could contact them easily. Living in a land of magic like Glint was going to be so different, and difficult for him since he didn't even have any real powers beyond shapeshifting. Plus, it was so far away from his brothers who would be living on the other side of the mountain. Without having magic, it would take Zann at least a full day just traveling to visit with them.

"Zann, I'm so glad to see you," called out his mother as Zann and Lira rode over the bridge toward her.

Glint was also too close to his mother, he decided.

"Be nice," whispered Lira as they crossed the bridge and headed toward the main cottage where Zann's mother now lived.

"I'll do my best." Zann stopped his horse and helped Lira to dismount. Then he turned and acknowledged his mother. "Mother," he said with a nod.

"Hello, Zann and Lira." His mother hugged Lira, and then she reached out for Zann. His body stiffened. He was about to push her away when he saw Lira shaking her head, telling him not to.

"We are happy to see you," said Lira.

"I am so happy you decided to come visit me, son. I never thought you would." Alaina's arms wrapped around him in a hug. Unfortunately, Zann couldn't bring himself to return the hug. His arms hung limply at his sides. "What brings you here? And so early in the morning?" asked Alaina.

By now, the curious fae folk all started to emerge from their houses and wander over to see who it was who entered the Whispering Dale.

"We wanted to come personally to thank you," said Lira.

"To thank me?" asked Alaina with a giggle. "Whatever for?"

"For your help with the battle yesterday. We never could have ended it if you hadn't helped. Right, Zann?"

"Mmmph," he mumbled, reaching up to pet his horse. "I'll take the horses to the stable."

"No need, for that. The fae will do it for you," said his mother. "You're our guest while here in the Whispering Dale."

"Nay, I insist," said Zann, taking the horses and heading for the stable.

Lira noticed the perplexed look on Alaina's face and figured she needed to say something to break this awkward moment. "It is a beautiful day," she said, trying to start out with small talk.

"He doesn't accept me and never will," said Alaina, staring at her son as he walked the horses to the stable.

"I'm sure he'll come around in time."

"Nay, I don't think he will, and it hurts me deeply. If I could go back and do things differently, I would. But the damage has already been done."

"Zann told me what happened," said Lira. "Being a mother myself, I would make sacrifices for my daughter as well, if I thought it was the best for her."

"Speaking of that, where is your daughter?" asked Alaina.

"Valindra is still back in Kasculbough. Zann and I will go to collect her tomorrow."

"Come, sit down," said Alaina. "I have prepared some limsta juice for both of you." She spoke of the green fruit that was both sweet and tart at the same time. It grew plentiful in Mura.

Lira followed Alaina to the front yard of her house where a small table was set up with three settings. Three glasses of limsta juice were already there as well as plates and spoons and a pie that graced the center of the table. A small vase of fresh cut flowers added to the enchantment of the spread.

"I've baked a pazzleberry pie for our visit as well," Alaina told her.

"You did?" asked Lira in surprise. "But how did you even know we were coming?"

All the fae who were curiously gathered around now, giggled. Still, they kept their distance, just watching from behind trees or rocks.

"I'm fae, my dear. We can read minds," answered Alaina.

"Oh, that's right," answered Lira.

"We'd better watch what we think around my mother, sweetheart," said Zann rejoining them, and giving Lira a quick kiss on the mouth. "Especially if we're anywhere near the field of lippenbur lilies."

"That was fast," said Lira.

"The fae are stabling the horses. They wouldn't let me do it," he explained.

"I told you, you are our guests," repeated Alaina. "Sit down, Zann. Please." She motioned to the chairs at the outdoor table.

They all sat, and Zann's mother served them pie and limsta juice, being the perfect hostess. They had a pleasant conversation, but most of it was just small talk involving flowers, children and the weather. Zann stayed quiet, and barely even looked over at his mother. Lira could feel the tension at the table and was starting to think that she had made the wrong decision by insisting that Zann come to see his mother and make amends.

"Nay, you didn't make a wrong decision, my dear," said Alaina, reading Lira's mind as she collected the dirty plates and stacked them.

"Huh?" Zann looked up in surprise and then frowned. "Mother, stop reading my wife's mind. It's not polite."

"I don't mind," said Lira.

"Well, I do." Zann stood up. "It's time for us to leave, Lira."

"Already?" asked Alaina. "I had hoped you would stay for a while and we could talk about mayhap planning a real wedding for the two of you."

"We're already married. We don't need another wedding," said Zann, his disposition still sour.

"Honey, it might be nice," said Lira. "After all, we were married so quickly that none of our family or friends were there to join us. This way, we could have a real celebration."

"We can have it right here in the Whispering Dale. Everyone will be invited," suggested Alaina, handing the stack of dishes to another fae who took them away.

"I don't think so. Lira, we should be going. We still need to visit your father," said Zann.

"Son, we really need to make peace between us." Alaina reached out for Zann but he stepped away.

"I'm not ready yet," he told his mother.

"I understand. It'll take some time, I'm sure." Alaina smiled slightly and nodded.

"How could you understand what I feel, Mother?" asked Zann. "You weren't abandoned as a child the way you did to us."

"Zann, please," whispered Lira, thinking Zann was being disrespectful and ungrateful.

"It's all right, Lira." Alaina looked back to her son. "Nay, Zann, I guess I don't really know how you feel because I don't know you at all. But then again, neither do you know me. If you did, you would realize that I didn't know either of my parents. I grew up as an orphan after giants killed my parents when I was only four."

"Four? That's the same age as Valindra," said Lira.

"What?" Zann's head snapped up. "I didn't know that."

"Nay, how could you?" asked Alaina. "We never speak."

"I'm so sorry, Alaina." Lira reached out and hugged her.

"How did it happen? How did you lose your parents, Mother?" asked Zann.

"Zann . . . don't," said Lira, not thinking it fair to ask his mother to have to relive that horrible day.

"It is all right, Lira. My son asked, and I want him to know." Alaina continued her story. "We were in a boat, fishing. The waters became rough and our boat washed up on the shores of the Isle of Denwop."

"Oh, no," gasped Lira, clasping her hand to her mouth.

"Weren't your parents elementals?" asked Zann. "Couldn't they have used the power of the wind to blow your boat back to Mura?"

"My father was half-human, Zann," Alaina told him. "He never had any real powers, I'm sad to say. My mother was a pure fae, but she didn't possess the powers of an elemental."

"So, were her parents elementals then?"

"They were. However, they died before I ever got a chance to meet them. Anyway, my mother was injured and knocked unconscious. She awoke just as a giant . . . devoured my father."

"Nay!" Lira gasped again and tears filled her eyes. "How awful."

"I will never forget how horrible that was to see." Tears filled Alaina's eyes too.

"Mother, I'm sorry. I had no idea," whispered Zann, his voice actually shaking.

"My mother hurried me off to a cave, but her injuries were severe. She didn't last but a few days. Then she died, leaving me all alone."

"So you were alone in a cave on the Isle of Denwop and you were only four?" asked Lira. "How did you survive? How did you escape the giants?"

"Well, the giants guarded the cave, so I couldn't escape. It was then that I discovered my powers, much earlier than I should have. It was done out of sheer desperation I guess."

"I can understand," said Lira. "The same thing happened to me when I regained my powers. It happened because I wanted to protect and help Zann."

"I didn't know anything about my powers or even how to use them," Alaina continued. "But I figured it out on my own. I used my powers to escape, and I made it to the shore. Thankfully, the fae were out in a boat looking for us, and they were the ones to rescue me. I swore from that day on that I would never, ever go back to the Isle of Denwop for any reason at all."

"That is a horrific story, Alaina," said Lira. "I am so sorry to hear the sad news about your parents."

"Thank you, my dear, but you need not feel sorry for me. You see, I believe everything happens for a reason."

"There is no reason in the world for that!" Zann said.

"Son, I am not saying I wanted my parents to die, and neither did I want to be an orphan. But I was alone, and I had to do what needed to be done in order to survive. I made a vow through the years that when I someday had children, I would make sure to never put them in a situation where their lives were compromised in any way at all."

"That's why you left us," said Zann in a low voice. "You didn't want us to see the struggle between you and father, because that would be a bad situation."

"Aye, that was part of it, Zann," answered his

mother. "You see, your father was a good man when I first married him. However, through the years, I think all the sin eating he did changed him somehow. After a while, he became violent and a threat to me. Yet, I could read his mind so I knew he would never harm you or your brothers. He thought the world of you. Sadly, he didn't feel the same way anymore about me."

"I still wish you would have stayed, Mother. We could have worked it out," said Zann.

"Mayhap you are right, son. I agree that perhaps my own childhood made me fear for my children just a little too much. But please realize that I also didn't want you and your brothers to ever have to watch if . . . if anything happened to me concerning your father."

"You mean if he ever hurt or killed you," said Zann.

"Yes. After seeing the death of my own parents, I didn't want that to happen to my boys at all."

"But mayhap we could have helped, even though we were young," said Zann.

"Nay, you were all too young to do a thing, but thank you. Once again, I am sorry for the decision I made. I never meant to hurt you, Zann. I hope you can someday forgive me."

There was silence for a moment, and then Zann spoke. "I can't say I totally forgive you, but would it be all right if today was the day we started to try to change that?" he asked.

Alaina looked up in surprise. "I would love that. Do you really mean it?"

"I do." Zann released a deep breath and held out his arms. "Come here, Mother. I can see what a fool I've been for the way I've been acting toward you, and I am sorry. I will try to change, I promise."

They hugged and laughed and cried. Lira joined in. The day was definitely getting better.

"Lira," said Alaina. "I didn't read your mind just now, I promise, but I can see the confusion inside you. Why don't you stop at the Pyramids of the Gods on the way back to Glint?"

"The pyramids? Why?" asked Zann, sounding like this was the last place he wanted to be.

"If you leave an offering to Hapsren, Goddess of the Home and Hearth, I think she will help to comfort you. Perhaps you will even find the answers you seek."

"Nay, we don't need to go there," said Zann, quickly dismissing the idea. "The last time I was there with Rhys, Darium, and Medea, a sea serpent tried to eat us."

"Zann, I think I would like to do as your mother suggested," said Lira. "I have been confused for a very long time now. Perhaps the goddess can help me find peace of mind."

"I can come with you to help chase away any sea serpents," offered Alaina with a smile.

Zann let out a deep sigh. "Nay, it's not necessary, Mother, but thank you. I will take Lira to the pyramids. If a sea serpent emerges, I will fight it off." He patted the hilt of his sword. "After all, I am her husband now, and it is my duty to protect her."

"Thank you," said Lira, giving him a quick kiss on the cheek.

"Thank you both for coming to visit me. I have really enjoyed our time together," said Alaina. "Zann, I hope now we have truly made amends."

"Well, not completely, but I think we've at least had a good start," said Zann, reaching out and giving his mother another hug. "If I still have issues that are unresolved, then Lira and I will visit the Whispering Dale more frequently until there are no more walls between us, I promise."

Lira's heart swelled with love to see the walls between Zann and his mother finally being removed. The only thing that worried her now, was that she had promised to visit her father today. Something told her that the visit with him wasn't going to turn out quite as well.

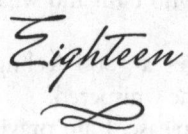

Eighteen

ZANN WATCHED as Lira laid her offering of flowers tied together with one of her hair ribbons, at the foot of the statue of the goddess, Hapsren. They stood next to each other on the shore of the small lake that encompassed the Pyramids of the Gods.

The people of Mura worshipped many gods and goddesses, but this lake with three pyramids was to worship Zoroct, the main god, Hapsren, the goddess of the home and hearth, and also Cnoir, the goddess of love and wealth. Each pyramid was a temple to one of them. Sometimes people entered the pyramids to worship, but after the last encounter Zann had here, he urged Lira not to go inside. Instead, she was worshipping from the lakeshore.

On the shore in front of the floating pyramids were three tall, stone statues of the deities. A long bridge led to each of the pyramids. Torches burned brightly in colors of red, yellow, and green, marking the doors of the pyramids, and also surrounding the lake.

Colorful lily pads with flowers floated on the water's surface.

"Hapsren, Goddess of the Home and the Hearth, I

lay my offering before you," said Lira, kneeling down. Zann rested his hand on the hilt of his sword and stood silently, watching for trouble. "I ask for your guidance to help me know who I am and what decisions to make in life."

Zann didn't get a good feeling about this at all. "Hurry up, Lira," he whispered.

"Shhh, Zann, please. I am praying to the goddess," Lira whispered back. "I ask also for your blessing on my marriage with Zann." She looked up at Zann. "Mayhap, I need to pray to Cnoir for that. After all, she is the goddess of love and wealth." Lira looked over at the statue that was situated on the other side of the statue of Zoroct. "I suppose I could pick more flowers for her."

"Nay, we're done here," said Zann, pulling Lira to her feet. "Get on the horse, quickly. It's time to go."

"Zann, you are acting as if you are scared. What's the matter with you?"

"It's not the deities I worry about, Lira. It's the monster lurking in the waters around the pyramids. Let's get out of here before it decides it's feeding time."

"Wait," she said, pulling against his arm. "One more thing." She went back to the statue. "Please protect my family and especially my daughter, Valindra. Thank you."

"You could have done that from atop the horse," grumbled Zann, helping her to mount.

"Zann, you are being silly. I wish I had gone inside the pyramids. There is nothing here to worry about."

"Say that to my brother's wife, Medea, and you might rethink your decision."

There was a loud splashing noise coming from the lake. When Zann looked up, he saw the exact thing he had been dreading. A pink sea serpent, as big as the pyramids rose up out of the water, its tongue shooting out of its mouth to taste the air. He knew this sea serpent only too well. It was the same one who came after Medea for stealing from the gods. They needed to get out of here fast.

"Damn it, I told you, Lira." Zann yanked his sword from his weapon belt, and climbed atop his horse. "We didn't steal anything," he called out to the sea serpent. "Leave us alone."

"Zann! It's – it's really a sea serpent." Lira's eyes opened wide in fright.

"Really?" he asked sarcastically. "Ride, Lira. Go! It's time to leave."

They rode away from the Pyramids of the Gods, and didn't stop until they were a good distance from the lake.

"Now, I'm glad I didn't enter the pyramids after all," said Lira as they slowed and rode next to each other after making some distance between them and the pyramids. "I wonder how the gods and goddesses think anyone is supposed to worship them when they have that thing guarding the lake."

"Who really knows what the gods are thinking. Mayhap they just don't like me. Well, it's over now," said Zann, shoving his sword back into his scabbard. "Let's go see your father. Although, I'm not sure that will be any less frightening then encountering the sea monster."

* * *

Lira held Zann's hand as they climbed the cliff leading to her father's home. They made their way over the little bridge hanging over the canyon, stopping right at his front door.

"I'm a little anxious about this. I haven't been very

nice to my father." Lira looked up to Zann with wide, green eyes.

"It'll be fine, sweetheart." It was windy this high up. He reached out and pushed a strand of her hair behind one of her pointy ears. "You were with me when I had to confront my mother, and I will be here with you when you talk with your father as well."

"I'm glad you made amends with your mother," said Lira.

"Well, I wouldn't go that far, but at least I think I understand her a little more now," said Zann. "Perhaps in time, things will be even better. But right now, we're here for you to confront your father."

"Yes," she said with a nod. "Things have been rocky between us for a long time."

The door to the house swung open. Elric stood there with his hands on his hips and a frown on his face. "Well? Are you going to come in or are you two going to stand on my doorstep yacking all day long?"

"Hello, Father," Lira said in a soft voice. Zann could feel her uneasiness.

"Elric, may we come in?" asked Zann, his loose hair blowing wildly in the wind. The weather was changing quickly since they left the Whispering Dale. Clouds blocked the sun, making it a dreary day. The wind was sharp and cold. Zann couldn't help wondering if the weather reflected his mood.

"Why do you ask to enter? Isn't that what I said, you big oaf?" Elric stepped to the side. "Get in here before you two are blown away."

Once they entered the house, Zann closed the door behind them. "Well, the nice weather we were having has certainly changed."

"There is much worse weather coming," said the elf. "You two need to be prepared."

"Thank you, father, we will," said Lira. "May we sit down?"

"There's the chairs," he said, holding out his hand.

Lira sat, and then the sage looked over at Zann.

"Zann, sit down," whispered Lira.

"I'm fine standing." Zann had no desire to sit on that tiny chair. For all he knew, his weight would snap it in half.

"Sit, oaf," snapped the sage.

"Father, his name is Zann, and he is my husband now," Lira told him. "Please, be nice."

"All right," said Elric. "Won't you *please* sit . . . you big oaf?" His request was followed by a crazy chuckle.

Zann looked over at Lira's pleading eyes and knew she wanted him to cooperate. He let out a sigh and carefully sat atop the small chair, hoping he wouldn't break it and end up on the floor. The wound on his bottom had finally started to feel normal again, and he didn't want to risk it. However, he did it for Lira.

"So, what do you two want?" snapped the sage.

"My, we are direct," said Zann, of course speaking of Elric only.

"Nay, you two are not direct at all," complained the sage. "As a matter of fact, you are wasting my precious time. There is something big about to happen and I need to prepare for it." The elf looked out the open window.

"Does this have something to do with the giants?" asked Zann, remembering Elric's earlier warning.

"Huh?" Elric turned around. "I didn't say that."

"Not now you didn't, but you told me before that the giants were going to come to Mura, running for their lives."

"Father, is this true?" asked Lira, sounding terrified.

"Did the gods tell you something, since you are their messenger?"

"Nay! I didn't say that. You didn't hear it from me. You are making this up, oaf." Elric slammed the shutter closed, then sped around the room in a blur. When he stopped, there were candles lit and he had a sumptuous feast spread out on the table before them.

"Ah, nice!" said Zann, happy to see roasted duck. Lately, with all the fae and elves around, he was lucky to get meat at all. He reached out to take some, but Elric jumped atop the table and slapped him on the hand. "What was that for?" asked Zann, rubbing his hand. His hand had been finally healing as well after the nick from the guard's sword he received in the dungeon of Evandorm, but if Elric kept hitting him, the wound would reopen.

"Before you eat, tell me what you want," said Elric in his wiry little voice.

"I don't want anything," said Zann. "I just came with Lira for moral support. Now, can I have some food?" He reached out for the food and once again got a slap in return. He felt like a child being scolded.

"Father, let Zann eat," scolded Lira. "He tells the truth. He is only here because I didn't want to come visit you alone."

"Oh. All right. Go on." Elric hopped off the table and sat in a chair, pouring himself some ale.

"The first thing I want to say is that I am not happy that you made that crown of power, using hair from magical people," said Lira.

"Yeah, yeah, I know that," scoffed Elric. "But I am proud of it. The braids were all magical. I had the kings' hair in there too." He grinned proudly.

"That's right, he did," said Zann, cautiously reaching out for a leg of duck. He grabbed it and quickly brought it to his mouth, glad he didn't get slapped again.

"Why did you even make that crown?" asked Lira. "I still don't truly understand the reason."

"I did it for you, daughter. You know that. After all, you were putting up walls and not embracing your powers. I wasn't sure if you were ever going to get them back."

"And, what if I didn't? What difference would it have really made?" she asked, nibbling on a piece of cheese.

"You need your magic to survive, Lira." Elric seemed to be trying to teach her something.

"No, I don't. Not really."

"You do if you are going to be queen. I was only trying to help the matter along."

"Well, your crown of power almost destroyed us all. You shouldn't have made it." Lira wasn't going to give up this fight, even if it no longer mattered.

Elric raised his chin and wrinkled his nose. "I didn't know the fool was going to wear the crown instead of you! And besides, you shouldn't have tried to destroy it."

"Tried?" asked Zann. "She did destroy it. I saw her put it in the fire."

"Uh . . . yeah, that's what I meant." Elric looked the other way.

"Father?" asked Lira, sounding suspicious. "What did you do? Please, don't tell me you kept the crown from being destroyed?"

"Great duck," said Zann, reaching for more, caring more about food than the crown.

"Have some pie. I made pazzleberry pie, too." The elf slid a pie in front of them.

"No thanks," said Zann, licking his fingers. "We already had pazzleberry pie at my mother's, before we came here."

"What? You went by the Whispering Dale? Why?" The elf squinted one eye and cocked his head.

"Father, it doesn't matter. What matters is that you and I have some things between us that we need to address."

"Oh, like you banishing me from the Queendom of Glint?" he asked in a sarcastic tone.

"I'm sorry about that," said Lira. "You are welcome to come back to the castle to live if you'd like."

"Nope." The sage crossed his arms over his chest and stuck his chin in the air. "I like it here better. Thanks anyway."

"Well, it's your choice," she said.

"Excuse me, but do you have any wine?" asked Zann, taking a sip from his goblet and peering down into the cup. "My stomach is a little upset from all the limsta juice that my mother served us, and this ale is only making it worse."

"She gave you limsta juice too?" asked the sage, sounding jealous if Zann wasn't mistaken. "No more ale for you." He snatched the cup from Zann's hand. "If you don't like it, then leave it." He thunked the cup down on the table so hard that the little ale that was left inside the cup splashed up on Zann's face.

"Thanks," grumbled Zann, closing one eye and wiping his face on his sleeve. "But I'm still thirsty."

"I want to make amends," Lira blurted out. "I want you to move back to the castle, and I want Valindra to know her grandfather while she is growing up."

"Really?" asked the little elf.

"Yes," said Lira. "I am ready to put everything behind us from the past. Are you willing to do that, too?"

"Well, I don't know," said Elric. "What about your brothers?"

"M-my brothers are dead, father."

"Nay," said the sage, shaking his head. He got up and went back to the window, yanking open the shutter. "They are not dead and they never were." He spoke, looking outside instead of at Lira. "I want my sons brought home first, and then I will forgive you for keeping them from me."

"Keeping them from you?" asked Lira. "I did no such thing. I saw Keevan and Korack get smashed under falling rocks. Rocks that I made fall! I killed them. Just come to terms with that because it is the truth." Lira jumped up, crying, wrapping her arms around her trembling body.

"Uh oh," said Zann, putting down the duck bones and wiping his hands on the tablecloth.

"Use the hand cloth, you fool," yelled Elric.

The wind outside picked up, pushing open a shutter and banging it against the wall.

"I think it's time we go, Zann." Lira turned and headed for the door.

"All right." Zann started to follow.

"Nay, you two are not leaving until I get my answer." Elric waved a fist above his head.

"Stop it!" Lira spun around in anger, and when she did her powers caused Elric to go flying through the air. He was about to be sent right out the window, but he counteracted the powers with his own. In a blur he was standing right next to them again.

"Uh . . . mayhap we can discuss this further at a later date?" asked Zann, knowing this was starting to become a harrowing situation.

"I'm done talking," snapped Lira, storming out the door.

Zann stood there looking at the sage and shrugged.

"Sorry," he said. He turned to leave, but the sage's words stopped him.

"It's up to you now, Zann."

"Pardon me?" Zann turned back to look at the elf. The little man seemed serious and solemn. Zann had never seen him this way before.

"Something bad, very bad is about to happen," he told Zann.

"Aye, you keep saying that, but won't tell me what it is."

"My daughter might not be able to stop it, especially where her daughter is concerned. It's up to you now, Zann. Don't let Lira down."

"Wait. What?" Zann shook his head. "I have no idea what you mean. And how does any of this concern Valindra?"

"Zann? Are you coming?" shouted Lira already heading across the bridge. "It's starting to rain. We need to hurry."

Over his shoulder he called out to her. "I'll be right there, sweetheart." When he turned back to question the sage further, the little man was gone.

Zann left the cottage and closed the door, feeling that knot in his stomach becoming even larger.

Nineteen

"**WHAT WAS** my father saying to you?" asked Lira as they made their way down the cliff and hurried back to the castle as it started to rain.

"I'm not exactly sure," said Zann, not wanting to worry Lira more. Especially if this really did concern her daughter. "He didn't really make any sense."

"He's like that sometimes."

"There you are, brother!" Darium and Rhys flagged him down from across the great hall.

"Thank you for helping out today," Zann told his brothers. "Were you able to get everything done before it rained again?"

"Aye, most of the cottages are repaired," said Rhys sitting down with his feet up on a bench. He had a tankard of ale cradled in his hands.

"There are still a few things that will need to be fixed yet, but Rhys and I are going to head back home." Darium's raven sat perched on the back of his chair.

"Did you get everything squared away concerning Mother?" asked Rhys.

"It is getting better between us." Zann scooted on to a bench and poured himself a mug of ale. "It'll just take a little more time, but, I'd say we made some good progress today. I understand her a lot better now."

"Good. Good," said Darium. "Before you know it, we'll be one big happy family again."

"Zann, I am going to check in with Sasha, and then I will pack a few things for our trip tomorrow," interrupted Lira. "I miss Valindra so much that I just can't wait to see her."

"All right," he said, reaching up to kiss her. Smiling, he watched her walk away.

"So . . . it looks like you're getting used to being married to the elf," said Darium.

"Are you staying married?" asked Rhys.

"I think so," said Zann. "Even though Lira didn't actually come out and say it, I know she will want to stay married to me. I don't want to ever lose her. I think I am falling in love with her."

"Are you staying here with her in Glint or coming back home to live?" asked Darium.

"I don't know yet." Zann took a deep draw of his ale and set the tankard back down. "I'm not sure I want to live in a castle with a bunch of elves, but I won't abandon my wife. Plus, Valindra needs a father. I am going to be her father now," said Zann, proudly.

"That's nice," Rhys answered. "But you really need to talk to Lira and decide where your family will live."

"She is Queen of Glint, brother," said Darium. "You can't expect her to leave her queendom."

"My wife left her kingdom for me," said Rhys.

"Lira's daughter is princess," Darium pointed out. "Someday she'll be the ruler of Glint."

"Aye, I know all this." Zann ran a weary hand through his long hair, not sure what to do. "The sage said something odd to me today, but I didn't tell Lira because I don't want to worry her."

"What's that?" Darium found a crust of bread on the floor and threw it to his raven.

"Well, he told me something bad was going to happen. It involves the giants . . . and I think mayhap Lira's daughter somehow, but I'm not sure."

"Bad?" Darium made a face. "How bad?"

"I don't know," said Zann. "He didn't elaborate. But I get the feeling all our troubles aren't over with yet."

"You mean your troubles, Zann." Rhys got up and stretched. "Darium and I are leaving. We've got wives at home, and I also miss my daughter."

"I understand," said Zann, getting to his feet.

"Are you traveling with us?" Darium stood up. His raven squawked and flew over to his shoulder.

"You two go ahead. I don't think Lira is quite ready to leave yet. Plus, I don't fancy traveling in the rain. I think we'll leave first thing in the morning."

"Well, if you're sure, then we'll be on our way," said Rhys. "I don't want to be away from Kasculbough for too long. King Sethor is bound to be upset since he didn't get the crown. There's no telling what he might try to do."

"Aye," agreed Darium. "And he wounded King Grinwald pretty badly when he stabbed him. I have a feeling there might be trouble between them when we return. I want to get back and find out what's going on."

"Aye, we all have our problems," said Zann, reaching out and clasping each of his brothers' hands in turn. "Safe journey, brothers."

"We'll see you soon," said Rhys, and he and Darium headed away.

Zann felt a shiver go up his spine as he watched his brothers leave. Part of him wanted to beg them to stay, but he couldn't understand why. Mayhap it was because of the sage's warning. Another part of him wanted to run after them and tell them he and Lira would be traveling with them. Everything seemed unsettling to him right now and he just wanted peace and quiet.

"Zann? What's the matter?" asked Lira coming up behind him.

"Nothing, sweetheart."

"Are your brothers leaving already? Mayhap we should travel with them."

"Nay, we'll go in the morning," he said, wrapping his arms around her. "It might be selfish of me, but I want one last night alone with you before we collect Valindra."

"I suppose that would be nice," said Lira with a smile, reaching up and putting her arms around Zann's neck. "Mayhap we could go to bed right now?" she asked in a playful manner.

"I don't see why not." Zann scooped Lira off her feet, loving the sound of her laughter as he carried her to the solar. He was happy to be spending private time with his wife, but on the other hand, he had a bad feeling that something was going to happen, and all he wanted to do was to protect her.

* * *

Zann tossed and turned, unable to sleep that night. He felt uneasy and worried, but didn't want to mention this to Lira. He looked over at her sleeping peacefully next to him. The light of the bedtime candle flickered against her smooth skin. Zann felt lucky to be her husband. He would protect her and her daughter and be the best husband and father that he possibly could.

He thought he heard a noise that sounded as if it

came from down the hall. There was a loud thumping noise and also something that sounded like children giggling. He wondered if some youngsters in the castle were awake instead of sleeping like they should be.

Zann quietly got up and hurriedly dressed, deciding to check since it wasn't safe for children to be wandering around in the dark. He was nearly ready to leave the room when Lira bolted upright in bed.

"Valindra!" she cried.

"Shhhh, you're dreaming, sweetheart." Zann went to comfort her, but she pushed his hands away and jumped out of bed.

"Nay, I'm not. I've had a premonition. She's in trouble. We've got to help her. It's the man in the portal again." Lira leaped from the bed and ran for the door.

"Lira, wait," called out Zann, hurriedly slipping into his boots. "Valindra isn't here. She's in –" It was too late. Lira had grabbed the bedtime candle and was running down the hall. Zann hurried after her.

"Sweetheart, slow down," he told her, noticing now that a few people in the castle were sticking their heads out of their rooms, curiously wondering what was going on.

"She's in trouble, I tell you," cried Lira.

"She's not even here. It was only a dream. Valindra is –" Zann stopped in his tracks when he followed Lira into a bedchamber and saw both Valindra and Rhys' daughter, Lily-Rae sitting atop the bed. Somehow he knew that magic is what brought them here. Most likely, Lily-Rae's magic. Next to them was a swirling portal, and in that portal was a man. "Oh, damn," he swore under his breath.

"Stay away from my daughter," Lira screamed at the man in the portal, dropping the candle and running for the bed.

"Sister," the man in the portal said in a sibilant whisper. "Sister, you have to help us."

"Go away," she cried out, reaching for Valindra, but it was too late.

The intruder had Valindra's arm and he was pulling her into the swirling mass with him. The little girl screamed, and Lily cried.

"Lira, get Lily," shouted Zann, racing right for the portal. "I've got Valindra." He grabbed her other arm as the little girl cried and screamed loudly. She struggled to try to free herself, but to no avail. The man in the portal already had a good hold on her. With one more tug from the dark stranger, Zann's hand slipped off of Valindra's and he took her away from him. "Damn," he spat.

"My daughter! Save her, Zann," cried Lira, cradling the crying Lily in her arms.

"I'll get her, don't worry." The portal hissed and sputtered and the swirling colors of red and blue became dimmer. The opening was collapsing and starting to close. Without thinking twice about it, Zann dove into the swirling mist after them, and the portal snapped shut behind him.

"Help! Guards, where are you?" shouted Lira, panicked to see that the portal had closed and both her daughter and Zann were gone.

"We're here, my lady," shouted a guard, entering the room with a torch in his hand. "What's wrong?"

"Lira, what's all the shouting about?" asked Sasha, hurrying into the room, tying closed her robe.

"My daughter has been taken by the man in the portal, Zann went after her," Lira blurted out.

"My lady, who is that?" asked Sasha, pointing to the crying little girl in her arms.

"Lily? Is that you?" Rhys rushed into the room followed by Darium. Both of them had tussled hair and their clothes were wet.

"Why are you two here?" Lira asked Zann's brothers. "I thought you left for Kasculbough earlier."

"We had to turn back because of the rain, and now I'm glad we did. Come here, Lily." Rhys reached out and took his daughter from her.

"Who is Lily?" Sasha demanded to know.

"She's my daughter," said Rhys.

"Well, why is she even here? Who brought her?"

"I have a sneaking suspicion my little witch has been up to her tricks again, using her powers of transportation," Rhys told her.

"She has powers? At that age?" asked Sasha in shock.

"Sasha, Valindra was with her when I entered the room," reported Lira.

"Ah, she must have brought your daughter here, too," said Rhys.

"They both must have missed their parents and wanted to be with them," said Darium.

"Well, my daughter is gone and so is Zann," yelled Lira. "Doesn't anybody care?"

"Zann is gone?" asked Darium, sounding half asleep. "Where did he go?"

"He went through the portal to save Valindra. That man stole her for good this time," said Lira.

"Did this man in the portal say anything?" asked Rhys, having calmed his two-year old daughter.

"H-he called me sister," said Lira, tears dripping down her face. "And he said he wanted me to help him."

"Sister?" asked Sasha. "Lira, what is this all about?"

"I'll tell you what it's about." Elric pushed his way through the crowded room, approaching Lira and the

Blackseed brothers. "That was Lira's brother in the portal – my son."

Gasps went up from the growing crowd.

"But I thought Keevan and Korack were dead," said the guard.

"They've been gone for four years now," added Sasha. "They can't possibly have survived."

"They're alive, just like I always knew they were," said the sage. "This proves it."

"But where are they?" asked Darium. "And what do they want?"

"The man asked me to help him," said Lira, strong emotions about choking her now. "They need my help. Oh, father, I think you might be right about this. I should have listened to you. We've got to help them."

"But we don't even know where they are," said the guard.

"I think I know exactly where to find them," said Elric, looking over at Lira.

Lira's heart leapt into her throat. This was the worst thing that could ever happen, because she already knew what he was about to say.

"Where?" asked Rhys. "Where are they?"

"The Isle of Denwop," said Lira softly, feeling as if all her nightmares were coming true once again.

"The Isle of Denwop? They're with the giants?" asked Sasha.

"I believe so," said Lira. "That is where I last saw my brothers. And now Zann and Valindra are there, too."

"It's not going to be easy to rescue them if that is really where they are," said Rhys. "Darium and I will help you but I've only fought off one giant before. We are not experienced at this at all."

"You may have more giants to fend off than you

think." Elric jumped up on a stool and pulled open the shutter that covered the window.

There was a loud noise outside that sounded like thunder. Lira swore she also smelled something burning. Smoke filled the air making it hard to see. And for a moment it almost seemed as if the earth shook beneath their feet.

"What was that?" she asked, running to look out the window. She could see the volcano on the Isle of Denwop. It was glowing red with plumes of white smoke trailing up high into the sky. The night sky lit up in an eerie glow.

"The volcano," shouted her guard, running to the window as well. "It's erupting!"

"That's right, you big oaf," said Elric, slapping the guard on the arm when he stood too close to him. "And now that their home is being threatened, all the giants of Denwop are headed in one direction . . . here."

"Zoroct's eyes!" cried Darium. "We've got to do something to stop this."

"Please. We've got to save my daughter and husband," begged Lira.

"And my sons," added Elric.

"Does anyone have any ideas of how to do this?" asked Rhys. "With the volcano erupting, we might not even be able to get onto the island."

"Then we need to find a way to open the portal again," said Lira. "It's the only way to get there."

"We need to find a way to put out the fire of the volcano," said Darium. "If we do that, mayhap the giants will stay put."

"Can't you do something about that, Darium?" asked Rhys. "You have powers of an elemental now."

"Of the air, yes. But this is way out of my league," he said.

"Mayhap your mother can help us," suggested Lira.

"Nay. Not with the fire from the volcano," said Darium. "Only an elemental of fire can do that."

"Then we're doomed," said Lira. "We don't have one of those, do we?"

"Not here," said Darium. "However, I'm sure my mother knows where to find one."

"And who can find someone to open the portal?" asked Lira. "Because unless we do, I'm afraid I'll lose Zann, Valindra, and both my brothers forever this time."

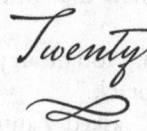

Twenty

ZANN LANDED hard on the ground, rolling over as the portal snapped shut behind him.

"Who are you?" asked the man from the portal, looking down at him.

Zann jumped to his feet, reaching for his sword, but unfortunately he hadn't had the time to don it. He was lucky to even be dressed at all, and not still clad in his night clothes.

"Father, help me," cried Valindra, struggling against the man's hold.

"Father?" asked the man, looking down at Valindra. When he moved his eyes off of Zann, Zann dove for him, taking the abductor to the ground.

"Let go of her," shouted Zann, punching the man in the face. Valindra screamed and cried some more.

"Stop it, please," begged the stranger, holding up his hands. "I am not going to hurt her."

"Then why did you abduct her?" snapped Zann, so angry right now that he wished he had a blade on him so he could kill him.

"I am Lira's brother, Keevan," the man croaked.

"What?" Zann got off of him, but stayed between him and the girl.

"I am her brother, I swear. I only took Lira's daughter because I knew that would bring her here to rescue us."

"Us?" asked Zann. "You mean you and the girl."

"And my twin, Korack."

"He's alive, too?" asked Zann, reaching over and picking up Valindra, holding her shaking body tightly against him.

"Korack is injured, and I'm afraid he will die. Please, won't you help us?"

"I need some answers first."

"Fine, but not here," said Keevan, struggling to get to his feet. He looked so thin and frail. Zann reached out and helped him to stand.

"Then where?" asked Zann.

"There is only one place to go where we will be safe from the giants. In the cave."

"They won't follow us there?" asked Zann.

"Nay. It's a small opening close to the ground and they can't fit inside. It's also what kept us alive all these years."

"The cave," repeated Zann, wondering if this was the same cave that his mother had told him about. Could it possibly be the same place she hid as a child?

"Please. We have to hurry," pleaded Keevan. "Usually the giants guard the entrance and the shore. But since the volcano has started to erupt, they are scattering and trying to leave the island."

"The volcano is erupting?" asked Zann, following Keevan and carrying Valindra who clung to him for dear life. If the volcano erupted, that meant the giants would have to leave the island. And if they left, there was only one place to go. Mura. "Damn," he said, realizing now that everything the blasted elf told him was coming true.

Oh, how he wished Elric had been wrong, and anything but a wise sage right now.

They hid behind rocks and trees, slowly making their way to the cave that held Keevan's brother. They were careful and quiet and kept watch for giants. In the distance Zann saw the volcano at the opposite side of the island smoking and shooting molten lava high up into the air.

"I'm scared, father," said Valindra, holding on to him even tighter.

"Shhh, it's fine. I have you, sweetheart. I'll protect you," answered Zann.

"Why is she calling you father?" asked Keevan, leading the way to the cave.

"I'm married to her mother now. My name is Zann Blackseed," he told him.

"Aye, Lira's husband died when we were trapped here years ago," Keevan confirmed. "How is my sister?"

"She's . . . fine," said Zann, not sure how to answer.

"The cave is just up ahead. Hurry, I see giants headed this way."

Sure enough, Zann looked up and his jaw dropped. The ground thundered under the heavy feet of the giants as they ran toward them, heading for the shore. They were even bigger than the giant that worked for King Sethor. They stood at least three times the height of Zann, and had huge builds on them that made them very bulky. There were men as well as women, and even a few children. Most of the giants had red hair. The men all had scraggly beards.

Zann ducked behind a tree, holding Valindra close. "Don't look," he whispered, holding her head to his chest. He didn't need the girl crying out right now and alerting the giants of their presence.

Once they passed, Zann darted out from behind the

tree and continued to follow Keevan. The air became thick from the smoke, making it harder to breathe. The volcano rumbled and the ground shook. This wasn't looking good at all.

"Duck your head. The entrance is right here," said Keevan, hunkering down. Just as he was about to go in, another group of giants appeared. To Zann's dismay, Valindra saw them and screamed.

"Humans!" came the low growl of one of the giants, looking in their direction.

"Get them," commanded another.

"Fast! In here," said Keevan, helping Valindra and then following her inside. Zann had just hunkered down to enter the cave when a giant reached out and grabbed his leg.

"Nay!" shouted Zann, his fingers scratching at the dirt as he tried to hold himself there and not be eaten by the giant as he was pulled away. The giant's grip got stronger. Zann was dragged over the ground and then lifted up into the air.

"Leave him alone!" screamed Keevan, emerging from the cave. "Let go of him, I say." Keevan threw a rock, hitting the giant in the face and only managing to make him angrier.

"Arrrrrgh," bellowed the giant, lifting Zann up higher.

What Zann would give for his sword right now. He struggled against the giant, as the beast brought him closer and closer to his mouth.

"I said, leave him alone!" Keevan did something next that surprised Zann. He threw a small fireball from his hand. It hit the giant on the leg before quickly fizzling out. It wasn't much and didn't last long, but it was all the distraction they needed. The giant cried out and dropped Zann. Zann fell to the ground, smashing into the earth.

"Oomph," he grunted as his face hit the dirt.

"Hurry, Zann," cried Keevan, running out to help him. Together, they made it back to the cave before the giant could grab either of them again.

Breathing heavily, Zann collapsed on the cave floor. "That was a close one," he said, feeling his heart about beating right out of his chest. He didn't even want to think about the fact he'd almost been eaten by a giant.

"Father," cried Valindra, running to him and throwing herself into his arms. "I thought the giant was going to eat you like it did to my other daddy."

"Nay, Valindra, that is not going to happen," he said, smoothing back the little girl's hair. "Keevan, you threw a fireball. Tell me, how did you do that?"

"I – I'm not sure," said Keevan, staring at his hand. "It has never happened before."

"He's getting his elf powers," said Valindra in a knowing way.

"Mayhap that's it," said Zann. "How old are you?"

"My brother and I were sixteen when we first came here. We've lost all sense of time living in a dark cave, foraging for whatever scraps of food we can get. We've both been tired and weak and sickly for quite some time now."

"You've been missing for four years," Zann told him.

"That long?" Keevan blinked and a sadness washed across his face. "No one has ever come to look for us," he said sadly.

"There are reasons for that, but it'll keep until later. Lira told me that an elf starts to come into their power at adulthood. It must be what is happening to you.

You've been so malnourished and weak that it must have taken longer to happen than it should have."

"Brother, what is going on?" came a small voice from deeper in the cave. There was a small fire burning near the entrance, but this man was further back and in the dark.

"Korack, this is Zann, Lira's new husband. And this is her daughter, Valindra," said Keegan.

A man dragged himself along the ground, making his way closer to the fire. Zann could see his face in the firelight now. He looked exactly like Keevan. But this man was even thinner, and had darker circles under his eyes. His leg was splinted and it didn't seem as if he could stand.

"Korack, what is it that is ailing you?" Zann put the little girl down and walked over to meet Lira's brother.

"I was injured by a giant months ago when I went out to collect food. My leg was broken and I was lucky to get away."

"I put a splint on his leg but I think he has an infection," said Keevan, walking over and pulling up his brother's pant leg for Zann to see. It looked awful. His skin was red and bumpy and pus oozed from somewhere but he couldn't tell where. "It has been getting worse lately."

"Oh," said Zann, inspecting the festering wound. A red line trailed up Korack's leg.

"I'm afraid I'm going to die," said Korack.

"Isn't there a way to heal it?" asked Zann.

"If I could get a hold of the Prunella Blue Curls herb, I could wrap his leg in it and he'd be better in a day," said Keevan. "I'm sure of it. But the herb only grows on the other side of the island. We've been trapped in this area for so long now, and we haven't been able to leave. Any time we try to escape, the giants find us and we rush back here for cover."

"How hard is it to get this herb?" asked Zann.

"I would have to go right through their village to get there. It would be a suicide mission, I'm sorry to say. I'm sure I'd never make it back alive."

"I'll get it," Zann offered. "Tell me exactly what it looks like and right where it grows."

"Nay," said Korack, shaking his head. "It is too dangerous, Zann. Just let me die. Abandon me the way our sister did to us."

Abandon. That word felt heavy in Zann's chest. He had been abandoned in life too. But this was different, and he wanted Lira's brothers to understand.

"Lira didn't abandon you. Not really," said Zann. "She thought you two had died along with her husband." He didn't want to go into the details since it didn't feel right to talk about it in front of the girl. "Besides, we're going to get out of here, I promise."

"How?" asked Korack. "There is no boat, and I can't even walk."

"He's right, Zann," agreed Keevan. "With the volcano erupting now, we are all going to die here. We'll never see our home or our family again."

"I want Mother." That only made Valindra cry louder.

"Stop it!" Zann commanded. "They will come for us. Lira and the others will save us."

"I want my mother, now," cried Valindra, clinging to Zann once again.

"How did you activate the portal?" asked Zann. "We can go out the same way we came in."

"I – I didn't do anything," said Keegan. "It just appeared. I was out collecting food one day and saw it. I was able to see through it and recognized Glint. I saw Valindra with Lira one day briefly, and I knew the girl was my sister's child. I had to get Lira's attention so I figured this was the best way to do it. That was why I tried to grab Valindra. I knew her screams would alert my sister. I had hoped Lira would realize we were still alive and that she would come for us."

"She won't come," scoffed Korack. "She'll leave us to die just like she did before."

"That's not true," said Zann. "Family means everything to Lira."

"Then why didn't she come looking for us when we first disappeared?" asked Korack with contempt in his voice.

"There will be time to discuss all that later. Right now, we need to move fast if we are going to get out of here before that volcano erupts."

"I agree," said Keevan.

"Keevan, why didn't you go through the portal into Glint instead of trying to pull Valindra back through it? If you had, you could have contacted your sister easily."

"I wasn't going to leave my brother behind. He is injured and vulnerable."

"I see," said Zann. "I will go find the necessary herb, and then together we will figure out a way to get off this island."

"You can't get the herb," said Keevan. "Forget it. It's a fool's task to go through the land of the giants."

"He's right," agreed Korack. "You'll never make it back alive."

"I think I know a way that I can. It'll be faster traveling and I will return quickly without being noticed."

"How?" asked Keevan.

"He's going to turn into a wolf," said Valindra with a sniffle.

"A wolf?" asked Korack.

"Valindra's right," said Zann. "Now tell me exactly what the herb looks like and the direct place where it grows. We have no time to waste."

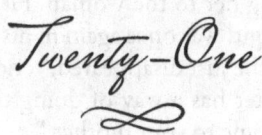

Twenty-One

"EVERYONE, ARM YOURSELVES FOR BATTLE!" cried out Lira, now fully dressed and donning a weapon belt of her own. She hurried out into the courtyard to see the sun just starting to rise. The volcano was glowing red in the distance and the air had filled with smoke.

"I'll lead the army into battle against the giants," said Rhys. "But I need someone to watch my daughter."

"Well, don't think I'm going to watch the brat, because I'm coming with you." Lira's father appeared in the courtyard dressed in chain mail and wearing a belt with weapons as well.

"Father? What are you doing?" asked Lira.

"My sons are over there and it's about time I save them."

"But you can't go to the Isle of Denwop. The gods forbade it," Lira reminded him.

"They did, but I don't care anymore. I'm going."

"You'll anger the gods, Father. Don't do it."

"So, mayhap they'll punish me, or take away my powers. Whatever they do, it doesn't matter. It'll be worth it to see Korack and Keevan again."

"I'll watch her, my lord," said one of the elven women, holding out her hands for little Lily.

"Be a good girl for daddy," said Rhys, giving her a kiss and handing her to the woman. He didn't walk far before the little girl was once again in his arms.

"I'm sorry, she just disappeared," cried the woman.

"My daughter has a way of doing that," said Rhys. "Lily-Rae, go home to your mother."

"No! I want to stay with you, Dada," Lily said with a pout.

"I can see this isn't going to work," said Rhys. "I can't fight with my daughter in my arms."

"Can you somehow call for her mother?" asked Lira.

"Nay. I don't have the power to do that," Rhys explained.

"I'll send Murk." Darium walked up with his raven on his shoulder. "Murk, go get Medea and Talia. We could use their help."

The raven opened its beak and squawked in protest.

"Don't give me trouble. Now go," commanded Darium, sending the raven up into the air.

"My queen, the warriors are ready." Sasha walked up, also dressed in chain mail and portions of armor. "I will lead them in battle against the giants."

"You?" asked Rhys with a chuckle. "Do you really think you can lead an army? You're a woman."

Sasha was at least a good twenty years older than Lira. However, she was also one of their fiercest warriors, which Rhys was about to find out.

"I'm a woman with more powers than you'll ever have," said Sasha, glaring at him. "I'll show you if you want to see."

"Sasha, nay!" cried Lira, but it was too late. Sasha held up her hand and used her powers to knock Rhys to the ground. He landed on his backside, still holding on to Lily. Thankfully she had not thrown a fireball at him or he'd be dead. Rhys grumbled, getting to his feet with his daughter clinging to him.

Then, Sasha screamed as she was lifted into the air, her arms and legs flailing about.

"Lily, put her down," Rhys told his daughter.

Sasha fell to the ground in a puff of dust.

"That child is powerful!" gasped Sasha. "Perhaps she should help fight the giants."

"We need to stop this and focus on our true cause. If we are going to save my family and also save Mura from the giants, we need to work together," said Lira.

"I agree," said Darium. "I'm going to ride out to the Whispering Dale and find Mother. She can help."

"I'm here, Darium," said Alaina, appearing with another woman at her side. "I am here and I have brought Brynn-Riletta from Lornoon. She is an elemental of fire and can help us control the volcano."

"Hello," said Brynn with a nod. Brynn's bright red hair looked similar to the color of the molten lava coming from the volcano.

"You can control fire? Really?" Rhys brushed himself off, still holding on to his daughter.

"I can. I get my strength from fire, and it cannot harm me," said Brynn.

"Good thing, since Sasha is in a bad mood," mumbled Rhys.

"Shall we go?" asked Brynn.

"Not without us." Medea magically appeared, holding the hand of Talia.

"Talia? Medea?" asked Darium. "I just sent Murk for you. How are you here already?"

"When I woke up and noticed the girls were gone, I had a feeling where they went. Lily-Rae, you are a bad girl." Medea took the baby from Rhys.

"Where is Valindra?" asked Talia.

"She's been taken through the portal, and our guess is that she is on the Isle of Denwop with Zann and my brothers," Lira explained.

"I think we have a lot to catch up on," said Talia. "But before you tell me more, let me call Murk back, as well as summon the other animals of Mura to help us." Talia used her powers as an elemental of the earth to do just that.

"I am worried for Zann and Valindra, and my brothers," Lira told the others.

"Don't worry," Alaina tried to calm her. "We have enough magical help that this shouldn't be a problem. If we all work together, our troubles will be over soon."

"You're right," said Lira with tears in her eyes. "Thank you all for helping me and my people."

"Mura is home to all of us," said Talia. "No one wants to see the giants destroy our land."

"Nay," said Lira, looking once again back up to the steaming, spurting volcano. "I just hope the giants haven't already killed my family."

* * *

Zann ran between the legs of the giants in his wolf form, trying to avoid their stampede as they ran for the shore. He hadn't had any trouble finding the Prunella Blue Curls herb, and now had a huge bunch of it clasped in his teeth. The air was becoming unbearably hot. It was getting harder and harder to breathe. Lava had already begun flowing down the side of the mountain, and it was moving fast. Zann had almost been overtaken by it when he grabbed the herb just before the lava covered it completely.

The giants were already at the shore and panicking,

trying to escape. Some were piled into their boats, and others swam, but they were all headed directly toward Mura. Zann needed to help fight them off, but first he needed to see to the safety of Lira's brothers and Valindra. The cave was low to the ground and the lava was heading right for it.

He made it back into the cave on all fours and dropped the herbs at Keevan's feet. Then he quickly shifted back into his manly form, lying on the ground naked and unable to move.

"Thank you," said Keevan. "I can't believe you got it."

"I can't believe he's still alive," said Korack.

"We need to move fast." Zann sat up and reached for his clothes, breathing heavily. "The giants are already headed for Mura, and the lava is coming this way."

"This herb works quickly and like magic," said Keevan, running over to apply it as a poultice to his brother's leg.

Zann finished dressing and looked out the cave entrance once again. He wasn't sure exactly how they were going to get out of here alive. He feared it was already too late.

After a few minutes, Keevan looked up. "All done. His leg is wrapped with the herb. Let's go."

"Can you walk?" asked Zann, running over to help Korack get to his feet. "We need to try to get to the water."

"I – I'm not sure," said Korack, wincing in pain as he now stood between Zann and his brother for support.

"Someone's coming," said Valindra, looking out the entrance of the cave.

"Damn it, no," said Zann, thinking she meant the giants.

To his surprise, he saw swirling colors just outside the entrance of the cave and realized that the portal was opening.

"Hurry," he said. "Everyone, get to the portal. This might be our only chance."

He and Keevan all but dragged Korack to the mouth of the cave where Valindra stood waiting. But before they could get to the portal, two people came through and then the portal snapped closed behind them.

"Mother? Lira?" Zann was happy to see them, but at the same time worried since now they would be trapped here, too. "What are you two doing here?"

"Son, I came to help you," said Alaina. "You didn't think I was going to abandon you, did you?"

"Lira," said Keevan, letting go of Korack and running to hug her.

"Mother," cried Valindra, running to Lira as well.

"Keevan. Korack," cried Lira. "I'm so sorry I didn't come for you years ago. I thought you were both dead. I'm so happy that you're not."

"Why didn't you send someone to find our bones at least?" snapped Korack, still holding on to Zann for support.

"We can discuss this all later," said Zann. "Right now we need to find a way to get off this island before we're fried to a crisp when that lava makes its way here."

"You don't need to worry about the volcano," said Alaina. "My friend, Brynn-Riletta who is an elemental of fire is taking care of that right now."

"Well, what about the giants?" asked Zann. "I saw them all in the water and heading directly toward Glint."

"That, we'll need to concern ourselves with," said Alaina.

"Can you open the portal, Mother?" asked Zann eagerly. "You must have already done so since you and Lira came through it."

"We didn't do that," explained Lira. "It just happened to appear and opened and we went through, looking for you."

Zann's heart sank. "So, then we really are stuck here."

"I suggest we all start making our way to the water," said Keevan.

"Aye," agreed Zann. "But I don't know how we're going to get across. Or how we'll fight off that many giants either. The way I see it, we need a miracle to get us out of here alive."

"Or just some powerful magic," said Lira with a smile. "And thankfully, that, we have, Zann. Don't worry, everything is going to work out fine."

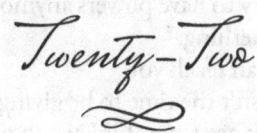

Twenty-Two

THE BATTLE between the giants and the magical beings of Mura had begun.

By the time Zann and the others made it down to the water, it was evident that some of the giants had already made it across and to the shores of Mura.

"The volcano has stopped!" Lira pointed and they all looked.

"Ah, yes," said Alaina. "I see Brynn-Riletta was able to control it. But it is so smoky that the giants don't even notice."

"Mother, can't you blow the smoke away? You can control the air," said Zann.

"I can, but it's a lot," she told him. "Zann, will you work with me to clear the air?"

"Me?" Zann didn't know what his mother was asking. "Mother, I don't have any powers except shapeshifting into a wolf, you know that. And unfortunately, I don't think my skill is going to help us right now."

"You are part fae, just like your brothers. Darium has discovered some elemental qualities lately, and Rhys has his power to heal himself. How do you know you don't have powers unless you try?" asked Alaina.

"I don't have any. I know it," he snapped. "Besides, I'm not in a hurry to have powers anymore. Now, please, Mother. Do something."

"Mayhap I can teach you."

"Nay. This isn't the time to be giving me lessons."

"Perhaps you are right. I'll have to go up to the volcano to do this since that is where the smoke is the worst." She disappeared to go do her work.

Zann helped Korack get down to the shore, but he could still barely walk. There was no way he'd be able to swim to shore. Neither would little Valindra.

"Lira, we need to get Valindra and Korack back to the castle. Do you have any powers that can help them do that?"

"I'm sorry, Zann. I don't have the power of transportation. I wish I did."

As soon as she said that, Medea magically appeared holding her daughter, Lily-Rae.

"Lily!" cried Valindra, excitedly.

"We're here to help," said Medea. "I can transport, bringing one person with me. Lily can do the same. So we can take you, two at a time, back to Mura."

"Take my brother Korack and Valindra first, please," said Lira. "Can you transport them directly to the castle?"

"Yes," said Medea. "Valindra, hold on to Lily's hand. I will take Korack's hand."

"And stay at the castle and don't go anywhere else, girls," Zann told the little ones so they wouldn't get the idea to go wandering off again. That's all he needed in the middle of a giant attack.

They dissipated, leaving Zann, Lira, and Keevan still stranded there.

Zann heard the growl of a giant, and once more found himself reaching for his sword. Yet again, he was reminded that he didn't have one. "Damn," he spat, spinning on his heels to see two giants emerging through the smoggy air.

"Zann, here. Take my sword," said Lira, giving it to him.

"Sister, give me a dagger. Fast," said Keevan.

Lira handed her dagger to him, but Zann noticed that it left her without any weapons to defend herself.

"Nay, Lira. You don't have a weapon now," he told her.

"I have my magic, Zann. I'll be fine," she explained.

"Get them," one of the giants said to the other.

Zann swung his sword, nicking one of the giants on the leg. Keevan managed to stab the other one on his knee.

"Arrrrrgh," they bellowed, angrier than ever now.

"Help!" cried Keevan, as the giant swiped at him and he ducked, just getting missed from the giant's heavy fist that came crashing down next to him as he fell to the ground.

"I'm coming, Keevan." Zann ran to help him, and was able to help hold off the giant. Then, just as it came for them again, the giant went flying through the air and crashed into a boulder, hitting its head and passing out.

Zann looked over his shoulder to see Lira smiling, having used her powers to move him.

"Thanks, sis," said Keevan, as Zann helped him off the ground.

"Nay!" he heard Lira scream. When Zann spun around, he saw Lira being held tightly in the hands of the second giant. He held her arms clamped to her sides, and she didn't seem able to use her powers on him now.

"Lira!" screamed Zann, bolting over to the giant,

slashing at it with his sword. Unfortunately, the giant was too big and too strong. It managed to knock Zann's sword from his grip. Then another giant appeared and grabbed Zann in his hands as well, lifting him off the ground.

As Zann was lifted into the air, he felt the giant squeezing hard. His head spun and he felt as if he were going to pass out.

"Lira! Zann!" yelled Keevan from the ground. He wanted to help them, but Zann realized it was too late. He and Lira were getting closer and closer to being the giants' next meal.

"Save yourself, Brother," yelled Lira.

"Nay. I won't leave you," Keevan shouted back.

"Go!" commanded Zann. "There is nothing you can do."

"Nay. I'll use my powers." Keevan meant well, but his powers were yet to be honed. He threw a fireball, but it fizzled out before it even hit the giant. Then, to Zann's horror, Keevan was scooped up by the leg, from yet another giant that seemed to come from nowhere.

"Nay!" shouted Keevan, struggling, flailing his arms and free leg, but not able to get free. "We're all going to die."

"I'm so sorry, Keevan," shouted Lira. "Please forgive me for not coming to look for you and Korack. It was me who caused Laeroth's death. I deserve to die for what I did, but you don't."

"I forgive you, Lira. I understand. And you didn't cause his death. Don't blame yourself."

"I love you, Zann," Lira said next, as the giant brought her up to its mouth to take a bite.

"Nay, leave her alone," Zann shouted, struggling, but unable to get loose. "I love you, too, Lira," he said, knowing these might be their last words between them.

"Enough with all the sentimental hogwash, you big oaf!"

Zann looked down to see Elric standing there with his hands on his hips and looking up to them from the ground. He was dressed in chain mail and wore a weapon belt with daggers, since swords were too long for him to hold. If Zann hadn't been on the brink of death, he would have laughed at this amusing sight.

"Elric, run!" shouted Zann, knowing the little man was no match for a giant. "We are all going to die. Save yourself."

"Nay! I will not leave my children. Or even you, oaf."

"Father, please. Go," cried Lira. "I don't want you to have to watch us being eaten." Tears streamed from Lira's eyes.

"No one is going to eat any of you if I can help it."

The elf was only the height of a child, and no match for the giants towering over him. Zann thought this was the stupidest thing the sage ever did. That is, until Elric took a hold of the giant's leg and lifted it up into the air with one hand.

The giant was so surprised that its arms went flailing about and he dropped Zann to the ground.

"Oooomf," Zann grunted as the air was knocked from him when he hit the ground. He looked over and noticed the crown of power on Elric's head. Elric repeated the process and Lira was released from the giant holding her as a prisoner as well.

"Father, you saved the crown of power from the fire after all," said Lira, getting up and running over to Zann.

"You're damned right I did. It's a little burnt but still seems to work just fine." He patted the crusty crown on his head.

"Father," cried Keevan, now about to be eaten by the third giant. The giant held him up above its head and opened his mouth wide.

"I'm coming, son. Hold on. This time, Elric used one of the other powers of the crown. With a wave of the sage's hand he sent the giant barreling backwards, falling to the ground. Keevan got away and ran over to join them.

"Elric, since you have the crown, you must have the power of transportation too. Take Keevan back to the castle," said Zann. "Hurry."

"Welcome back, Son," said Elric, taking a hold of his son's arm. As he transported with him, they disappeared from sight.

"I'm glad your father didn't burn the crown after all," Zann told Lira, seeing her sword on the ground and picking it up. All three giants lay on the ground unconscious.

"Father saved me," Lira said with tears in her eyes. "And Keevan tried to help us. They both almost lost their lives because of me."

"Lira, there will be time for soul-searching later. Right now, I think we'd better go." Zann nodded towards a horde of giants, running right toward them.

The two of them ran to the shore, only to see the giants fighting on the other side of the water on the banks of Mura. The elves and fae, and even Darium and Rhys were trying to hold them back. Everyone used their powers, but the giants were too many and too strong.

"If we're going to get out of this alive, we're going to need a little more help," said Zann.

As soon as Zann said it, he saw Murk up in the sky, leading a flock of raptors over the water. They started to dive bomb the giants, clawing at them and pecking at their eyes. The giants swatted at them and covered their heads.

As the giants on the island got closer to Lira and Zann, the elemental powers of nature helped them further. Vines reached out and tangled around the giants' legs, knocking them to the ground and holding them there.

Even the stricat, one of Mura's fierce felines that could fly, flew overhead trying to push the giants back. It was much like a lion with wings, big and very fast and strong.

Lira used her powers from the shore, holding out her hands and blasting the detained giants with fireballs to keep them from coming any closer. It all helped to slow down the fight, but they still needed more power on their side.

"If only something could make the giants realize that the volcano is no longer active. Then, mayhap they'd come back to Denwop and leave the fae and elves alone," said Zann.

Lira heard the loud sound of flapping wings coming from overhead. She also heard something that sounded like flames being shot through the air. She looked up to see, of all things, a dragon with someone riding it. There were no dragons on Mura. The only dragon she'd ever seen was when the witch, Medea, came through a portal recently riding one. But the dragon had been sent back through the portal, and she wasn't expecting to see it ever again.

"Zann, look!" Lira pointed up to the dragon that was swooping lower, still breathing fire. "There's a dragon with someone riding it."

"Yes!" Zann exclaimed, whooping loudly and raising

his fist in the air triumphantly. "That's Marco. He is Medea's brother-by-marriage and that's his dragon. Medea must have opened the portal back to England to get him."

"But how could she control a portal?" asked Lira.

Zann quickly explained. "After our last episode with the portal, we obtained a crystal key from the gods. It enables people to travel through the portal back and forth to England, where Medea's family lives.

"It's working," shouted Lira. "The dragon is scaring the giants back to Denwop."

Lira and Zann were watching the dragon and didn't see yet another giant come up behind them. Lira once again felt the giant's fists close around her, trapping her arms so she couldn't use her magic on it.

"Zann!" she cried as it lifted her into the air. "Help me."

"Lira!" he screamed, spinning around to realize what had happened. "Turn invisible," he told her. "Mayhap that will trick the giant."

"I – I can't," she said. "I can barely breathe and feel like I'm going to faint. Zann, I don't want to die."

"Leave her alone!" screamed Zann, sounding angrier than he ever had.

The giant squeezed even harder and grunted at Zann.

"I – I can't . . . breathe." Lira felt as if she were about to die. Then, she thought she was dreaming, because she saw Zann waving his arms like crazy. Hail and rain pelted down from the sky, bouncing off the body of the giant, but somehow not even touching Lira.

The hail was big, and hit the giant hard. The giant didn't like that. He used one hand to block more hail from hitting his head, and when he lost his tight hold on her, Lira used it to her advantage. She pushed away from the beast and went falling to the ground once again.

"Lira!" Zann ran over and grabbed her hand, dragging her to her feet.

The sound of flapping wings from overhead caused them both to look up to see the dragon landing on the shore. The giants left on Denwop all ran inland in fear.

"Zann, do you need a ride?" shouted Marco, waving from atop the dragon.

"Ride a dragon?" asked Zann, sounding excited. "Yes, we do!"

He and Lira ran to him, and mounted the dragon.

"Hold on to Marco tightly, and I'll hold you from behind," Zann told Lira, putting her in between him and Marco. With a command from Marco, the dragon's head lifted and it snorted loudly. Its wings started flapping, creating a cold breeze.

"I'm scared," cried Lira, holding tightly to Marco.

"I've got you, don't worry." Zann's face pressed up against the side of her head and his arms clasped tightly around her waist. "Relax and enjoy the ride," he told her. "It's not everyone that gets to ride a dragon."

"Here we go," Marco shouted over his shoulder, directing the dragon up into the sky.

Lira's heart raced, but once they were away from the dragons she started to relax. Still, she kept her eyes squeezed shut.

"Open your eyes, Lira. Look how beautiful it is up here," said Zann.

Slowly, Lira's eyes opened and she saw the most wonderful sight. They were up in the clouds looking down at Mura. She could see the fields of lippenbur lilies in the Whispering Dale and when she peered further out she even saw her castle in Glint.

"Oh, Zann. This is amazing," she said, letting out a

deep breath. The dragon turned back toward the water now.

"Look," called out Marco. "The battle is breaking up."

Sure enough, the giants had stopped fighting. They turned around and slowly headed back to their own island, realizing the volcano was no longer active. The dragon flying overhead also frightened them, and as Marco dipped down, they looked up in fear and ran back to their boats.

Marco turned the dragon and headed back to the castle. The volcano was still now, and the sun broke through the sky creating a rainbow that this time ended right at Castle Glint. Lira smiled, feeling happy for the first time in a long time. She lifted her face to the sun and closed her eyes again, feeling the wind against her face and blowing her hair. She had never felt so alive or so free.

"We're going to be all right, Zann," said Lira, turning and resting her head against him as they rode atop the dragon back home. "Everyone worked together, and we are all going to be fine from now on."

Thankfully, the battle with the giants was finally over.

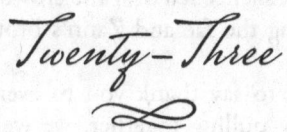

Twenty-Three

LATER THAT DAY, everyone gathered back at Castle Glint, where Lira made sure there was a feast prepared to feed all who had helped to keep the giants from invading the land. The sun shone brightly, and the sky lit up in colors of bright white and vibrant blue.

No more giants tried to come to Mura, but instead stayed on their own island where they belonged. This time no one was killed, but there were a few dozen injuries.

"If I can have everyone's attention please." Lira stood on one of the castle's balconies, while everyone gathered in the courtyard below. Even the dragon was still here, but Marco kept it far from the others so they wouldn't be scared.

"Lira, I'm here," said Zann coming up behind her and slipping his arms around her waist. He gave her a quick kiss behind the ear.

"Zann, I have an important announcement to make. Actually, I think we should go down into the courtyard to do it."

"All right," he said, seeming confused.

Lira felt anxious, and hoped what she had to say was going to be accepted by all.

Once they got down to the courtyard, Lira held up her hand and a silence fell over the crowd. Everyone was there, including the fae and Zann's brothers and their families.

"I wanted to say thank you to everyone for your help today. By pulling together, we were able to save the land of Mura from being taken over by the giants."

Cheers went up from the crowd. "Hail, Queen Lira," shouted one of the elves.

"There's more," she said, getting the crowd to still once again. "Today, I am happy to say that my brothers, Korack and Keevan have finally come home."

More cheers were heard.

"We're happy to be here," said Keevan, raising his tankard in the air. Korack sat on a chair with his leg elevated, but the herbs were already taking hold and he would heal completely. He didn't seem to quite forgive Lira yet, but she knew it would take some time. After all, she had been angry with her father for the last four years, so she knew how he must feel.

"Father, are you here?" asked Lira, looking around the crowd for him. Then, she saw him sitting amongst a group of elven women with the crown of power on his head. She wasn't sure if anyone would ever be able to live with him again now that he held so much power. "Father, thank you for saving my life today," she told him.

"That's what a father does," he said, sounding like he had drank a little too much wine.

"And Medea, thank you, too. And your brother Marco who showed up with the dragon in the nick of time."

Marco stood up, lifting his hand in the air. "I'll be

giving all the children dragon rides before I go back through the portal," he announced.

That got a nice reception from the children, but wasn't quite accepted by their parents.

"If Marco needs a break, I am a dragon lord now, too, so I can take over for him." Rhys stood up and addressed the crowd. When he did, Lira could see that he had a big, deep cut on his face from fighting the giants. Blood dripped down his cheek.

"Oh, Rhys, your face is hurt," said Lira.

"It is?" His hand went to his cheek. He used his power to heal himself, and suddenly the cut disappeared. "Nay, there is nothing there, Lira."

"I guess not," she said with a giggle. Then she continued. "I also want to thank the fae for coming to our aid today. Especially Zann's mother and her friend, Brynn-Riletta who is an elemental of fire. Brynn helped to stop the volcano from erupting more than it already had."

"It was my pleasure," said Brynn. She was a beautiful woman with long, red hair. "And I invite you all to visit me and my family at Lornoon someday."

"Why not?" asked Zann. "It's close enough and we don't have to take a portal to get there."

That made everyone laugh.

"Speaking of portals," said Darium. "Did we ever figure out how that portal appeared or if it will come back again."

"I think I can answer that one," said Zann's mother, Alaina. "I believe that Lira's brother, Keevan made the portal appear, but didn't even know it. His elven powers are starting to emerge now and will get even stronger as he regains his strength and health. He must have wanted to contact his sister so badly, that he somehow made it happen."

"I did that?" asked Keevan, sounding so excited. "Well, mayhap I did." He looked very proud of himself, but his twin looked upset since he didn't have his powers yet and it was years past due.

"Sit down and stop gloating, brother." Korack waved his hand through the air, and when he did, Keevan was knocked to the ground.

"Hey!" said Keevan. "That wasn't nice, Korack."

"Did I do that?" asked Korack looking at his hand. A smile slowly spread across his face.

"You sure did," said Lira. "It seems now that your leg is healing, your powers are emerging too."

"I did do that, didn't I?" Korack studied his hand in amazement, smiling from ear to ear. This was the first time Lira had seen him smile since they returned from the island.

"I'd also like to thank my aunt, Sasha," said Lira.

"Me?" asked Sasha, seeming surprised that she would even be mentioned.

"Please join me up here, aunt."

"Whatever for?" asked Sasha.

"Please," begged Lira. "I have something I want to give you."

"Well, all right." Sasha joined them.

Lira looked over at her daughter and little Lily and nodded. "All right, girls. Bring the present here."

"A present? For me?" asked Sasha. "Whatever for?"

"Here you go, Mother." Valindra handed her a large box covered in purple velvet. Little Lily-Rae clung to Valindra's dress, watching with wide eyes.

"Aunt Sasha, I want you to have this." Lira handed the box to her aunt.

. . .

Zann watched over Lira's shoulder, not sure what she was up to. Then, Sasha opened the box and gasped. She held up a beautiful gold crown with jewels embedded in it.

"Lira, this is your mother's crown," said Sasha. "It is the crown of the Queen of Glint. Why in the world are you giving it to me?"

"I am giving it to you, because you are my mother's sister, and I feel that you would make a much better queen than I would."

Gasps were heard and then silence in the crowd.

"Lira? Are you really giving up your title?" asked Zann, not understanding why she would do such a thing.

"Zann, I know you don't really want to live in an elven village, just admit it," said Lira.

"Well, I . . . well, I . . ."

"What he means is, hell no," said Rhys, making them all laugh.

"I am your husband, Lira." Zann took her hands in his. "I will live wherever you want me to. I don't want you to give up your crown just for me."

"I haven't felt comfortable being queen for quite some time now."

"But you did wonderfully today in leading and helping your people."

"Mayhap. And I am glad to feel as if I've redeemed myself in some ways. But in other ways, I feel as if I will never be able to pay for the damage I've done."

Zann realized the death of Laeroth still weighed heavy on her mind. Mayhap getting out of the castle and starting a new life as anything but the Queen of Glint would help Lira heal the hurt she still felt.

"I just want to be a wife and mother, not a ruler and leader," she told Zann.

"So, you're saying you want to stay married to me then?" asked Zann, just to make sure.

"Of course, I do, Zann. I thought you knew that. I think I would also rather live with you on the other side of the mountain, instead of staying here in the land of Glint."

"Where exactly do you mean?" asked Zann. "It's not like we can go back to Evandorm. Lira, I don't even have a home anymore to take you to."

"You have a home at Kasculbough, brother," said Rhys.

"Or in the Whispering Dale," said his mother.

"I can help you two build a cottage next to mine and Talia's in the Goeften Forest," offered Darium.

"Well, there you go," said Lira with a smile. "It looks like we have more than enough places to choose from now."

"But what about your daughter?" asked Zann. "She is Princess of Glint. You are going to deprive her of that privilege?"

"I have already talked it over with Valindra." Lira pulled her daughter to her in a hug. "She said she wants to be with you and me no matter where we go."

"I see," Zann answered, still not sure this was the right choice for Lira.

"So, Aunt Sasha, will you accept the title of Queen of Glint?" asked Lira.

Everyone remained silent, waiting for the woman's answer.

"I am honored," Sasha replied. "Of course, I will accept the title of queen. But only if you promise to ask Valindra again when she becomes of age if she'd like to be queen of Glint, because she is the rightful heir."

"How about if when you die, she will take your place then?" asked Lira.

"Of course. But I don't plan on dying anytime soon." Sasha smiled. "Unless you know something that I don't?"

"Nay, I know nothing, and neither do we want you to die, My queen." Lira took the crown and placed it on Sasha's head. "Please welcome Sasha, the new Queen of Glint," she announced.

The crowd cheered for her and clapped.

"Lira, are you really sure about this?" whispered Zann, still not able to understand how anyone could give up a queendom. He wanted to make sure Lira wouldn't regret it.

"I am certain," she said, looking out to the crowd for her father. "Father? Are you out there?" she asked.

Everyone looked around, but he was gone.

"He left," she said in a mere whisper. Zann could feel her pain.

"I'm sure he'll be back," he told her.

"Nay, I'm not so certain about that." Lira looked over to Sasha next. "My queen, I hope you are happy with your new title." Lira bowed to her, something that Zann was sure wasn't easy for her, since everyone had been bowing to her up until now.

"Lira, I would be happier, only if you agree to be my advisor," said her aunt.

"But I won't be here in Glint. It wouldn't be proper, or a wise thing to do," Lira explained.

"Then mayhap we can have two advisors," suggested Sasha. "That way you can still be involved in the elven realm when you come back home to visit."

"I would like that, thank you," said Lira. "But can I suggest three advisors to the queen instead?"

"Three?" asked Sasha. "Do you have someone in mind?"

"I do. I would like both of my brothers, Keevan and Korack to fill those positions."

"Well, I would have to say I agree," said Sasha, with a nod and a smile.

"So do we," said Korack now standing next to his brother, looking as if he felt much better. By the smile on Korack's face, Zann guessed that he had forgiven his sister.

"Clear the way, clear the way, coming through," came Elric's voice as he walked up to the front with a knight from Evandorm with him. There were some concerned whispers amongst the crowd to see one of their enemies back on elven soil.

"Father, where were you?" asked Lira. "And what is that man doing here with you?"

"I was gone but I'm back now," said Elric. "Were you looking for me for some reason?"

"I wanted to tell you that you no longer have to live on top of the cliff by yourself. You belong in the castle, so I hope you will live at Castle Glint from now on, even though I will no longer be here."

"Nope, sorry. Not interested." Elric dismissed the idea with a wave of his hand.

"What?" asked Lira, looking like she was about to cry. "Why not?"

"Because, I have a job, if I must remind you. I'm the cook at Evandorm and that is where I'll be living now."

"Evandorm?" asked Zann. "I don't understand. They are our enemies now."

"Go on. Tell them," Elric said to the knight standing next to him.

"Hello, everyone. I am Sir Thomas from Evandorm. I am head knight there." The man looked nervous to be around those his people had just fought.

There were mixed reactions from the crowd that he

was even there at all.

"I wanted to apologize for the recent battle, but we were only following our late king's orders. I assure you, none of us wanted to fight you. We lost many of our loved ones as well."

"Late king?" asked Rhys. "What are you saying?"

"Did something happen to King Grinwald?" asked Zann.

"Yes," said Sir Thomas. "He was mortally wounded by King Sethor during the battle, and just this morning he passed away."

"Really?" asked Zann. "So he was worse off than we all thought. Who is King of Evandorm now?"

"No one," said the knight. "His heir died in the battle as well, so that leaves us with no king. We need a ruler."

The crowd murmured to each other.

"We are afraid that King Sethor is going to try to claim Evandorm for himself now," Sir Thomas continued. "None of us want that. That is why the people of Evandorm have decided that we need to find someone strong to lead us that does not come from Macada Castle."

"What about you?" asked Zann. "You seem like a good warrior. Mayhap you can be their ruler."

"Nay, I can't be a king. I am just a knight," protested Sir Thomas. "I have spoken to the people and knights of Evandorm. We have decided that it would be beneficial to have a leader who has magic, actually. That will keep Sethor from our door."

"Magic? But I thought you didn't condone magic at Evandorm," said Darium.

"That was only King Grinwald who held that belief. Those of us who are left have seen the power of magic and know it is what will keep us safe in the end. That is why when our head cook returned just a little while ago, we all discussed this and came to a decision."

"Head cook?" Zann looked over at the elf.

"That's right, you big oaf. It's my position," snapped Elric. "You know that. I have a job now."

"I'm surprised you didn't convince them that you'd be a good king of Evandorm while you were at it," mumbled Zann. "Or did you?"

"Actually, he convinced us that you and your new wife would be the perfect rulers of Evandorm," the knight told Zann.

"He did what?" That surprised Zann, since he didn't think the sage even liked him.

"Father? Really?" asked Lira. "You said that?"

"Daughter, you are a queen without a queendom now," said Elric.

"Mayhap so, but you weren't even here. How did you even know that?"

"I'm a sage. I know things. Besides, I could see it coming for a while now, Lira. You were not happy ruling here. Now that you have given the crown to Sasha, you need a place to live. So, what do you say?"

"I – I don't know what to say," said Lira. "I am not sure I really want to be a queen again."

"You won't be holding all the responsibility this time by yourself," said Elric. "Remember, they are king-doms, not queendoms on the other side of the mountain. Your husband will be ruling with you. Even if he doesn't deserve it."

"Zann, what do you say about all this?" asked Lira.

"I say it's a lot better than living in the back of the kennels," Zann answered with a chuckle. "I would be honored to take the position, but only if you were at my side as my queen."

"What is your answer, daughter?" asked Elric. "We

are all waiting to hear."

"Zann? What should I do?" asked Lira seeming excited about the offer, but hesitant to accept it.

"Sweetheart, I know you weren't happy being queen, but mayhap that could change if you had a king at your side to go through it with you," said Zann. "I would be willing to do it, if you would."

"I . . . I suppose so," she answered. "Yes, I think I would like that as well."

"Great!" said Zann, feeling excited about his new role. Never in a million years did he ever dream he would end up being a king, like his brother. "I like this whole idea of us being king and queen of Evandorm," said Zann. "But can we continue to call it a kingdom instead of a queendom?"

Lira laughed, and gave him a hug. "I wouldn't want it any other way."

"Then it's settled," said Elric, clapping his hands together, getting the noisy crowd to be still again. "Tomorrow, you are all invited to a scrumptious feast at my daughter's new home, Evandorm Castle."

Zann cleared his throat.

"I mean, my daughter and her husband's new castle. I will cook up a feast like you've never had before."

"Elric, that's a generous offer, but is a feast really necessary?" asked Zann.

"It is if we're also going to celebrate your wedding that I, of course, will officiate once again." The elf grinned and straightened his chef's hat. "This time it'll be done right, and followed with a true celebration."

Zann groaned and looked over to his brothers who were both laughing heartily now.

"To the King and Queen of Evandorm," said Rhys, holding his tankard high in the air.

The crowd cheered for them. Zann felt even happier

than when he'd managed to bring forth rain and hail. Things were looking up after all.

Twenty-Four

ZANN STOOD in the courtyard of Evandorm the next day, wearing a long purple velvet robe and a gold crown embedded with jewels of yellow, red and green. This was the adornment of the king, and it felt like naught but a dream to him. The coronation ceremony went smoothly and now the wedding was about to begin. Zann felt so lucky to have a title, a kingdom, a new home, and a new family all rolled into one.

"Are you happy, brother?" asked Rhys. He and Darium stood at his side. The courtyard was filled with not only the people of Evandorm, but also some from Kasculbough. Some of the elves came too, such as Sasha and Lira's brothers and father. Not all of the magical beings traveled here for the wedding, but a few of the fae made the journey, including Zann's mother and Talia's family.

"I feel as if I am in a dream and will be disappointed when I awake to discover none of this is true and I'm still just a huntsman," said Zann.

"You, son, are destined for great things." His mother joined them. "And now that your elemental powers have started to emerge, who knows what you can accomplish."

"Aye. I thought I was going to be naught more than a damned wolf for the rest of my life," Zann answered with a chuckle.

"I cannot believe I have two sons now that are kings of Mura," said Alaina.

"Well, you're Queen of the Fae now, so I think that tops even this," Zann told her. "Mother, I wanted to say thank you for not abandoning me when I was trapped on the Isle of Denwop."

"So, you forgive me now? Completely, I mean?"

"I do," Zann answered. "I see that I was wrong to judge you, and I only hope we have made amends."

"We have as far as I'm concerned."

"I admire you for your strength," Zann told her. "I can see now that you would only do what you thought was the best for your children. I can only hope I can make the right decisions for my family when Lira and I start having children as well someday."

"I am proud of all my sons and love you all so much." His mother encompassed all three of her sons in a hug.

"Darium, mayhap we should seize Macada Castle for you," suggested Rhys.

"No, thanks. I don't want to be a king," Darium answered. "Besides, Talia is an elemental of the earth so the best place for us to live is in the forest."

His raven squawked and Darium held out his arm. The bird landed on it and Darium looked into its eyes. "Murk says that Lira is ready and the wedding is about to start."

"The bird told you that?" asked Zann in surprise.

"Can you talk to animals now the way Talia can?" asked Rhys.

"Nay, not really. But you both know I can read minds on occasion, and that is just what I did." He sent his bird back up into the air. "Let the music and the wedding begin," he called out.

The musicians started playing a cheery tune. Darium and Rhys and Alaina stepped back as Sasha led the way down the stairs of the keep. Valindra and little Lily followed, throwing flower petals onto the ground. Lily stopped and looked back at the petals and held out her basket. The petals rose into the air and went back into her basket, making everyone laugh.

"Lily, you need to leave the petals there," said Medea, running out and collecting her daughter.

Next, came Lira, holding on to the arm of her father. Actually, since Elric was so much shorter, she had her hand on his shoulder instead.

"She looks beautiful," whispered Zann, watching his wife walk toward him, dressed in a long, green velvet gown that showed off her strawberry-blond hair. In her hair she wore striking lippenbur lilies, the flowers of the fae. Zann could smell the strong scent from where he stood, and was already getting randy. Lira did nothing to try to conceal her pointy ears, and neither did she need to hide them anymore.

Everyone in Evandorm knew she was an elf. The people here accepted elves and magic now. With King Sethor being outnumbered, since Zann and Rhys made up two of the three kings of Mura, they didn't think he'd cause any more trouble for those who had magic.

When the music stopped, Lira took Zann's arm. Her father climbed atop a wooden box, standing in front of them to conduct the ceremony for the second time. He wore the crown of power almost everywhere he went now. Zann figured it made him feel even more important, even though Elric always pushed the fact that he was a wise sage.

The gods of Mura weren't happy with him and so Elric was no longer their messenger, although they let him keep his elven powers. Zann figured now that Elric wasn't tied to the gods anymore, that is probably why he resumed his position of head cook. Either way, Lira would get to live with her father, making up for the time she'd lost.

Her brothers were happy with their new positions of advisors to the new queen. And with Elric's ability to transport, as well as Medea and Lily's, none of them would have to spend much time traveling to and from the magical lands by hiking over the mountains anymore. They would be able to get there instantly with the help of the others.

Elric officiated at the wedding, surprisingly not even using the words 'big oaf' once during the ceremony. That alone made Zann happy.

"The rings, please," said Elric.

Valindra stepped forward and handed him a small box. "Here you are, Grandpa."

"Why, thank you, granddaughter," he replied looking like he enjoyed every minute of it.

"Lira, I love you, and love that you are my wife." Zann reached out for one of the rings and slipped it on her finger.

"I love you, too, Zann. And I am more than happy that you are my husband." She put a ring on his finger as well.

"You're welcome," said Elric.

"What?" asked Zann.

"I am the one responsible for your marriage, but I'll take no credit for it."

"I think you just did," said Zann, making the crowd chuckle.

"All right, hurry up and kiss so I can serve the food," complained Elric. "I added a special ingredient to the pazzleberry pies that you are just going to adore." In a wave of his hand, Elric had the tall white chef's hat on his head, crammed right over the crown of power which he refused to take off.

"I will gladly kiss my wife," said Zann, dipping Lira down and kissing her so passionately in front of everyone that she had to stop him.

"Zann," she whispered. "I think we'd better save the rest for later. After all, there are children present."

"I'm sorry," said Zann, bringing her back to a standing position. "It's just that when I'm around you, my love, I cannot control myself. You make my mind filled with happy thoughts."

"So you're happy then, Zann?" she asked.

"More than you know. Are you happy too, Lira?"

"I don't think you need to ask. Just look at my smile."

Elric started zipping around again in a blur, setting up tables of food in the courtyard for the festive celebration.

"How do you feel about my father living here in Evandorm with us, Zann?"

"I think I'll get used to it," he answered. "However, if he starts stepping out of line thinking he's in charge since he constantly wears that crown of power, I might have to make it disappear."

"Zann, you wouldn't."

"Nay, I wouldn't, but it sure is fun to think about it. And the best part is, I do believe your father has finally stopped calling me and my brothers big oafs."

ONE YEAR LATER

"HURRY, EVERYONE," called out little Valindra, running through the courtyard, shouting. "Come see my new baby sister."

Zann walked out into the courtyard with Lira next to him. She insisted she was going to walk out there and not be carried, even though she'd just birthed the baby this morning.

"King Zann and Queen Lira, rulers of Evandorm," announced Elric, holding on to his crown of power and bowing before them. This was something that Zann never thought he'd see the sage do. The irritating elf had actually turned out to be quite a nice fellow after all.

Zann's brothers and their families were here waiting to see the new baby. So was Zann's mother, as well as some of the fae and the elves. Lira's brothers had been there since sunrise, wanting to support their sister and see their new niece.

"I present, Princess Leandra," said Zann, holding the baby up high so everyone could see her. "She has been named after Lira's late mother."

"Zann, be careful so you don't drop her," warned Lira.

"You know that would never happen, my love."

"Can I see my new cousin?" asked Lily, now three years old. She jumped up, but was too short to see anything.

"She has such light hair," remarked Alaina, leaning over to kiss her new grandchild.

"Aye, it is nearly white, just like Zann's," said Lira.

"I want to see!" Lily jumped up and down.

"She has beautiful green eyes and cute pointy little ears just like her mother," said Zann, in awe, drinking in the baby's beauty.

"We are happy for the two of you." Rhys peeked over at the newborn as he held his baby boy, little Lucio that Medea birthed just recently. He had been named after Medea's father.

"Aye, we all have two children now," said Darium. He approached with his son, Thistle, in his arms. Talia was next to him with Thistle's twin sister, Cricket. These were typical fairy names as well as names from the earth.

"Yes," said Talia. "I do think that the Blackseed boys have broken the tradition – or should I say curse, of only having boys." She giggled, in her cute little fae way.

"I can't see. I can't see." Lily continued to jump up and down, trying to get a look at the baby in Zann's hands.

"Babies, I like," said Darium. "But I can only hope we'll never see another portal."

"Portals aren't bad," remarked Medea. "After all, that is the way Rhys and I met."

"And the way we visit her family," added Rhys with a nod.

"I want to see the baby." Lily continued to jump up and down in anticipation.

"Some portals are bad and others are good, as I am

sure Darium can attest to." Zann spoke while smiling at his new baby girl. "My little princess is so precious that I cannot stop looking at her." Suddenly, the baby was gone and he was standing there with nothing in his arms.

"Where is she? She's gone! What happened to her?" he cried, turning a full circle looking around. "Zoroct's eyes, I hope she hasn't been sucked through another portal."

"Zann, relax. She is right there," said Lira, calmly.

He turned to see little Lily-Rae holding the baby in her arms. Lily was small and it looked like she was about to drop the newborn.

"Sorry about that," apologized Medea. "I guess we weren't paying attention to Lily and she really wanted to see the new baby. So, she just transported her new cousin over to her."

"I guess it's all right," said Zann, hunkering down and putting his arms around Lily, helping her to hold the baby. "I'm now living the life of magic, so what did I expect? I guess it'll just take me a while to get used to everything, that's all."

"You're not sorry you have such a magical family, are you, Zann?" asked Lira.

"Nay, not at all," said Zann. "I am filled with tons of emotions about it." He felt overjoyed to be not only a husband and father but also king. He also felt extremely lucky to be alive, and thankful that he'd made amends with his mother.

Rhys and Darium walked over, and Zann stood up to talk with them.

"Well, look at the that. The Blackseed boys are all together again," said Elric. "We've got the three big oafs all in a row."

Zann groaned, knowing it had been too good to be

true. Elric would most likely never change, and somehow Zann was all right with that.

"Father, that's not a nice thing to say. I thought you weren't going to call them that anymore," scolded Lira.

"You're right. I'm sorry, daughter," grumbled Elric. "I've been watching them for a while now with their magical women, and all I can say is that the Blackseed brothers have been *Bedeviled*, *Bewitched*, and **Beguiled**."

Afterword

I hope you enjoyed Zann and Lira's story and will take a moment to leave a review for me. It was fun creating the world of Mura. I have made a very detailed map that I would love to share with you. It is in color, and also shows the land of Lornoon, the home of Brynn-Riletta, the Elemental of Fire. Click **HERE** to see it.

If you'd like to read Brynn's story, you can do so in The Dragon and the Dreamwalker - Book 1 of my Elemental Magick Series.

Rhys' wife, Medea has come through the portal from England, but has shown up in the last three books of my **Tangled Tales Series**. Her first appearance is seen in **Lady in the Tower –Rapunzel,** where you will also find the dragon lord, Marco.

Another of my paranormal fantasy series that you might be interested in involves Greek myths. It is my Greek Myth Fantasy Series that was inspired by watching *Xena: Warrior Princess*, and *Hercules: The Legendary Journeys.*

Portals are magical and can take us to faraway places or realms we've never dreamed of before. You never know what you will find, what will come through from the other side, or to where you might be whisked away. Your imagination is the limit!

To find out more about my books that include the genres of fantasy, paranormal, medieval, small town contemporary, western, and more, please visit my **amazon page** or my **website**.

May you always find magic in your life!

Elizabeth Rose

About the Author

Elizabeth Rose is an Amazon All-Star, and bestselling, award-winning author of nearly 100 books and counting! Her first book was published back in 2000, but she has been writing stories ever since high school. She is the author of fantasy/paranormal, medieval, small town contemporary, and western romance. You'll find sexy, alpha heroes and strong, independent heroines in her books. Sometimes her heroines can even swing a sword.

Her earlier fantasy romance novels started out with her **Greek Myth Series**, inspired by the TV shows *Legendary Journeys of Hercules* and *Xena: Warrior Princess*. One of the books, **The Oracle of Delphi** was featured on the History Channel during a documentary of the Oracle. Elizabeth joins Oliver Heber Books with her **Portals of Destiny Series** which brings back characters from some of her other fantasy series, making guest appearances.

She loves adding humor to her work, because everyone needs to laugh more in life. Her **Bad Boys of Sweetwater: Tarnished Saints Series,** focuses on 12 brothers, a bunch of kids, and lots of humor. This small-town romance series was inspired by people, places, and things in her own life. The location is the lake and small town of Michigan where she grew up visiting her grandparents.

Living in the suburbs of Chicago with her husband, Elizabeth has two grown sons and one granddog – so far. A lover of nature, she can be found in the summer swinging in her 'writing hammock' in her secret garden, creating her next novel. Her secret garden is what inspired her medieval series, **Secrets of the Heart**, which of course centers around a secret garden too!

Visit elizabethrosenovels.com where you will find book trailers, sneak peeks at upcoming covers, excerpts from her books, as well as original recipes of food that her characters eat in her stories. If you'd like to sign up for her newsletter, join her private readers' group, or follow her on social media, just copy and paste the following links.

Join Elizabeth's Newsletter
Join Elizabeth's Facebook Group

Also by Elizabeth Rose

Tangled Tales Series

Lady and the Wolf (Red Riding Hood)

Just a Kiss (Frog Prince)

Beast Lord (Beauty and the Beast)

Touch of Gold (Rumpelstiltskin)

Lady in the Tower (Rapunzel)

A Perfect Fit (Cinderella)

Heart of Ice (Snow Queen)

Elemental Magick Series

The Dragon and the Dreamwalker

The Duke and the Dryad: Earth

The Sword and the Sylph: Air

The Sheik and the Siren: Water

Greek Myth Fantasy Series

Kyros' Secret

The Oracle of Delphi

The Thief of Olympus

The Pandora Curse

<u>Once Upon a Rhyme</u>

Mary, Mary (Mary, Mary Quite Contrary)

Muffet (Little Miss Muffet)

Blue (Little Boy Blue)

Dark Encounters
Familiar
The Caretaker of Showman's Hill
The Curse of the Condor

www.ingramcontent.com/pod-product-compliance
Lightning Source LLC
Chambersburg PA
CBHW021345130726
47899CB00019B/3255